The Human Race

Tahnee Fritz

The Human Race is a work of fiction. Names, characters, places, and incidents are the products of the author's imagination or are used fictitiously. Any resemblance to actual events, locales, or persons, living or dead, is entirely coincidental.

For Dad

Part One

I hate what's become of the world. Most of the humans do. There is so much violence and blood and meaningless death. It's not even the normal kind of death where your heart stops beating and your loved ones put you in a hole in the ground. A boring way to spend eternity, but if you are lucky, that's what you'll get.

It's just not like that anymore.

The world has changed.

Depending on what happens to you, causing your heart to stop beating, there's a pretty decent chance you'll come back as one of two horrible things. Each monster is disgusting, covered in filth and blood, and they *always* stink of death. They both have the power to destroy your entire life in only a few seconds. All it takes is just one bite or a single scratch from either beast and you might as well kiss your human life goodbye.

It's as simple as that.

I guess I should shed some light on how the world got

this way. About five years ago, these *brilliant* scientists decided they needed to create the ultimate cure. *For the life of me I can't remember what the cure was actually called.* It was supposed to be the one thing allowing us humans the ability to live for years longer than a normal lifespan. The one thing that would eliminate our constant worrying of what new diseases we could catch. It was meant to be the cure for cancer, diabetes, chronic asthma, *hell* even the common cold was on the list of what this thing was going to fix. But, like all of the other wonder drugs ever to hit the market, this one had a side effect. A really, *really* bad side effect.

Now, this cure worked at first. People were getting healthier and their lives seemed to be getting better. No one needed to pay for medicine anymore and pharmacies across the globe started closing their doors for good. Everything appeared to be perfect. Then there came this little boy who suddenly burst into flames while at the park with his mother. The first reported side effect. If I remember right, this boy had some form of leukemia and his mother took him to one of those magical scientists with the cure. He died from severe sunlight exposure with boils and burn marks all over his tiny body. No one could explain how or why it happened.

Soon after, numerous cases of this really bad sunburn were reported all across the world. People were quick to blame the miracle cure for this issue. Mainly because the humans who experienced these problems were injected with it and those who weren't were fine in the sunlight. The cure was taken off the shelf and the world waited to see what came next.

Another added side effect. This one's a little bit worse.

An older woman out in California decided one night, she wanted to go a little crazy. She wound up biting her husband while he slept and drank every ounce of his blood. There was a picture of that woman in the paper a few days after the incident. She had this eerie appearance. Her skin was deathly pale, kind of translucent, and her eyes were hazed over a lot. Even her hair had changed to this gloomy grey color.

Everyone began noticing this new effect happening all over the place. Reports of people going crazy and they stopped being themselves completely. They never went out in the sunlight anymore and craved the taste of blood over anything else. Offer them a doughnut, they'd reach for your wrist instead. If you weren't sucked dry, you were doomed to become one of them. A vicious new lifecycle.

The name "Vampire" hit the streets after more and more reports piled in. These aren't like those cozy vamps you see in the movies. You know, the ones that glitter in the sunlight or fall hopelessly in love and change their ways. The ones in the real world, the world that I live in, are pretty damn horrifying and *cannot* come out in the sunlight. Their pale skin starts to boil and blister and this nasty, yellow puss oozes out. It's really gross when you see it happen up close and personal, but that is the fastest way to kill one of them. You'd have to have perfect aim with a gun or crossbow and hit them in the heart on the first shot. Even then you have to get really close in order to hit the target and that is definitely not one of my favorite things.

These vamps can be tricky sometimes. They can fool with your mind. If you catch them in the right time of night, they can look and act like a normal human. They can even speak. Not loud or in complete sentences, but enough to get your mind to think they're still human. That's why you have to pay attention to the details or you'll wind up dead. I've learned how to tell the difference between the vamps and the living. First of all, their eyes can give it away. Most of them have grey or hazed over eyes and it looks like they might have cataracts. Vamps' skin is so pale, it seems like it glows in the right lighting. Another dead giveaway. It's a shame there are hundreds of people who have fallen victim to a vamp because they couldn't see the difference.

A truly sad world this has become.

To add to the end of the world, the original group of scientists attempted to fix this problem. I find it quite humorous that the government and the rest of the world allowed the same group of people to attempt to cure what they started in the first place. One would think they would have found someone else to do the job, but apparently no one chose to think of the obvious issue with this. Those guys got it wrong the first time. God knows they're bound to screw it up again.

So naturally, it didn't take long for the next batch of monsters to come along. In fact, it happened right on the operating table. They injected some young man, a victim of the original cure, with this new magic liquid, then waited. And waited. Eventually his hand started to twitch and a very slight amount of color returned to his skin. Not much, but enough for them to believe the new cure worked. They did tests with a UV light and his skin didn't boil like it should have. Everyone thought it worked and they got super excited.

They failed to see that the boy's heart never started to beat again. They looked past how his eyes changed from grey to the darkest shade of black.

The scientists thought wrong.

When they noticed these new problems, it was already too late. That boy snapped his eyes open and ripped through the straps holding him to the table. He leapt into the air and landed on a young woman who didn't have the chance to scream for help. He sunk his teeth into her skin and started ripping her to shreds. She didn't come back as one of them. She was one of the lucky ones.

From what I've heard about this story, the other doctors in the room tried fighting back. None of them had guns and the security guard only had a Taser which pissed the boy off even more. He attacked, he bit, game over security guard. That's all it takes is one bite. In seconds, you can find yourself writhing on the floor in pain as your body dies yet you somehow stay alive at the same time. Thus beginning another horrible lifecycle taking over the world.

This new disease seemed to spread a lot faster than the vampire outbreak. It took much less time to die and come back as a zombie than it did to slowly die and change into a vampire. I've seen them both take effect on people and both ways seem excruciatingly painful.

These zombies are definitely different than the vamps. They are so far gone they don't have the ability to speak or move very fast at all. They can't comprehend what you tell them and I *highly* doubt they care. Even if they tried, they could never pass as a living human. Most of them begin to rot soon after they're bit and their skin starts to peel away. Not a single part of them is at all what their human self used to be. They don't care who you are when they attack and they don't care if you try to fight back. They'll come at you with every-thing they've got and, if you're not prepared to kill them, you might as well face the facts that you're going to be one of them soon. Very soon.

As you may not think, these two creatures tend to stay away from each other. I haven't heard of either one infecting the other and I would absolutely hate to see the product of that. It would probably be some super zombie-vampire thing. Something that still looks and has the ability to act human long enough to trick you so they can eat you and drink your blood before you have time to react.

Horrible thought. I'll probably have nightmares for the next few nights. *Way to go brain.*

My theory on why they don't bother each other is because they both smell dead. From what I remember seeing in the movies, vamps get weak when they drink dead blood and zombies can tell when you're already one of them. It makes sense they would leave each other alone.

After the outbreak of both monsters, the world went so far downhill not much could bring it back up. If people didn't die from being bit or sucked dry, they died the stupid way. Trying to get away in a hurry and not looking where they're going. Getting into car accidents or fights over food happened constantly. Then the obvious suicide of millions who didn't want to risk becoming a monster. I'm so glad that thought never popped into my head.

Technology started to dwindle, another obvious. It only took a couple of years for the power to go off completely. You were considered very lucky if you had a working generator and really had to guard yourself. Like get yourself a tank or build a moat or something to keep thieves at bay. Cars and trucks died right along with everything else. Some still work, but most people just walk or ride a bike if they need to get somewhere. Vehicles of any kind are noisy and attract attention of the wrong kind.

It's not a fun place to live at all.

So, like I said, the world has been like this for about five years. I don't see it getting better any time soon. *Or ever.* I'm nineteen now and I've seen way too many disgusting things for more than one lifetime. Makes every horror movie I've ever watched seem like a kiddie flick. Things just don't gross me out too much anymore, which is pretty bad considering how I'm a girl and all. It's also a good thing that I can handle seeing things this planet never should have gotten introduced to in the first place. It's a key to survival.

Humans have also broken up into two different categories. Those that choose to stay in groups and rebuild cities and towns. They have their own means of protection and would do just about anything to keep their homes safe. They have plenty of guns and resources to last a while and they actually want to keep the human population higher than the monsters.

Then, there are the travelers. The ones who stay on the road at all times of the day and night looking for a safe place away from the bad guys. We have our own means of security, whatever weapon is nearest at the time we need one. We have to stay fit in order to get away in a hurry. The need to know how to protect our lives as well as the ones we're traveling with is priority number one. We are often looked down upon for reasons I can't quite understand. I guess people think we are too undomesticated and only know how to scavenge for things. The people who think this are idiots if you ask me.

It doesn't matter which group you're a part of, though. Either one is subject to an attack by the vampires or the zombies. We're all doomed to look over our shoulders for the rest of our short lives.

It isn't an ideal life, but it's the life the humans have to deal with now.

As for me, I stick with my dad. He's the only family I have left and I'd like to keep him around. He's a funny guy sometimes, always tries to make the best out of the worst possible situations. We have been traveling north for a few months trying to get to Canada. He's got it in his head that the monsters aren't up there. I can almost guarantee they are. The zombies might not like the cold, but the vamps don't care. I don't even think they can feel the cold.

So this is my life in a nutshell. We went south at first to find my grandparents and found them dead. We lost a lot of very close things along the way, but it hasn't destroyed us. Now we're heading north. A long walk from Florida to Canada and we aren't even halfway there. Let's hope we can make it.

***

It's morning. The only way I can tell that is through a small hole in the shack we stayed in overnight. It's cloudy outside, blocking most of the sunlight. I can hear the pitter patter of rain drops on the tin roof. I'm not a big fan of walking in the rain. I don't have an umbrella, it takes up too much space and is a pain in the ass to carry. That and I wouldn't want to run into a vamp or zombie while carrying one. We could always try to find a car for us to "borrow" for a little while. Most of those are either destroyed, empty on gas, or the battery is dead. Good things like that are hard to come by anymore. Which is why we stick to the old fashioned form of getting places, walking and staying in random buildings at night.

My dad and I always take turns overnight to keep watch. A way for us to stay safe and alive when the sun goes down. We've been doing this for a while so it's gotten to be a habit. I take the first watch and at one in the morning I wake him up so he can finish out the night. We've had a problem with the vampires a few times. Nothing dad's gun couldn't handle. He's a pretty good shot when it comes to killing them. Hits them right in the heart almost every time, whereas I miss quite a bit. Unless I'm really close to them, like a foot away, there's no sense in me wasting my bullets when I know I'll miss. I prefer not to get *that* close.

The shack we chose to stay in for the night is behind an old gas station. I think they used it to store pop cans and bottles for recycling. It still has that sugary smell and stick-iness all over the floor. We only have one sleeping bag to take turns using and never bothered finding a pillow. That's just another thing that will take up too much space. We travel light. We only have one change of clothes, each of us has a jacket, and there's a few other odds and ends in each of our packs. Dad carries the food while I have some old keepsakes in my bag.

I would love to spend time looking for different things. Like some new clothes for instance. The malls and stores are just so empty nowadays, it's really hard to find any-thing that suits us or anything we like at all. I got lucky and found my amazingly comfortable black boots when we were in Florida. They were just sitting on the shelf of an old shoe store ripe for the picking. So I picked them, tossed my old raggedy tennis shoes over a telephone wire, and enjoy my new, knee-high suede boots.

It's the little things in life you have to enjoy when there isn't much of a life left.

I roll over in the sleeping bag and look up at my dad. He's staring out through the small peephole in the door. I can't tell if what he sees outside is good or bad. His facial expression never really changes. He always looks calm and peaceful, like nothing bad has happened to the world or our family. A little bit of that has rubbed off on me and I only take things too seriously when monsters are around. Thinking like that has managed to keep us two alive for five years now and hopefully it doesn't fail any time soon.

I sit up and push the sleeping bag off me. I stretch my arms over my head and let out a small yawn. The watch I've always had on says it's seven in the morning. I can't tell what day it might be, but I know summer is almost here. The rain is always a good indicator to tell us when summer is approaching. Dad's hoping we make it as far north as possible before winter hits. He really thinks we'll be safe up there.

That is the only thing I have my doubts on. Even if there are no zombies or vampires up north, the winter will kill us. We wouldn't have any warm shelter besides a tent or shack somewhere. We don't have any coats or heavy clothing to keep us from freezing. I'm sure food is pretty scarce up there as well and neither of us are the best when it comes to hunting. But, I stick by his side and hope for the best. If he's wrong, we'll find somewhere else to survive or die trying.

He finally looks away from the peephole and turns to me. A small smile crossing his aging face. Wrinkles took over the corners of his mouth and forehead soon after the outbreak of the undead. His once brown hair faded to shades of grey and is wearing thin at the top of his head. He hides his bald spots with a red Cardinals hat which he found in an old sports bar. I've seen them play once and they destroyed their opponent. A good past time of me with my family, when I had a family anyway.

"Good morning, Bridget." He says with a smile.

"Morning, dad." I say right back.

I get to my feet and go to my backpack sitting on a table in the corner of the shack and open it. Inside, I have our old family photo album. I can't bring myself to look in it, but I can't bring myself to throw it away either. It would be too much like forgetting I ever had anyone other than my dad. I never want to forget what I once had before the world turned to hell. I also have a pair of jeans and a t-shirt. Nothing nice, just something to change into when these clothes get too nasty to keep wearing. I have a black hoodie with fur lining the hood. It's my favorite thing to wear mainly because it doesn't have holes and looks new. There are a few other odds and ends I keep in my bag, like my old IPod and a couple of books to read when I get bored. Things my dad says is a waste to keep, but like the photos, I can't throw them away. To go along with my girly side, I have a hair brush and even some old makeup which I only use when I am able to take an actual shower. The kind with soap and changing into clean clothes afterwards. A rare occurrence when you're on the road.

I take the hairbrush out and start brushing away. My hair is pretty boring and brown, kind of long, to the middle of my back. I trim it every once in a while, when it gets too out of hand. It's always wavy, just like how my mom's was. I wince at the few snags the brush catches and I can hear my dad snickering. On the handle of the brush is the pink hair tie I stole from my sister a while back. I take it off and pull my hair back into a pony tail. My bangs are parted off to the side and don't get pulled back with the rest of my hair. When I'm done, I shove the brush back in my pack and zip it closed.

I turn back to my father and ask, "So, anything for

breakfast?"

He shrugs, "Same thing as usual, Bridge."

I force a smile, "Yay," then think of the apples we found a few days ago. They've served as our breakfast, lunch, and dinner ever since we came across the orchard and stuffed a bag full of them. At least it's something to eat so we don't starve.

He lifts the bag from the floor and tosses me a green apple and takes a red one for himself. Both of us bite into our meal and the crunch echoes through the shack. Other than the rain beating on the roof, that's all we can hear. I glance down at our sac of apples and notice we are running low. Enough for maybe another day or two, depending on how we ration them. We'll need to find more food soon meaning we'll have to risk going into an abandon building. A place with no lights and could possibly be teaming with vamps or zombies. Depending on the situation, that could be an exciting risk.

My dad must have noticed me staring at the bag of food, "We'll find more soon, Bridge. We should get to the next town today and be able to trade and stay someplace for the night."

I nod, "Okay, dad. It just sucks that we have to walk in this rain to get there."

"It's not *so* bad. We've walked farther in worse." He replies.

I smile, recalling the horrible storm we had to walk through two winters ago. Snowflakes the size of golf balls, wind blowing so fast I could feel the tears freezing to my face. We forced ourselves to walk an hour in that storm just to take shelter in the back of an old box truck. We stayed in that truck for two days waiting for the storm to blow over. The snow was up to our waists by the time we started walking again. Making it almost impossible to move at all, but we managed to make it through.

"How much further till we get to the next town?" I ask, taking another bite of my apple.

"All day. We won't get there till dinner time and I'm praying we can trade something for meat." He responds.

"Have you heard any rumors about this town?"

"Not any bad ones. I think it's just a small one, maybe a handful of people. Nothing like Florida where the cities are crammed full of people. That's what'll get you killed fast." he says.

"I like the small towns. People are always really friendly there." I say.

"Yep," he finishes his apple and tosses the core on the ground. "Finish up and get your things together. We need to get moving soon. Make sure your gun is loaded as well."

I nod, then quickly finish my apple. I toss the core to the floor with his and wipe my hands on my jeans. I get back in my pack and grab the black hoodie from inside. It's the only thing I have to keep myself somewhat dry and warm in this weather. I slip it on and zip it up then pull the hood over my head. Neither of us sleep without our shoes on, unless we are safe in a town with more than just us. That way if we need to make a quick getaway, we don't have to fight with putting our shoes on to do so.

Another tip of mine to survive the apocalypse.

Dad rolls up the sleeping bag and wraps it in a garbage sac to keep it dry, then straps it to the bottom of his backpack. He slips a grey sweatshirt over his head and puts the hood up. The two of us fling our bags over our shoulders, instantly weighing us down a bit. Next, we go to our guns.

They sit side by side on the table. His a semi-automatic that has seen its fair share of bloodshed. Mine is relatively new. A nine millimeter that's a silvery black color. We bartered for it right before we left Florida. Dad thought it was about time I had a gun of my own and found this small one with plenty of bullets to keep me going. The perfect gift for a nineteen year old girl who lives in a world with zombies and vamps.

I lift my gun from the table and make sure the safety's

on so I don't accidently shoot myself. I've seen that happen before and it's not pretty. Then I make sure it's loaded with all ten bullets and smile.

"Ready to go?" he asks, after he has his own gun in his grip.

"As ready as I'll ever be, pops." I say with a smile.

I follow him to the door and wait for him to unlock it. He takes one last look through the peephole before pulling it open.

***

It isn't raining as bad as the sound on the tin roof made it seem. The drops are huge but it's really only sprinkling. The sky isn't even that dark. The storm must be letting up. The clouds are still grey, but the wind isn't howling like it was last night. There were times I thought the whole shack would blow over.

Thankfully it didn't.

We walk away from the shack and head for the street. The town we stayed in overnight has been abandoned for a while now. Many of the buildings have been burned down and are merely charred remains along the roads. I know there are monsters hiding somewhere in the buildings that are left standing. Vamps are probably watching us from the dark corners as we walk in the middle of the street. They might not like the daytime, but that never meant they slept through it. They're just planning their next attack on whatever victim gets in their way. So far, it hasn't been us.

I don't know which I hate the most of those two beings. They're both pretty scary and mean and, well let's face it, disgusting. Both can't really stop themselves from being the way they are. They can't control what they do or why they do it. Almost makes me feel sorry for them. Then I think of what they've done to this world and to me and the sorrow disappears.

I will admit that I kind of like the zombies a bit more. Those ones are really easy to predict and outrunning them is a breeze. They are slow and uncoordinated and *much* easier to kill than the vamps. If you don't have sunlight, you're basically screwed. Still a tough decision on which monster to hate the most. One day I might have an answer. Today's just not that day.

We stay on the main street for a while until dad gets his map out to make sure we're going the right way. I'd hate to get going and find out we're lost. That's how we ended up turning around and heading south again for three days. It wasn't until we got to one of those green signs along the highway, the ones that say which city is coming up. We saw one that said Orlando 87 miles and had to turn around from that point.

We got to the northern border of Georgia and we're about to cross into Tennessee. The town we're headed to is there somewhere, a few hours away I guess. I'm glad dad knows where we're going, because I have no clue. When it comes to reading maps or taking directions of any kind, I'm not good at all. I get all befuddled and lose my spot and then I just get aggravated and take it out on the world.

I'll stick with my gun and leave the navigating to someone else. Shooting is more my style. The very first time I shot a gun was right after this pandemic began. One of those zombies was in the backyard of my childhood house and I picked up my dad's gun and shot it right in the head. I've never been more proud of myself until that very moment. I just can't believe it took my dad so long to get me a gun of my own. It's hard having to borrow his whenever we get into a jam.

We turn onto another street in the town, this one will lead us to the highway. As we walk, I look around at the buildings on either side of the street. Quite a few of the windows are busted out and a few have smoke damage covering the window frames. If it weren't for the burned buildings, the abandoned cars, and the few rotten bodies strewn all over the place, this wouldn't have been a bad town to live in. I'm sure at one point it was teaming with life and people were always happy to go through their day. Walking down the streets with smiles on their faces and not a care in the world. That's not this place. It's filled with death and despair. It's nothing now. A desolate land I'm glad to be rid of soon.

Dad spots a red minivan stranded in the middle of an intersection. The drivers' window is busted out and the passenger door is wide open. I know what he's thinking. Maybe the keys are in it and maybe it still has a full tank of gas with an undead battery. I'm thinking the same thing and hoping for it too. A nice ride in a car would be like heaven right now regardless if the engine's roar would attract zombies.

He closes in on the van, his gun raised out in front of him in case we see movement. I stay a few feet behind him with my fingers wrapped tightly around my own gun. I've never gotten nervous about approaching a random car or even going inside a building. I know those things are hiding everywhere we go and it's always the thrill of a good adventure that drives me forward. One of the reasons I never complain about going across the country with dad.

I watch as he peeks inside the broken window and looks through the vehicle. I rush up to him when he waves for me to come. The smell of decay burns my nose when I get close enough and I quickly cover my face with my hand. Slouched over in the drivers' seat is what's left of a human. It's so badly decomposed I can't tell if it was a man or a woman. Maybe if the head was still there I could get a clear answer on that. There's just nothing left except a black, gooey hole in its neck.

"Want some jerky?" dad jokes, nodding to the corpse.

I grimace and shake my head. There's not much left to the body other than the dark brown muscles and the bones poking through. One of its hands is still wrapped around the steering wheel. Dad's right though. It does look like a giant piece of beef jerky. Not a flavor I'd be willing to try anytime soon.

"The keys are still in the ignition." he says.

I stare at the body again and take a deep breath, "I think I'd rather walk than force myself to help you take that thing out of there. Other than that, I doubt it will start anyway. That person probably died with the car running."

He nods, "Most likely. Let's just keep going."

"Don't get me wrong, dad, I do hate walking and would love to find a car. Just not that one. It's much too gross for me."

"Oh, quit being such a girl, Bridge, you have seen worse." He says as we start walking again.

Another point for dad at being right on something.

The zombies themselves look far more disgusting than the corpse in that van. Most of them have dried blood covering the front side of their body. It's soaked into whatever clothes they were wearing when they got infected. If they were wearing any clothes at all. I've seen one with its left eye dangling out of its socket, a brown mucus pouring from the hole. The zombie I'll never forget, would have to be the one with the bottom portion of its jaw completely gone. It used to be a woman wearing this bright pink dress, stained with blood of course. Her tongue hung out of her mouth, draping onto her neck like a necklace. I'm not even sure how she would eat a human without the bottom part of her jaw. But, she came after us with a hunger that died the second my bullet entered her brain.

These are much better memories to relive than any old slumber party with my friends. I *honestly* don't think I could get anymore sarcastic than that.

The on ramp to the highway isn't much farther. A couple more blocks and we will be putting plenty of distance between us and this town as possible. We've gotten lucky and haven't run into any monsters in this town, but I know we will once we get back on the highway. For some reason, zombies tend to roam the highways and interstates looking for a fresh meal. Granted, there are normally more of them hiding in towns and houses, but we see our fair share of them on the highway. Vamps tend to stick to the cities and the woods so they have a place to hide during the day. The one good thing about traveling when the sun's out.

I let out a yawn as we ascend up the ramp. A few scorched cars are crashed against the concrete wall to our right. I don't bother to look inside those for the remains of their owners. With any luck, they died in that crash and aren't roaming around as one of the monsters.

There's a black sedan at the top of the ramp with its trunk popped open. The front end of it is completely under the back end of a truck. I can hear the rain drops hitting whatever is in the trunk, it sounds like plastic. Dad goes up to the car and stares at what's inside. I walk to his side and look down at the few white grocery bags. All of them still full of their contents.

I turn to dad and he smiles at me, "Shall we hunt for treasure?"

"We shall." I reply in a regal tone of voice.

The first bag I rip into is filled with the blackened remains of whatever food was once in there. It smells awful so I don't bother touching anything to find out if any of it is still good. I toss that bag aside and grab another. This one is much better than the first. No food or fresh bottles of water, but I find something so amazing I feel like I could cry. There are three bottles of the most wonderful thing I've seen in a while, all a different type. Shampoo, conditioner, and body wash. This person must have ran out of everything when they bought this and, luckily, no one's stumbled upon until now. "Soap." I say my heart filled with glee. "This doesn't get traded when we get to that town, by the way."

Dad chuckles as he continues going through the bags. He isn't having much luck. Whatever food left in the bags has long since expired and all that's there is a black pile of mush. The wrappers are even black and disgusting. He gets down to the last bag and we *finally* find something good. Four cans of soup, two chicken noodle and two beef stew, a box of noodles we could trade at the town along with the jar of spaghetti sauce. Dad's not much into boiling noodles like that. He likes to the easy meals to prepare. If we're lucky, our find will get us a dry place to sleep for the night.

"Turn around so I can put what we're not going to trade in your pack," dad orders and I obey.

Once he has my bag zipped up, with the food and my amazing new soap inside, I spin around again so I can put the noodles and sauce in his pack. He likes to hold onto whatever we can use to trade for things. I know the reason for that, I just don't like to think about it. He says he wants me to hold onto the food just in case something happens to him. That way he'll know I won't starve when he's gone. I'm glad he plans ahead for this, but I hope and pray it'll never come down to it. I don't know how long I'd survive without him.

***

We've been walking for about an hour and nothing exciting has happened. No zombies and no other humans. The rain picked up for about ten minutes and we waited under an overpass until it let up. It actually stopped completely when it did, but the dark clouds remain to block out the sun. At least I'm able to take the hood off my head and let the breeze blow through my hair. We check every decent looking car we pass, hoping one of them would start for us. They're all completely destroyed or the keys are gone and neither one of us knows how to jump start a car. There was one that still had gas and the keys were still in the ignition, but the engine wouldn't turn over. It was a blue Mustang and it would have been a fun car.

Dad reaches behind him and pulls the bottle of water from its holster on the backpack. He was able to fill it up with rainwater as we waited under the overpass. With pollution practically nonexistent anymore, the rain isn't very toxic. I guess the atmosphere is cleaning itself up while the living creatures on the planet suffer. A little ironic if you ask me. Humans spend millions of years inventing new things, killing our atmosphere and the planet, then we create the one thing that is wiping us out while cleaning up the planet in the process.

You're welcome Mother Earth.

"Thirsty?" dad asks and I take the bottle from him.

I only take a small drink in order to conserve it. No saying how long it will be before we come across fresh water again. We don't venture into the woods looking for lakes or anything. It's dark in there and the trees block the sunlight so the vamps can come out and play whenever they want. Too risky for us.

I hand him the bottle and he puts it away, "Hey, dad, what day do you think it is?"

He shrugs, "I don't know. It feels like a Thursday so we can guess that."

"How does it feel like a Thursday when you don't know what day it is either?"

Again, he shrugs, "It's like when I was at work and I just get that feeling that in one more day I'll be able to relax with my family at home."

"Maybe it feels like that because we're going to make it to that town today." I reply.

"Probably, but it's better than feeling like a Monday. Those are almost as bad as Sunday."

This is what our conversations consist of now. *Boring.* Mainly back and forth small talk about what day it is or what month it is or how far we've traveled and boring stuff like that. Nothing fascinating happens anymore to give us something different to talk about. We have run into people who actually keep track of the day and month thus ending part of our boring conversations for a while. We met a guy in Florida right before we started walking north. He said it was March 2019, about five years after the wonderful cure. Hard to believe I was only fifteen when this all happened.

I remember the day I first found out about it. I was in the backyard with my older brother. He was practicing his pitches for baseball and I was there to toss the balls back to him. He could throw the ball so fast, it took the bark off the tree and left a good sized dent in the trunk of it. Then the cure came along and ruined everything.

Our mom came running outside screaming at us to come in. She said it wasn't safe anymore and we couldn't play outside. The news was on and I saw the monsters on the screen. Zombies chasing people through the streets of New York and vampires hunted whoever was out at night. Security cameras showed the evidence of the attacks and was enough to get my family panicking. My older sister came home from college because they were shutting the place down. It was a scary time and leaving the house made every-thing worse.

We tried to wait it out, hoping for the best every day. A few of the neighbors stayed behind with us while the rest drove off in search of safety. It wasn't until the next door neighbor's house got broken into at night and they all ended up dead. Well, one was for sure dead and her husband came back as a vamp. That was our cue to leave and dad thought it was best to head to Florida and find his parents.

That trip brings up too many horrible memories and I don't want to recall them right now. I close my eyes, fight back my tears, and walk onward with dad.

"You alright over there, Bridge?" he asks.

I open my eyes and nod, "I'm fine, just thinking."

"Care to elaborate?"

"Not this time." I'm sure he knows what I'm thinking about.

He nods and we keep going. A semi-trailer blocks the road ahead of us, so we cross the median to get around it. Before we get to the other side, I can smell a familiar aroma drifting through air. I've gotten pretty good at sniffing these things out. Their deadness floats on the air, finding its way up my nose. Not the best smell on the planet, but at least it's a sign something worse is about to come our way.

There's three of them standing on the other side of the overturned trailer. They're staring at the wheels on the bottom of the chassis, probably trying to figure out if the rubber would taste good or not. Zombies can be such idiots some-times.

Dad doesn't see them at first and is about to walk out to where they could see him. I quickly grab his arm and yank him back so we can hide behind a parked car. We don't make a sound. Noise would draw the zombies to us.

I peek my head around the car so I can get a good look at the zombies. I know they're gross, but something about them makes me want to see what they look like before I blow their heads off. Of the three of them, one is a man and the other two are women. The man is wearing a bloodied suit and his pants are ripped off at one of the knees. The only thing left of that leg is bone and I'm surprised he's still standing. One of the women is half naked wearing only her bra and underwear. A nice gouge is missing from her stomach and blood drips from her mouth. The other woman seems relatively clean compared to the other two. She must be a newbie out to learn the ropes with the ones who turned her. Poor girl. This will be all over with soon though.

I sit back and lean against the car with dad, "I've been itching to kill a zombie lately. Can I take the lead on this one, dad?"

He sighs, "A father's only dream is to hear his daughter ask to kill some zombies. Go for it, sweetie. Make this old man proud."

I smile and roll my eyes. He is so *cheesy* sometimes.

There are a few times when we come across zombies or vamps on our journey and we like to make a game out of killing them. The zombies are really easy to tease. You just have to get their attention, let them lumber on over, and when I can see the black haze of their eyes, *Kablam!*, they're dead. I kind of get a little excited when it comes to killing those things. They're just so easy.

The vamps are fun when we are looking for food during the day and we find one hiding in the shadows of a building. I think they get too hungry sometimes and forget about the sunlight and chase after us all the way outside. In a matter of seconds, their skin begins to boil and turns a bright red color. The worst thing about watching them die, is the horrible scream they let out as they fall to their knees and let the sunlight burn the hell out of them. But, like I said, it's fun to lead them on and let them think they're going to get a good meal.

I slip the bag off of my shoulders and leave it on the ground next to the car. I stand up, turn the safety off, and ready my finger on trigger of the gun. I take a deep breath and step out from behind the car. I reach up and tighten my pony tail. It's been a few days since I've had the extreme pleasure of destroying the things that have taken so many human lives.

There were only two zombies last time and we took them out in a matter of seconds. We didn't really take the time to tease them at all.

I walk across the highway toward them and enter the grassy median. The weeds are so tall they reach my knees. I've walked through thicker weeds on this journey with dad, so these are nothing. I freeze when I get to center of the median. The three of them are still hovering together, not giving me the time of day. I'm surprised they haven't smelt me by now. Normally zombies pick up on humans faster than the vamps. These ones must be too in tune with staring at the tires to even look my way. Like I said, they are idiots.

With the gun clutched in my fingers, I open my lips just enough to let a whistle escape and I play them a tune that sounds like birds chirping. It doesn't confuse them at all and they turn their mangled bodies toward me.

Let the groaning commence.

The sound they create used to scare me. It gave me nightmares for months. But after listening to it for so long, I guess I got used to their songs. A demonic melody that literally wakes the dead. I think they only moan to let others within range know there's food nearby. I don't get why they would do that when they would have more to themselves if they just stayed quiet. All I can hope for right now, is that the three of them are the only ones around here.

The half-naked woman leads the pack with her arms stretched out in front of her. A typical zombie look, but she's the only one doing it. She lets out a horrible screech and moves her legs as fast as she can. The man moves slightly faster, even with a messed up leg. He sort of limps as he walks and I can hear a crunching sound coming from his boney leg. The third lags behind and her song isn't as loud as the others. She still has the black, bloodlust lurking in her eyes as she slowly saunters behind the other two.

I wonder what she used to do when she was a human. Her clothes depict a fairly decent looking older woman, maybe in her late thirties. Maybe she was a teacher before all this happened. She probably loved waking up early and going to school to mold the young minds of today. Too bad something had to come along and ruin her life.

Much like the other two, she can't control what she has become and for a tiny second it pains me to have to kill them. I know there's no cure for either the zombies or the vamps, but part of me has always wished there could be one so I wouldn't have to keep killing them. Their human selves could be in there somewhere, trying to fight what they've become. It's doubtful, but no one will ever know.

They're closing in on me, about fifteen feet to go. I can smell the death on them even more now and I scrunch up my face in disgust. They're practically screaming at me, riping me apart with their black eyes. Blood oozes out of the man's mouth as he lets out another bellowing moan. He's the first to lunge at me and the first one I raise my gun to. The blast echoes all around us and he falls to the grass with a hole in his head. A brown slime gushes from the wound and his eyes stare up at the sky.

His death doesn't faze the others, it only makes them move faster. I take a few steps back and aim my gun at the naked one. Her arms are still reaching out for me and I pull the trigger. Another direct hit to the head and she falls face first on the ground. A smile crosses my lips and I stare at the third and final zombie.

There's something different about her this time. She notices the other woman dead on the ground and stops rushing at me. Her blackish eyes look from her dead friend then back to me. It's almost like she's weighing the options, considering what she's about to do. Even if she doesn't come after me, I still have to kill her. It's the only way to keep these things under control.

"Just pull the damn trigger, Bridge!" my dad's voice calls from behind me.

I know I shouldn't be lingering about killing this one.

She might seem like a newborn zombie, but she's a zombie nonetheless. She's still a man-eating monster who's doomed to wander the planet killing innocent humans with no control over what she's doing. A monster that needs to be stopped no matter how confused I am by her reaction to the death of the other woman. Zombies don't have feelings and therefore shouldn't stop to weigh the options of coming after their dinner.

I stare at her for a few more seconds. She forces herself to take a small step closer to me. I hold my gun up high and take a deep breath. Her eyes take a sudden change to something a lot more malicious. Blood seeps out through her gritted teeth and she lets out a screeching wail, sounding more like a banshee than a zombie. Just as she leaps with her arms reaching out for me, I pull the trigger a third time. She falls to the ground at my feet and I loosen my grip on the gun as I lower it to my side. My eyes look down at the ground and stare at her lifeless body right in front of me. Her bruised arms stretched out in front of her and a gaping hole in her head. The bullet passed right through whatever was left of her brain.

Her body twitches a tiny bit and startles me just enough to get me to shoot her again. I got her in the head and some of that brown mush squirts up into the air. Lucky for me, it doesn't touch my skin.

"You alright?" dad asks.

I roll my eyes and turn around to head back to him, "I'm fine. Just weirded out by that last one."

"Yeah, it did seem to hesitate before lunging at ya. I almost had to rush over and show you how the master does it." He jokes.

I shake my head as I step onto the concrete, "You're the master alright. The master at almost getting caught by those things a few minutes ago."

"Oh be quiet." He says as he hands over my backpack.

I swing the bag over my shoulders. I look over to dad

who is currently staring down at my feet with a smile. I raise an eyebrow and glance down to see what's so funny.

"Are you kidding me!" I shout. "I got that goddamn brown crap all over my boots."

Dad gets a good chuckle out of my sudden whininess for my boots. I wouldn't complain at all if they were old and beat up. I *just* got these right before we left Florida. They aren't supposed to get ruined yet.

"Don't worry, when we get to a puddle you can wash them off. I'm sure that shit won't stain your precious boots." The smile on his face makes me roll my eyes at him.

"You better be right because you were wrong about it not staining my last good pair of jeans. I could never get the smell out of them and I had to throw them away." I say as we start walking again.

"Oh, quit being a girl. You'll be alright." He says, then puts his arm around my shoulders and we move onward.

***

A few hours ease by and it's after lunch. I'm ever so thankful for having a watch to keep track of time. It's one I found raiding my grandparents' house when we were in Florida. Nothing special, just a knock-off brand with rhinestones around the face of it. A few have fallen off since I obtained it. It's the kind you wind up whenever the battery starts to die. I make sure I wind it up at least every other day. It might not matter, but it's a nice thing to know what time it is and right now it's time for me to eat.

My stomach growls and it's loud enough to catch my dad's attention. He smiles and laughs a bit. He's always good about keeping the mood light and making fun of me when I'm having issues. At least he stopped giving me crap about my boots since I was able to get the zombie blood off of them.

"What's for lunch, dad?" I ask, already knowing the answer.

He rubs his chin with his thumb and forefinger for a second to think about it, "Hmm, maybe we'll stop off for some fast food at the next exit. A hamburger sounds pretty good right now."

I nod, "Yes it does. One with extra pickles and loaded with the good stuff. Lettuce, mayonnaise, and so much cheese."

"That does sound like an amazing lunch to me. You're buying this time." He says and we both smile.

"As long as you pay for our steak and baked potatoes next time." I retort.

"Totally." He takes his bag off and digs inside for the sack of apples.

We could stop and boil a can of soup, but that would take too much time and it's best to save that for dinner. There are only a few apples left, two for each of us and we decide to eat the rest of them for our lunch, instead of rationing them. Nothing *near* as good as a hamburger or pizza or steak or *anything* that isn't fruits or vegetables. The last time I ate something other than fruit and the occasional can of soup, was at least a year ago. This nice family let us stay with them for two nights during a rain storm. They made the best sandwiches I've had since this whole thing started. They made their own bread and had a few cows they kept for the meat. It wasn't much, but it was far better than what we were used to.

I finish with my first apple and start on the second. I

can still hear my stomach growling, but it's growing faint. I can't wait to get to that town so we can rest in an actual bed and be around living people for once. The dead aren't as fantastic as they seem. That's mainly because they're dead and we have to shoot them right away. My dad can be kind of annoying, too sometimes. I know that's bad to say, but when you're around the same person day in and day out for god knows how long, you start to get sick of them. I love my dad more than life itself, but I would do just about anything for other human contact.

"How much longer till this town? I'm getting tired of walking." I ask.

He shrugs, "Shouldn't be much farther. We'll get there before dark, about suppertime."

"How do you know this is a nice town? We've never been there and those rumors you heard aren't always true."

"We just have to trust what we hear, Bridget." He replies. "When you can't look places up on the internet, you have to trust what others tell you. I've been told this is a nice town. The people are friendly and stick together to keep each other safe. We'll just stay long enough to rest, get supplies and more food. After this place, it's a pretty long walk to our next stop."

"Longer than three months?"

"Not quite that long, but long enough." He shows me a sly smile, "There are a few bigger towns and cities along the way that I'd rather not stop at. I've heard too many bad things about those places and we're safer if we stick to the smaller towns."

"Good plan." I add, then take the last bite of my apple.

I toss the core on the ground and wipe my hands on my jeans. Then I reach for the bottle of water and take a drink. The bottle is about half empty and still slightly cold. I glance up to the sky and stare at the grey clouds for a second. It hasn't rained since that downpour a few hours ago. Maybe a few sprinkles here and there, but nothing to get us soaked.

I actually prefer the grey clouds over a nice sunny day. It matches the depressing mood of the rest of the planet. In my mind, there's no point of enjoying a beautiful sunny day when millions of zombies are out to destroy you. Same with the full moon and bright stars at night. They aren't enough to take away the horrid nature of the vampires waiting in the shadows to attack you and drink your blood. I think the weather should match the mood of the planet. Dark and dreary. Then again, we would never see the sun if that were the case.

Dad finishes his second apple and tosses the core and the empty sack to the ground. No sense in holding onto the trash, it only takes up space in our bags. Space we could be using to store things we find to trade for good food.

We pass by another pile of cars and trucks. This time it looks like the van at the front of the wreck lost control. It must have rolled, causing about ten other cars to collide behind it. A few of them were really nice cars at one point. A convertible, a really nice black sedan, and a bright blue sports car I would have loved to drive. Unfortunately, it is sandwiched between a rusty Corolla and some kind of SUV.

"Makes you wonder what happened to cause that accident, huh dad." I say as the two of us stare at the wreckage.

"Some people are idiots and can't handle driving with a zombie or vampire attacking them." He replies.

"Yeah, they should have taught that in drivers' ed." I joke. "Not like it would have made a difference to me since I never made it to that class."

"I'll still taught you how to drive. It's not my fault vehicles just don't work like they used to anymore." He replies.

"That's for sure." I say. "Walking is okay, though, at least we don't have to get out and push things out of our way."

"Or worry about other humans trying to steal the car

away from us." Dad adds.

We pass the accident and we're on a part of the highway with trees surrounding both sides. It looks like it goes on for miles and for some reason the woods always seem to make me nervous. I'm sure that reasoning has something to do with the fact that my first encounter with a vamp was in the woods.

I'll never forget that night.

My mother thought it was a good idea to get off the road and camp amongst the trees for the night. Us girls slept together while my dad and brother kept watch. There was one vamp in the area which they didn't see. It was more than our family needed and more than my brother could handle. I remember waking up to the sound of his blood being sucked out of him while my dad was frantically loading the rifle to take another shot.

The vamp was pale and its eyes an eerie grey color. It's hair was white and glistened in the firelight. When my dad finally got the gun loaded, it let out a horrible screech as the bullet entered its gut. The next shot went through its heart and it fell dead on top of my brother. We buried Charlie at the campsite with a cross to mark the grave and vowed to never go in the woods at night or any time of day again.

As I stare at the woods now, all I can think about is how they're in there watching us, wishing they wouldn't burn if they came into the daylight. The grey clouds let just enough sunlight through to kill them instantly if they ever tried. At least during the day there's always something to protect us from one of our enemies.

"Quit staring at the woods, Bridge," dad says, "I know they're in there too, but you can't let your mind think about them. That's how you let your guard down and something worse happens."

I nod and quickly turn my head away from the trees. I hate thinking of my family, other than my dad. I hate when the rest of them pop into my head like that. I can always feel the horrible rock in my throat and it lingers there for a while, even after they've left my mind. I know it's normal to miss the people you care about, but I just wish those feelings would go away. I wish the joy I get out of killing zombies and vamps with dad was enough to make me stop missing them so much. Unfortunately, the world doesn't work that way. I'll always be stuck with these feelings.

At least I still have dad. It's been the two of us for about a year now, even though it feels like longer. He and I have gone through a lot together since we left our home in West Virginia. There were five of us when we left and over the years of traveling and walking across the country, our pack has dwindled down to just the two of us. Things shouldn't have turned out this way. The world shouldn't have turned out this way.

"You okay over there, Bridge? You seem a little lost in thought." Dad says.

"I'm fine, just thinking about stuff." I reply, thinking always seems to get me in trouble.

"You're thinking about them, aren't you?" he always knows what's on my mind.

I swallow the lump in my throat and nod, "I miss them and I really wish they were here."

"Me too," he says, "Although I'm sure right now your sister would be whining about her feet hurting from walking for so long."

I smile, "Yeah and she'd force Charlie to carry her for a while. Which he would because he was too sweet to turn anyone down."

"Yep and your mom would be trying to get you to act more like a girl and stop shooting a gun."

"I guess killing zombies and vamps for the sake of humanity isn't ladylike enough for her." I kid.

"She never was big on that. Always thought the humans were still alive in there somewhere. That someday they would come back and everything would be fine again.

Even after Charlie, she always looked at them like they still had a soul." Dad says, "I saw that same look on you right before you killed that third one back there."

I glance over at him and he turns his head away from me. He only does this when he's tearing up and doesn't want me to see him cry. He has it in his mind that he has to be the tough guy for both of us. That he has to be the one who doesn't think about what happened to our family. How we lost everything we care about in the world because of those damn monsters. He doesn't realize that I'm plenty tough and he can let his feelings show every once in a while.

I turn away from him and think back to that female zombie, how she hesitated before coming at me. Maybe she did still have a soul somewhere deep inside that non-beating heart of hers. Maybe her hesitation was her human self trying to show up again. If there is still a soul in those zombies, what kind of soul would be left? The kind that knows what they've done and wouldn't want to live with that knowledge? Or the kind that has been so deteriorated by the disease there's not much soul left? Either way, I think I did whatever human was left in that woman a favor. Not just for her, but for my family. A sort of payback for what's happened to them.

"I don't think they have much of a soul left anymore, dad. Whatever they do have, isn't human anymore and I don't think they'd want to live like that. Killing them saves them in a way and I don't think mom saw it like that. She was the kind who only saw the good in people and couldn't see that there's no good left in these creatures. Whatever good they might have had at one point, has been stolen from them and I don't think they'll ever get it back." I finally say after a few seconds of silent walking. "And God help the man who comes up with the cure for all of this. Who the hell knows what would come next."

I see a smile come across his lips and he looks my way. There's a slight hint of red to his eyes and he wipes whatever tears were in them away with his hands.

"First vampires, then zombies, probably some sort of hideous mixture of them both if someone ever tries curing them now." Dad says with a sly smile.

"Let's hope we don't have to find out any time soon." I reply.

***

Another long day of walking practically over and my dogs are barking. I'll never get used to walking nonstop for miles until we come to a stopping point that's safe enough for us to spend the night. I'll never get used to trying to find that safe place either. Sleeping under the stars is what we normally do. We *can* get lucky enough to find an old shack or small house that we've deemed monster free. Still, I'd do anything for a few nights in a nice town, in a comfy bed where I can sleep without worrying for once.

I'm sure dad can tell I'm getting a little excited about getting to this new town he's been telling me about. I've only asked him a hundred times when we're going to get there and he's only told me a hundred times that we'll get there when we get there. I don't mean to be a constant pest about it, I just really want to get there. Being able to speak to another human being will be so rewarding after a walk that seems to be never ending.

We pass by an old green sign sticking out of the ground on the side of the road. All three city names on the sign are crossed out with black spray paint. That's a way for travelers to tell those places are not safe and empty of living beings. All of those places are still miles away and the place we're looking for isn't too far ahead, according to dad.

"How much farther did you say?" I ask, getting a little worried we won't make it by sunset.

"The man who told me about this place said we'd be real close when we find the sign with the markings on the back. He told me all the cities on the front of that sign will be crossed out in black paint, just like the one we're passing now." Dad replies and both of us turn around to see the back of the sign.

A smile crosses his face when he sees the message painted against the silver back of the sign. I'm hoping he can figure out what it means because to me it's just gibberish.

"What does 'S4N' mean, dad?" I ask as I read the back of the sign.

"It means there's a safe place four miles north of here. They do it like that so the vamps won't figure it out." He says.

"Clever."

He nods then we turn back around and keep walking, "What time is it, Bridge?"

I lift my hand and glance at my watch, "Almost five."

"Okay, we should get there within the hour." He says.

We keep walking, moving a bit faster than before. I know he wants to get there sooner than risk us being out after dark. It's one thing to have zombies to deal with, they're easy to predict and easy to kill. When the vamps come out to play, life gets a little harder to defend. They have advantages where we do not. I've heard they can see in the dark and can hear humans coming from miles away. They can smell and catch us before we can even react. I've even heard of them jumping a few feet into the air to land on the humans who were trying to kill them. Like I said, things get even worse at night.

About twenty minutes pass by and we come across

another sign on the side of the highway. This one just has a giant "S" scribbled on it and I can only assume it means we're really close to the town. There's an off ramp packed with abandoned vehicles leading down a slight hill. We take that exit. Out of habit, I keep my gun ready and peer into every car we pass just to make sure there's nothing hiding inside. A few have their owners still decomposing in the drivers' seat. They are so far gone, there aren't even flies buzzing around them anymore. Doesn't mean I'm not still going to be on edge.

We make it to the bottom of the ramp and stop at the sign. Dad looks both ways before we keep going. To the left isn't pretty. What looks like an explosion has charred the way with a dozen burnt cars stuck under an overpass. Body parts, mainly bones, are scattered about in the street and in the grass. I can see a few black skulls lying about, their bodies are somewhere else in the mess. I can't tell what the cause of the blast could have been, but I have a feeling it was planned out.

The way the cars are all shoved under the overpass, like they're trying to block something. Maybe zombies or vamps were trying to get through and the humans needed a faster way to keep them out. A bomb seems to do the trick just about every time.

To the right looks much better. A few more cars are stranded in the middle of the street, almost like they're still driving. I'm sure the people who once owned them were probably on their way to work or school or to visit their families. They most likely didn't expect things to go array and they had to leave their vehicles in order to escape whatever madness came their way.

I follow dad along this stretch of road and start to notice a very odd smell coming from the way in front of us. Not really an *odd* smell, just not something you want to smell when you're approaching a place you really want to be. It is the familiar smell of smoke, ash, and a putrid smell of death.

As I inhale through my nose, I start getting a really bad feeling about what we are walking into.

"That doesn't smell right." Dad says, under his breath.

He completely read my mind.

He starts to pick up the pace and I follow close behind. We go around a slight bend in the road and are faced with a hill we have to climb. The smell gets stronger as we ascend up the slope and pass the abandoned cars. Dad stays a few feet ahead of me and I nervously clutch my gun. Who knows what could be waiting for us on the other side of this hill.

Dad makes it to the top and stops moving. His head angled downward at whatever lay in front of him. I pull myself up the rest of the hill and get a good look at what he sees.

Black smoke billows from piles of charred wood. Trash and remnants of clothes and blankets are littered all over the place. Ash floats through the air like snow falling from the sky in winter. The few buildings that remain standing are blackened with smoke coming through the open windows. Burnt bodies are scattered all over the streets and in between piles of rubbish. We found the town we were hoping to find. There just isn't anything left of it.

"Dad," I whisper, "what do we do now?"

He doesn't say anything. He simply swallows his pride and takes a step forward. I stay close to his side as we venture into the town. The smell is much stronger and I have to cover my mouth and nose with my hand in order to keep the stench away. I keep my eyes wide open, peering from left to right, keeping watch for any signs of movement. A few grey pieces of paper blow around in the wind and ash dances at our feet. My hands are shaking and my heart beats faster in my chest. I'm used to being afraid, just not afraid of a ghost town like this.

I move closer to dad, brushing my arm against his. All I can think about is seeing a half-burnt zombie bursting out of one of the buildings to come after us. There's no telling if any are hiding in the rubble or lurking around the out-skirts of town. It really wouldn't surprise me if we see one.

I hear a noise ahead of us and I jump a little. It sounds like a stick breaking under someone's foot. Dad hears it as well and we stop moving. He lifts his gun and aims it straight ahead of us. We hear the noise again, this time louder and definitely footsteps. They don't sound labored, like a zombie, and it's still too early for the vamps to come out.

"Show yourself!" dad shouts.

I keep my eyes staring at the empty road in front of us, expecting to see a whole army of monsters come out of nowhere. Instead, we see a man walking out from beside a building with a rifle aimed right at us. The man is probably the same age as my dad and his clothes are dirty and covered in soot. His jeans are torn at the knee, but there's no scratch or bite mark from what I can see.

After the man walks out, a few more people follow him. Six others to be exact. A young boy about the age of ten carries a baseball bat in one hand and a teddy bear in the other. Three other men around the same age as the first all come out wielding pistols as well. An older woman has her arms wrapped around the shoulders of a girl who seems to be the same age as me.

"You humans?" the first man who came out shouts at us.

Dad nods, "Yeah, and you?"

The man lowers his rifle and nods, "Yeah, we're all human."

My heart slows a tad and dad lowers the gun in his hand. The man starts walking toward us, the small group of people right behind him. The others put their weapons down as we approach one another. Finally, we find other living humans to have some sort of contact with.

"What happened here?" dad asks.

The man shakes his head, "I don't know. We got here

a couple hours ago and found this place burnt to hell. I think the vamps did it. The zombies aren't talented enough to burn a small town down like this."

"Shit." Dad exclaims. "Those bastards are getting crafty."

"Names Jim and this is my family." The man motions toward the others. "My wife, Dena, and my daughter Sherry. My three brothers, Jack, Brian, and Wayne and my nephew Dillon."

Dad nods, "I'm Phil and this is my daughter, Bridget."

"Nice to meet you." Jim says with a small smile.

"Same here." Dad replies.

"You know, we're actually going to camp right outside town. There's another place about half a day's walk west of here and we're wanting to get a fresh start in the morning." Jim states, "The two of you are welcome to join us. We don't have much food to share, but we have plenty of water and enough guns to keep us safe through the night."

Dad's never normally the type of guy to voluntarily stay with strangers we meet on the road. He'd rather not risk getting robbed in the middle of the night or wake up dead.

"I think we will take you up on that." Dad says, totally surprising me. "We have a couple cans of soup we can spare for dinner tonight and it would be nice to sit down with other living people for once."

"Thanks, that's much appreciated. We have some chicken leftover and some old bread we got a few days ago. Not much, but enough to keep us healthy." Jim adds. "Follow me and I'll show you where we made camp."

The small family turns around and heads back to the building they came from. I am still a little wary about going with them. I've heard about running into strangers on the road out here. The ones whom you think you can trust and they wind up literally stabbing you in the back and take everything you have. I can't come up with a logical excuse as to why dad wants to go with them and camp for the night. I guess he's still a little shocked about finding the town in shambles to make a clear decision for us. We'll just have to see how it goes.

***

Well, we didn't get stabbed or shot or robbed, at least not yet anyway. This family is actually really nice. The kind of family I used to have before things went to hell and the world fell into turmoil. Jim, the one who introduced everyone, used to be a basketball coach at a high school in Atlanta. His brother, Jack, the bald one, he used to be a doctor. A good person to have around, especially out here on the road. Jack's son, Dillon, is really quiet and only seven years old. Jim's other two brothers used to be lawyers and even had their own practice in the city when the so-called cure came around. They had a lot of complaints when the cure decided not to be a cure anymore. Jim's wife, Dena, was a stay at home mom who also ran a daycare out of their basement. Their only daughter, Sherry, with her long blonde hair, is a little on the eccentric side.

She sits next to me around the fire. It's in the center of a circle made out of old wooden beams from the buildings. We use them as benches so we can sit while we eat our meal of chicken and a small amount of soup to dip our bread in. Actually, the best meal I've had in a while.

"So, Bridget, how old are you? I'm eighteen, just turned eighteen I think. Not real sure when my birthday was.

We ran into this guy a few weeks ago who was trying to keep track of the days and months and whatever and he thinks it's May and my birthday is in March and I was thirteen when this happened so that means I'm eighteen now. How old are you?" Sherry finally takes a breath after talking a mile a minute.

"Umm, I'm nineteen, but if it's really May then I'll be turning twenty in three months." I reply, then take a sip of my soup, I talk much slower than she does.

"That's so cool. You know I haven't been around another girl my age for a *long* time. It's so nice we ran into you guys out here. I can finally have someone to talk to about anything. Instead of Dillon over there," she motions to the little boy, still clutching the teddy bear, "he doesn't have anything interesting to talk about, ever. All he wants to do is hang onto the stupid bear he found a year ago in an old toy store. He can't go anywhere without it in his hand. Even takes a bath with it, when we are able to do that."

I force my best smile as I listen to her nonstop talking. I turn my eyes to dad who is sitting across from us with the other men his age. He sort of laughs when our eyes meet then goes back to talking to the others. I glance up at the sky and notice how dark it's getting. Soon we'll have to keep quiet and try to fall asleep with the ever present risk of being sucked dry by the vamps. It's never easy to sleep with that on my mind.

"So, Bridget, is it just you and your dad out here alone? Where's the rest of your family?" Sherry asks and I turn my eyes back to her.

"Uh, yeah, it's just the two of us. He's the only family I have left." I reply.

"What happened?" she suddenly got really quiet and sympathetic.

I shrug, "They're gone. I don't really like to talk about it."

She nods, "That's okay, I understand. We can change

the subject."

"Okay."

"So, tell me," she begins, then gets quiet again, "when's the last time you had sex?"

That's one hell of a subject change. It catches me off guard and I'm sure I have the dumbest expression on my face as I stare back at her. Sex is never something my dad and I bring up on a normal day. He doesn't ask me about it and I'd rather not talk to my dad about that sort of thing. I'm not a prude or anything, waiting for my wedding day will never happen. Not only because I'll probably never have a wedding, but I highly doubt I'll ever find a guy out here in this wasteland that's worth giving up my life for. Sex is something I would like to experience at least once in my life, but I don't think doing it with some random guy on the side of the road is how I want to experience it.

I keep my eyes glued to Sherry's and say, "I haven't done it yet."

She smiles, "Really? A hot girl like you has never had sex? The last town we stopped in for the night, I wound up finding this super awesome guy who showed me around town. We made out for a bit and I ended up staying the night in his little apartment. I know, it sounds worse than it is, but I like to live on the edge and go for the things that I want. When I'm in the mood for it, I really like to find the right guy to fulfill my demands."

I shrug, "I guess I just haven't found the right guy yet. I haven't found any guy really."

"Yeah, I hear ya on that. It is slim pickings out here and I don't think it will get any better unless we go off to a big city or something. I don't know how you and your dad are, but we try to stay away from cities. Bad things happen there."

"We don't go there either. We stay on the road and stop in towns when we have the chance." I say, then slurp down the rest of my soup.

"Where are you headed?"

"North to Canada. Dad thinks we'll be safer up there."

She raises an eyebrow out of confusion, "I've never heard of that before. I'm pretty sure these demons are everywhere and I don't think the cold will keep them out of a place. Especially if there's food for them."

"I know, but he thinks we'll find safety and I don't have the heart to tell him otherwise."

"Yeah, there were times when I would have loved to stay behind in one of the towns we've come across. Just let my family go on without me, but I love them and they love me, even with all of my quirks and faults. I can't bring myself to stay in one place and hope things work out for them. If bad things happen to my family, then I'm going to be there to let the bad things happen to me as well."

I smile, "That's a good way to look at things."

She smiles even bigger, "I know, I can surprise you sometimes and say something really unexpected."

Sherry does have her quirks and talks *way* too much, but I can honestly see myself being friends with this girl. She's really easy to talk to, amazingly listens to every word I say, even if it's not a lot. She doesn't talk down to me like some of the other girls my age have done before. There might not be very many humans left in this world and of the few that are left, some can be kind of cruel and hurtful. You would think the high school drama would have died right along with high school. Not everything changes though.

***

I had a decent, peaceful night's sleep for the first time in months. I don't know if it had something to do with the company or that I didn't have to wake up in the middle of the night to take my watch. The only time I woke up was when Sherry decided she needed to go to the bathroom and demanded I go with her. That will always be something us girls have to do together. Not only do we feel safer nowadays when we do things like that in packs, but it brings back a little piece of the world we once had.

I open my eyes and see the sun shining above us in a bright blue sky. The air doesn't smell fresh or clean. Burnt wood and death still lingers in the area. I can't wait to get out of this town and get away from that horrid stench. It isn't the best thing in the world to wake up to in the morning. I would much rather have the smell of bacon and eggs burning on the stove instead of burnt bodies lying in the streets.

I sit up in the sleeping bag. Dad let me use it all night while he took turns keeping watch with the other men. They let us women and the younger boy sleep the whole night. I haven't been able to do that since we left Florida. I stretch my arms above my head and let out a slight yawn. I look around me and notice Jim handing out small chunks of bread for breakfast. It's all they have left to eat and I know their food supply is running low, much like ours. They probably came to that town for the same reason we did, supplies and food.

I stand up and grab the sleeping bag to begin rolling it up. Next, I shove it back in the plastic bag and strap it back to dad's backpack. We kept our bags together on the ground next to me while I slept. Sherry, who slept by me the whole night, stands and I help her fold her blanket so she can stow it in one of their packs. While she's busy with that, I take the time to fix my hair. It got a little frizzy while I was sleeping. I take the hair tie out and smooth all the loose hairs so I can put it back in a ponytail. It's much easier to take care of when it's out of my face all day.

Dad walks over to me and hands me a small piece of the dry bread, "Jim is wanting to know if we would like to join them on their way to the next town. What do you think?"

I shrug as I take a bite, "They seem pretty cool to me and it would be kinda nice to walk with other people for once."

He smiles, "Did you make a friend?"

"I think so. Sherry is definitely different, but I could see myself spending more time with her." I reply.

"Then we'll go with them. We need to get some more supplies anyway." Dad says.

He lifts his bag from the ground then walks back over to Jim. I pick mine up as well and put the straps over my shoulders. I take the last couple bites of my bread as Sherry comes back over to me. The bag she carries is bright pink with an array of feathers dangling off one of the zippers. Mine is simple and boring, a black bag with no decorations on it at all. A good sign that I'm not much of a girly-girl.

"So, are you and your dad going to come with us?" she asks in a hopeful tone.

I nod, "Yep."

She squeals, then jumps up and down in excitement. I smile and try not to seem too surprised at her sudden happiness. When she calms down, she wraps her arms around me and gives me a really squishy hug. The kind I used to get from my mom when I was younger right before she dropped me off at school. The kind of hug that always told me she would miss me.

After everyone is all packed up and the fire suffocated by dirt, we head on our way to the next town. I'm told we will get there sometime in the afternoon so it won't be as long of a walk as I'm used to. Dad walks with the guys his age, Sherry's mom walks hand in hand with the little boy, Dillon, and I walk alongside Sherry. We stay at the back of the group and I have my gun in my hand in case we run into trouble.

Sherry doesn't have a weapon. It doesn't surprise me considering how she is surrounded by strong men who can take care of whatever problem they might run into. All I have is my dad and we take care of things together.

"I'm really glad you guys are coming with us. It'll make this trip so much better now that there's someone else my age I can talk to. You have no idea what it's like to talk to only your mom and four older guys who think they know everything. Dillon doesn't even talk too much." Sherry explains.

"Yeah, it is kinda nice to have someone other than my dad to talk to. You can't imagine the conversations we have sometimes. Most of them are about the weather or us trying to figure out what day it is." I say.

She giggles, "So, have you ran into any monsters out here? We haven't been on the road for very long and only had one run in with a zombie. Uncle Brian took care of that nasty thing though."

"Yeah, we've come across quite a few zombies out here. Yesterday I killed three of them."

"What about vamps?"

"The last one of those we saw was about a week ago. We were rummaging through an old gas station for some food and stuff. It came out of the freezer and was dumb enough to chase us outside in the sun. Thing fried in like a minute." I say with a smile.

"Ewww," she grimaces, "I hate seeing those things out in the sun. They are gross in general, but when they burn up like that, it's so much worse."

I wonder how she's lasted this long after seeing so many disgusting things. The vamps aren't that bad when you look at them. They still look somewhat human. It's the zombies that are far from pretty. Most of them are so disfigured with body parts missing or a good majority of their innards hanging out through a hole in their gut. Makes having a nice dream almost impossible after seeing one.

"You remind me of my sister." I say with a smile.

"Should I take that as a compliment?" Sherry asks.

I nod, "Yeah, she was great, but she was always disgusted by every little thing we came across. I swear she threw up at least once a day because of the awful things we'd see."

Sherry was quiet for a second, then, "I'm sorry you lost just about your entire family, Bridget. I can't say I know how you feel because I'm surrounded by mine. The closest I can get to relating to how you feel, is when I lost my best friend. Our families stuck together for a year after things got bad. Then one night, we found this old house and decided to stay. Her parents went out to patrol the area and never came back. She was so depressed about it, she ended up killing herself. I can at least find comfort knowing she died at her own hands instead of at the mouth of one of the monsters."

"That's horrible. This place sucks." I say.

"Damn right about that." Sherry runs her fingers through her blonde hair, "You know, I used to want to be a ballerina when I grew up. All I ever wanted was to dance on stage with thousands of eyes watching my every move. I took so many lessons and was in so many recitals. That was the best time of my life and I hate thinking how it was all for nothing. You know what I mean?"

I nod, "Yeah, I wanted to be journalist. I was the youngest person on the high school newspaper and wanted to be the editor one day. The best time I ever had was going around the school reporting things and getting to the bottom of whatever was in the school food. I don't think all that time I spent doing the one thing I love was for nothing. Sure I'll never get the chance to be a big time journalist or anything, but I'll always have the memories of when I was a good one at school. I wouldn't trade that for anything."

"I guess you're right, Bridget." She does a ballerina twirl on her heels. "Maybe one day, when we find a safe place to spend the rest of our lives, we'll be able to do the things we love again."

"I don't know. Being a journalist was great when I was younger, but killing zombies and vamps is a much better waste of time." I joke.

She and I share a laugh together and continue following the others. I used to wish for the day when we'd find a safe place out there in the world. Somewhere to live and be happy without the threat of zombies or vampires. After being trapped in this world with those monsters for almost five years, I lost the will to believe a safe place out there exists. That no matter where we go, we will always run into them. We will always have to defend ourselves and kill what used to be innocent people just to save our skins. Even if there is a safe place out there somewhere, I don't think I'd even fit in with a normal crowd anymore. It's been so long since I've lived a normal life, I think I have forgotten how to do it. It would be easier for me to continue on this long, arduous road with dad always by my side instead of forcing myself into an uncomfortable world with strangers.

That might sound odd to some, but I really don't care what they think. Let them think I'm weird for enjoying the thrill of shooting a zombie in the head or luring vamps out into the sunlight. Those things aren't going to kill themselves, so someone has to do it. Why not let a nineteen girl who grew up in the suburbs do the job. This one is extremely good at it.

***

It's been a couple hours since we left the blackened town and the sun in the sky has warmed up the world around us. I take my hoodie off and shove it inside my backpack. It's much cooler without that thing on. My red t-shirt still looks somewhat new, just a small stain on the bottom from when I was trying to clean my gun. Black grease doesn't come out very well. My shirt isn't as clean or nice as Sherry's navy blue shirt with a crazy flower design on the front of it. She obviously knows how to stay clean better than I do.

The wind blows through my hair and I take in a deep breath through my nose. A familiar scent catches my attention and I go on full alert. This little gift of mine has come in handy on quite a few occasions. While on this journey with dad, I've gotten good at sniffing out the horrible scent of something that's dead, even when no one else can smell it. It's not the rotting on the ground type of dead either. It's the still walking around on two legs trying to eat whatever living thing they can find type of dead. They have a very particular odor which I have trained myself to get used to in order for us to know when one of them is close by. They sort of smell like old, dried blood mixed with feces along with vomit. They just smell like something that will never stop decaying, whereas the actual dead just smell dead . That smell doesn't stick around forever like it does with zombies. I'm really only good at it when we're downwind of whatever monster is nearby, but every so often I catch it when I least expect it.

I take in another long inhale through my nose and the smell intensifies. They can't be too far ahead of us and I know we will run right in to them. I rush away from Sherry who begins to protest and join my dad with the other men.

"What's the matter, Bridge?" dad asks.

"I can smell them. The zombies, they aren't too far ahead." I reply.

Jim and his brothers turn their heads toward me, "What are you talking about? I don't smell a thing." the bald one, Jack, states as he breathes in through his nose.

"Trust me on this, I can smell them." I say.

We walk onward and get to a bend in the road. A few cars are parked along the side and kneeling behind the last car in the line, are two of those damn zombies. On the ground next to them, is the twitching remains of whatever human they made a meal out of. I can hear the slurping sounds as they munch away at the person's flesh. Not a pretty sound to hear. Another not so pretty sound to hear, specifically when there's a zombie or vamp within hearing range, is the sound of a loud gasp coming from Sherry right behind us.

The slurping stops as well as our walking. One of the zombies gets to its feet and lets out a throaty moan when its black eyes come across our group. The other one is still busy devouring whatever it can of the human on the ground.

The zombie starts walking toward us, blood and pieces of skin dripping from the corners of its mouth. I can't tell if it is a man or a woman. The clothes are baggy and the hair is too long to tell. It's face is too bruised and bloodied to get a clear shot at trying to figure out what gender it was at one point. Not like it matters all that much anyway. In a few short minutes, it'll be just as dead as the person it was snacking on.

"What do we do?" Jim whispers.

I glance at my dad and smile. The kind of smile begging him to let me do what I'm best at. He rolls his eyes and waves me onward. Another chance to show off my amazing zombie killing skills in front of our new friends.

I turn to Jim and his brothers, "Don't worry. I got this."

I walk away from them and head toward the zombie. I notice one of its legs is broken between the ankle and the knee. The bone is sticking out, but that doesn't stop it from trying to run at me. If it were a normal human, they would be screaming out in immense pain at even trying to walk on a leg that badly damaged. Zombies don't notice pain, at least they don't care about it if they do.

It lets out another bellowing moan as I get closer to it.

Just a few more feet and I can get a good shot in. No sense in wasting bullets when I know I'm too far away to get a good shot. I raise my gun and stop walking. It still comes at me, anger burning in its black eyes, blood dripping from its face. I still can't tell what gender it is, but in three seconds it *really* won't matter. I take a deep breath, count slowly in my head. *One, two, three.* The gunshot echoes all around us and is instantly followed by the thud of the monster falling to the ground. A perfect shot right to the head.

Next, I turn my eyes to the second zombie. The instant it heard the gunshot, it stood up from its prey. This one I can tell is a man, one with a good sized hole in his chest. It looks like a fresh wound too, brown mush is still oozing out of it. The person on the ground over there must've tried fighting back and failed, miserably. This one grits his brown teeth, squishing out whatever part of the human he was eating between them. He lets out a few grunts and begins sprinting toward me. Normally these things don't run that fast, but this one seems to be in good shape and is actually running at a decent speed.

I raise my gun one more time and point it at his head. Something tells me not to pull the trigger just yet. Why not have a little fun for once? I lower my aim a tad and take a shot. The bullet goes right through his throat and he falls to the ground. Brown mush squirts out of the wound I created as he twists and turns in the street. Whatever moans he tries to make come out raspy and muffled.

As I watch the thing squirm on the ground, an image I haven't thought of in a while pops into my head. The morning my sister, Maggie, was killed at the hands of a zombie. About two years ago, on a morning much like this one. We had just made it to Florida and were out exploring, trying to scavenge a little bit. One of them came at us by surprise and attacked my sister. It got one bite on her neck and she started to make the same sounds as that zombie on the ground in front me. Dad got a good shot at the zombie who bit Maggie, but it was already too late for her. She lay in the grass, tossing and turning, the poison already coursing through her veins. We didn't get the chance to say goodbye and dad had to take the pain away from her. He made the right choice. There was no stoping what she was about to become.

"Bridget, take the next shot!" dad's voice broke through my thoughts and I stare at the zombie.

It manages to roll onto his stomach and is trying to pull himself up to his feet. Anger courses through my body as I think of my sister. She didn't deserve to die like that. She was a good, kind-hearted young woman who I looked up to at one point in time. I quickly take a few steps until I'm standing within arm's reach of that thing. In my heart, I know he used to be a normal person. Someone who had gotten in the way of a zombie and came back as one himself. He didn't deserve that. He reaches his arms out, still making raspy moans and tries to grab at my ankles. I aim my gun at his head and he looks up at me.

In his eyes, I see pain and suffering. The kind of look that is begging me to end the horrible life he had been given. I steady the gun in my grip and close my finger around the trigger. Another echo from the gunshot and this one's head falls to the ground

Another zombie dead and for good this time.

I stare down at my kill, the puddle of its black blood growing at my feet. I lower the gun and listen to the footsteps of the group coming up behind me. I wonder what they think of me after seeing me take down two zombies alone. A hero? Maybe because I was the only one brave enough to go for the shot. Dad would have done the same if it were our family. He never would have hesitated like the others.

I turn my eyes toward the feet of the person the zombies were munching on. The left foot is twitching. I lift my feet and head for the body. Whoever it is, or was, would be much better off completely dead. Turning into one of those monsters has to be extremely painful and is not what anyone on the planet should want.

I can hear the raspy breathing coming from whoever is lying on the ground. I step around the back end of the car and stare down at the body. A woman, maybe in her thirties or early forties. I can't tell with all the blood on her face. A gaping hole in the middle of her stomach reveals whatever is left of her organs along with some of her intestines strung onto the concrete. Her eyes are rapidly moving back and forth and I can already see the black haze taking them over.

Dad walks up next to me and stares down at the woman. I'm sure he's thinking the same thing I am. *How the hell did she survive that?* Most of what's in her stomach is either gone or hanging outside her body. She has to be in an intense amount of pain and is probably in shock so she doesn't know what's going on anymore. I can't help but feel sorry for her. She was probably on the road to the next town and got mixed up with those two zombies. Or they were travel partners and failed to tell her they had been bitten. Whichever it was, it's not a good way to have your life come to an end.

"I got this one, Bridge." Dad says as he angles his gun at her face.

I look away and stare at our feet. The sound of his gun echoes around us and her foot stops twitching. Dad puts his hand on my shoulder and leads me away from the gory scene. Sherry and her family are standing a few feet away with their eyes wide as they stare at us. I can't tell if the look on Sherry's face is that of disgust or excitement. Her mouth is hung open, but there's a slight smile on one side. Any second she would let us all know what she's thinking.

She takes a step closer and says, "Oh. My. God. Bridget. That was awesome! You were like a freaking hero just now, going up to those things and blowing their heads off like it's nothing. *Ugh*, I wish I had your bravery."

I look at the ground and shake my head. At least she wasn't disgusted and grossed out by what I just did. Being thought of as a hero tickles my fancy a bit.

"I think we should keep going." Jim says. "With all that noise from the guns, someone or something had to hear it. We don't need to run into anything else out here."

He leads the group again and dad joins the other guys. I lag behind with Sherry who links her arm with mine. I smile and walk alongside her, following the others.

***

We make it to the next town just before suppertime. Luckily there's still a town here to make it to. Nothing special about it. Looks like it was at one point the main street in a bigger town or city. The welcome sign has been hand written, apparently they renamed whatever this place was, and it is now called Nash Tenn. Obviously a mixture of Nashville and Tennessee, but according to dad we aren't even close to where Nashville should be. Maybe that city died over the last few years and the founders of this one wanted it to live on in some way.

The buildings that make up the strip of the small town are nothing but old brick or wooden buildings, many with boarded up windows. Some had just been recently built and turned into apartments or houses for the people who live here. My eyes pass over the buildings as we walk by them. There are two right at the entrance to the town, one on each side. They are built up higher than the others, serving as watch towers. I can see two men standing in each tower with big guns in their hands. They stare down at us as we enter their town.

Past the towers, are a few shops and even a small restaurant. Next door to the restaurant, is a fenced in area with cows and chickens roaming around. The food source. In the middle of the street, people have set up small stands trying to sell or trade whatever they can to make a living. We walk past one with a young woman trying to sell handmade clothes. Another with an older man selling wooden carvings that he made himself. More useless things that would just take up too much space in our bags.

People walk right on by us as we make our way down the street. Most ignore us, but there are a few who send snarling glances. I guess these people don't care for newcomers in their precious town. I notice how they are dressed differently than we are. The women and younger girls are all wearing dresses with their hair done up nice and neat in buns, not a strand out of place. Sherry and I are comfortable in our jeans and t-shirts and I'm sure our hair doesn't look too pretty. The men and boys here all wear jeans with button down shirts. The men in our group are wearing jeans too, but they are covered in mud and grime. Their shirts are soaked in sweat and all of us are in desperate need of a shower.

I catch a few odd glances from some of the girls around my age. They all appear to be prissy with their upturned noses and flowery dresses. I can't imagine trying to run away from vampires or zombies wearing one of those things. Fighting one off would just look ridiculous.

"I feel *way* out of place here." I say to Sherry.

"Me too. All these girls look really mean and bitchy." She replies quietly.

I smile, "Yeah, they do."

We keep walking, following the guys. We pass a few more shops, one for clothes and another for bags of rice and oats. Then we get to the housing and apartments. People sit on their porches or on the balconies of their apartment and stare at us as we walk down the street. There's a large building on the right hand side with a man in a black suit standing right outside the door. It's an old hotel, a small one too. The lights around the old marquee are busted out, except a remaining few. It doesn't seem like the town has electricity so that sign probably hasn't worked since just after the cure got out of hand. The glass windows are boarded up with small holes in the wood so people can see out to keep watch. This building screams eerie, but it's right where we are headed.

The man standing outside the building approaches us and says, "Welcome travelers. You look like you're in need of a place to stay the night." His deep southern accent makes me smile.

Sherry's father steps forward and says, "That would be nice. We have been walking for quite some time now."

"Well, come on in. I have plenty of rooms available and you couldn't have picked a better night to come to Nash Tenn." The man states. "My name is Henry Johnson, owner of this fine establishment and curator of the big event tonight."

He takes a bow, then leads us in through the blacked out doors to the hotel. We follow and step inside the small lobby of the building. The red carpet under our feet is stained brown and torn in a few places. The walls are a faded yellowish color with gold trim and candle holders hung all over the place. The front desk is made of mahogany wood with a young woman sitting in a chair behind it. She passes us all a huge grin as we follow Henry Johnson through the place.

He leads us up a flight of stairs to the second floor, then turns left down a hall. Candles are spread out to light up the way, some in glass fixtures on the walls and others hanging from the ceiling in old chandeliers. We walk to the end of the hall where we stop next to an old ice machine.

"I have two rooms available for your large group." Henry pulls a key out of his pocket and unlocks a door to our left, then pushes it open. "As you can see, there are two beds in this room as well as the other. We also have cots on hand in case some of you prefer to sleep alone. We managed to get the plumbing to work so ya'll can take a shower and get cleaned up. The water is cold, but it'll still get the job done. As for payment, I just ask that you attend our little event tonight and have a good time. I would also appreciate if ya'll would clean up after yourselves in here, like keep the beds made and your dirty clothes off the floor. If you choose to stay another night, we'll talk about payment then, but enjoy yourselves tonight."

"What's this event you keep bringing up?" Jim's brother, Brian, asks.

Henry smiles and clasps his hands together, "Oh, it's just down the street under the big tent they're setting up. We have a bit of a show to put on and we are more than excited for it. This doesn't happen very often and this town tends to make a big deal out of it."

"Why at night?" dad chimes in.

"That's the only time it can be done and you will see why, sir." Henry digs in his pocket and pulls out another key, then hands both keys to Jim, "Ya'll can use the room across the hall as well. Have a good evenin'."

He leaves all of us to stand alone in the hall. Each one of us has a real dumbfounded look on our faces. Almost seems too good to be true and I'm really curious as to why he gave us the rooms for free. Normally, inns and motels on the road want at least some food or something rare as a trade to stay overnight. Something this amazing, there's got to be a catch.

"Okay, my family will stay in one room and, Phil, you and your daughter can have the other." Jim states.

Sherry steps forward in protest, "No, I wanna stay in whatever room Bridget is in."

"Sweetie, I don't think our new friends want us encroaching on their lives any more than we have already." Jim replies.

Dad shakes his head, "You haven't encroached on our lives at all. You helped us out when we needed it, why go our separate ways already. Let the girls stay together for the night. It might be good for both of them to have normal teenager time at least once in their lives."

Jim moves his eyes between Sherry and my dad. He's thinking about the decision and I find myself really hoping he says we can stay together. The last actual sleepover I can remember having, was right after the "cure" was released to the public. I had a few of my old girlfriends spend the night and it was a blast. We played truth or dare most of the night and made prank phone calls to some of the guys in our grade. I know spending a whole night with Sherry won't involve any of that, but it will still be much better than spending another night alone with my dad for company.

Finally, Jim opens his mouth and answers, "Okay, Sherry, Dena, Bridget, and my nephew Dillon, will have this room. We will take the room across the hall. Not ideal, but I think you're right. They should have some girl time."

Sherry lets out a happy squeal while a pretty big smile crosses my face. Jim hands the key to his wife and she goes to the door to unlock it. The guys start tossing their bags all over their room and get comfortable on the beds. Dad stays in the hall and stares at me.

"I think I'm gonna go find a shop to trade for supplies and get us some dinner. I'll find out what time their little show is going to start so we can go together." He says.

"I'm going with you." Jim adds.

I nod, "Okay. I think I'm going to make good use of the working shower and get cleaned up."

Dad sniffs the air and jokes, "Yeah, you are getting a bit ripe."

"A few months on the road will do that to you." I say. "And you smell pretty gross yourself."

He smiles then leans forward and plants a small kiss on my forehead, "I love you, Bridge."

"I love you, too, dad." I say, realizing this will be the first time in a very long time that we will be apart for more than a few minutes.

He walks away from me, with Jim by his side, and I turn around and watch him leave. I worry, of course, thinking I'll never see him again. That's why we always make sure we say we love each other before we go anywhere alone. Just in case we never get the chance to say it again.

***

Henry Johnson was absolutely right about the shower. The water is freezing cold and the pipes let out loud groans whenever the water gets turned on or off. The pressure itself isn't so bad, not a waterfall like I would love, but it gets the job done.

I have candles spread out in the bathroom to light up the place. It's just your typical hotel bathroom. The walls are a faded yellow color and the white tiles have started to turn grey from years of dust and grit getting stuck on them. The mirror is cracked in a couple spots but doesn't mar my reflection.

I use a small amount of the soap we found and feel cleaner than I have felt in a while. I actually smell like a girl again, an ocean fresh girl. After I dry myself off, I wrap the white towel around my body and step onto the small mat on the floor next to the bathtub. Goose bumps cover my arms and legs after the short, cold shower. My wet hair hangs over my shoulders.

I stare at myself in the mirror, shadows dancing across my face from the flames of the candles. I step closer to get a better look at myself. There are a few freckles across my nose and cheeks, under my brown eyes. My hair is starting to get long again, almost time for me to trim it up a bit. On my left shoulder is the scar I got when I was ten years old. I flipped over the handle bars on my bike after trying to jump this ramp my brother built in the driveway. Mom was so furious at Charlie and worried beyond belief when the doctor said I fractured my collar bone. I had to get surgery and keep my arm in a sling for a few weeks, but it was worth it. Charlie and I had a lot of fun that day.

A smile comes to my face as I think back to the wonderful times I spent with my family. Times I'll never forget. I used to terrorize the hell out of my sister. Steal her clothes, her makeup, and hide them all over the house just to make her stay home even longer to hang out with me. She always acted like she was mad about it, but I could tell she really liked spending time with me. I'm sure she'd love me right now for finding soap and shampoo in that car yesterday. She wasn't much into getting dirty or not taking a shower for more than a day. She was the girly-girl in the family.

My backpack is sitting on the floor next to the toilet. I sit on the closed lid and start sifting through the bag for my fresh pair of clothes. Another pair of dark blue jeans, the skinny kind so my boots will fit over them easily, and a black V-neck shirt with a few white stars printed on it.

I get dressed quickly and slide my boots over my feet. I put the watch back on my left wrist and glance at the time, just past seven. Then I go about shoving everything back into my bag. I dry the soap and shampoo bottles off and put them at the bottom with my other clothes on top. I offered to let Sherry and her mother use it, but they had some of their own. Something they were able to trade for when they left the last city they visited.

Before I walk out of the bathroom, I stare at my reflection again. My hairbrush is sitting on the grungy counter next to the sink and my hair tie. I run my fingers through my wet hair and bring it back into a pony tail again. One of these days I'll have a reason to let my hair hang down.

I stuff my brush in the bag and zip it up. Then I open the door and walk out into the main room. Sherry is sitting on the floor at her mother's feet getting her blonde hair pulled back into braided pigtails. She smiles up at me, then winces as her mother tugs at her hair again.

"I could do yours next, Bridget, if you want me to." Dena suggests.

I shake my head and politely say, "No thanks. I like it like this, it's easier to take care of."

"Your father came back. He said that event starts at sundown and apparently the whole town is going to be there. Other than a few people to watch for those creatures out there." Dena says, tugging on Sherry's hair again.

I nod, "It must be one hell of a show if the whole place is going. Makes me wonder what they have going on in this town."

"I know, it could be like a weird church thing or something." Sherry adds.

"I've never been to church." I comment like it's nothing.

Both of them give me an odd look. Even the little boy, Dillon, who's playing with his teddy bear on the other bed, turns his head and passes me a confused look.

Church was never forced on us. It was a choice in my family and all of us chose not to go. That and over the last few years I've really begun to question my beliefs in a higher power. If there were such a thing as God, would they really cause this to happen to the people they created? Would they really allow a horrible thing like zombies and vampires to advance to the top of the food chain? The human race is endangered now and I really find it hard to believe that someone in the sky is in control of it all. I used to think a god was behind everything, but things happen, you lose people you care most about, and you begin to change your mind.

"You've *never* been to church?" Sherry asks, both her eyebrows raised.

I shrug, "My family never went to things like that. We'd go there for weddings and stuff, but never for an actual church service."

"Don't you believe in God?" Dena asks.

"Not really. I have no reason to given all that's happened to this planet and my family. I like to think if someone is in charge of it all, he'd give me a break and quit with the bullshit." I reply.

Dena shakes her head and lets out a sigh, "I know you have lost a lot of close people in your life, but you can't blame God for that. He's the reason all of us are here. He chose us to survive this thing. How can you think God didn't keep us around for a higher purpose? How do you know that God didn't leave you alive so you can do something better with your life?"

Again, I shrug. There's no sense arguing with someone who is apparently a diehard Christian. They tend to stick to their beliefs no matter what and always try to win the argument. I know what I believe in and to me it's the right thing. If there is a god out there, he sure has one strange sense of humor and needs to lay off the death for a little while.

A knock comes to the door and I turn my head. It's a soft knock, nothing too angry sounding or like the person on the other side of the door wants something other than to see how we're doing. Still, every time I'm behind a closed door, I can't help but wonder who or what is waiting on the other side. With two man-eating creatures roaming around, you never know what you'd open the door to. I take the few short steps to the door and twist the knob. I let the door swing open and see my dad's smiling face staring at me. He hasn't had the chance to get cleaned up and, knowing him, he'll probably wait. After all, there are four other grown men he has to share a room with.

"How was your trip through town?" I ask.

He shrugs as he walks into our room, "Not bad. Got a few things so we can head out again tomorrow. More ammo, some food, stuff like that. How was your shower?"

I follow him to one of the beds and sit down next to him, "Awesome. I think you need to take one now. The soap is in my bag if you want to take one here. We're all done in our bathroom."

"Yeah, I probably should before we go to that thing tonight. Jim is taking one across the hall anyway. So, if you ladies and young man don't mind, I'm going to hog your bathroom for a bit." Dad says with a smile.

Dena chuckles and shakes her head. She's just finishing up with Sherry's hair, not a strand out of place. Other than her jeans and t-shirt, she'll fit in perfectly with the other girls in this town. I'm proud to admit that I never will. It's good to not fit in once in a while.

***

The sun has set and our little group is on our way down the street to whatever event is going on. Sherry's mother decided to stay behind with Dillon, but the rest of us are a little curious to see what this town has going on. I'm actually a lot curious. I've never been to something like this before. I might even be a little giddy about seeing what this place has to offer. That doesn't mean I'm going to go without my gun. I have it tucked safely in my jeans behind my back with my shirt to cover it. You never know what could jump out at you, even in this seemingly safe town.

There are quite a few people walking down the street toward the big tent that is setup at the other end of town. It's so massive it takes up enough space to build two good sized houses. The people here seem really excited and probably know exactly what is going to be under that tent. The girls are all traveling in groups, whispering and laughing amongst themselves. The boys walk together, staying relatively quiet, but wear smiles on their faces. Quite a few men wander the streets with shotguns and rifles, keeping watch and making the rest of the townspeople feel safer at night. Must be nice to have this kind of security at all times of the day and night instead of just yourself and your father to rely on.

We make it to the tent and have to walk past a couple guards at the entrance. Their eyes are busy scanning for vamps and zombies so they pay no attention to the people entering through the open flap.

Inside are dozens of metal folding chairs set up in rows on the grass. People are filling them as they come. The chairs are facing a stage-like platform at the other end of the tent. Torches illuminate the wooden platform and a section of it is blocked off by a black curtain, hiding whatever they don't want the rest of us to see. There are a few tall torches standing at the back of the tent behind the rows of chairs so everyone can see where they're going.

Sherry leans close to me and whispers in my ear, "What do you think it is?"

"I have no idea. Hopefully nothing horrible." I reply.

We choose a row of chairs at the back and sit down. I'm sandwiched between my dad and Sherry who is sitting next to her father and his three brothers are on the other side of him. My heart is beating pretty fast not only because I'm nervous about whatever is going on, but from being surrounded by a hundred or so random people I've never seen before. I feel a little claustrophobic being trapped in a room with all of these strangers. If something bad were to happen and we need to make a quick getaway, there's the good possibility of getting trampled by some of these people. I'm used to not having to take a risk like that, so being in this large of a group is really keeping me on edge. I hope this night goes by quickly so I can get back to that nice, cozy bed waiting for me back in our room.

The rest of the people file into the tent and choose places to sit. Many of them search for a place up close to the stage, but all those chairs are taken. A good majority of the town is here and all of them are staring up at the stage. My eyes are glued to it as well, patiently waiting to see whatever surprise this place has to offer.

After the crowd quiets down a bit, a familiar face walks onto the stage. He's wearing a black suit and tie with a top hat on his head. It's Henry Johnson and he reminds me of a host I'd see at a circus. The huge grin on his face even screams that this is going to be a good show, much like a circus. He's even carrying a cane as he walks to the center of the stage.

"Welcome!" he waves his arms out and smiles to the cheering audience. "I'm sure all of you are wondering what I have in store for you this fine evening. I must say, it took a lot of effort to make this night happen and I am more than pleased with how things have turned out so far. This will be far better than what we brought out last month. We all know how that night ended."

Laughter comes from the crowd and Henry begins walking back and forth across the stage, working the audience.

"Tonight, ladies and gentlemen, I have something all of you are dying to see. An up close and personal look at something which has taken a while for us to get our hands on. This is nothing like those zombies we brought out, those were boring and predictable. I'm sure all of you can remember the monotonous moaning they let out that night. We were all disappointed in their act last month." Henry exclaims.

My heart is racing faster now and I have a gut feeling what they have hiding behind that curtain. If he's saying they had zombies here a few weeks ago, there's only one other thing they could have gotten their hands on that would surprise anybody. Why they would want to capture those demons, is far beyond anything I can comprehend.

"Fellas," Henry turns his attention to a few men standing off stage, "if ya'll would please bring out our main event." He looks back to the audience, "No sense in keeping ya'll waiting when this is what you came here for."

I can feel my hands shaking and I'm starting to find it hard not to reach for my gun. Why would this town be fascinated with keeping zombies or vampires as their prisoners? Why would they celebrate like this? Why ask myself questions like this when they're only making me more nervous? This place is the exact opposite of what a safe town should be.

The crowd is cheering at the top of their lungs as we watch two large men roll something on the stage. A black sheet is draped over it, but I can tell it's some sort of cage. The bars underneath the sheet stick out a little, letting the cloth dip between the gaps.

I glance over to Sherry. She's huddled up with her father, scared out of her mind. She told me they haven't had many run-ins with the vamps and I'm sure they were hoping they wouldn't have to face them any time soon. Especially not in a town they hoped to stay the night in. I look to my dad and his eyes are focused on the black sheet.

"Dad," I whisper to get his attention, "I think this might have been a bad idea."

He nods, without turning his head to look at me, "I was just beginning to think the same thing."

I turn back to the stage and Henry is so excited, he

doesn't want to wait any longer. He grips a corner of the black sheet and with one quick jerk of his wrist, he rips the cover off and reveals a large metal cage. My jaw drops as I stare at not one, not two, but three pale vampires reaching their arms through the bars of the cage. The crowd around me cheers and claps their hands only making the vamps more excited. Even from where I'm sitting, I can see the long, white fingernails on their hands as they try reaching for any-thing within distance. Their sharp teeth glowing in the light from the torches. I really want to pull myself out of that chair and leave before anything bad comes this way, but the cur-iosity of wanting to see what happens is pinning me in place.

My eyes dart from one vamp to the next. One is an older man with a bald head. Dried blood on the corners of his mouth. His clothes are torn and he's not wearing any shoes. The one standing in the middle is a woman. Her hair a light blonde that's almost translucent. She is letting out a loud shriek trying to press her face through the bars. The third is a young man, probably my age. His hair is a light shade of brown and the purple veins in his forehead and neck stand out against his pale skin.

All of us can see the hunger burning in their eyes. They reach out for food, for blood, and they are so close to it, but they just can't grasp it. Their arms aren't long enough to grab one of the men a few feet away, but they still reach for him. And he just stands there with his arms folded across his chest, laughing at them. I know they're vampires and horrible creatures who literally suck the life out of human beings, but they were at one point a human being themselves. They lost who they once were the day they were bitten and transformed into those bloodsuckers up there. They don't deserve to be locked in cages and mocked for amusement. In my opinion, they all should be killed.

With a smile on his face, Henry stands off to the side of the cage and speaks to the crowd again, "Now as I have said before, it was quite a feat to capture these things. It took ten of our good men to setup the perfect trap. If you were closer, you would be able to see the burn marks on their bodies from the sun. These vampires sure are stupid when it comes to hunting their food. They'd do anything just to get a taste of us."

He laughs. The crowd laughs. I sit in the back of the room staring in shock at what these people find entertaining. I don't think they realize just how dangerous the vamps in that cage really are, especially when they're hungry.

I keep my eyes on the cage. It rattles and shakes with every move the vampires make. They shriek and shout at us, screaming words I can't quite understand. It sounds like they are yelling "food" or "hungry". I can see their lips moving and I know they are capable of speech. Being this far back and having to listen to the entire crowd cheer, it's kind of hard to hear what those vampires are screaming for.

"Who wants to be brave enough and see how close they can get to the cage?" Henry shouts to the crowd.

A few people jump up and run to the stage. It gets harder to see what's going on as they rush up there. I stand in order to get a better look and the rest of our row stands with me. The vamps start shaking the cage even more as their food source comes closer to them. I can see the deranged looks on their faces even from all the way at the back of the tent.

Two young girls approach the cage first. They don't get very close before getting scared at running back to their seats with playful grins on their faces. An older man gets a little closer and smacks the bars of the cage with his wooden cane and laughs about it on the way back to his seat. With every person who gets close, the cage moves a little more. It doesn't seem stable or strong enough to hold them and if I strain my ears just enough, I can hear the metal of the bars clanking together. It's only a matter of time before things get out of control.

A few more souls brave Henry's challenge and chicken out before getting close enough. Then a teenaged girl with bright red hair stands alone on the stage. She stares at it while those behind her urge her to get closer. She takes a few baby steps to close the gap between her and the cage. She's closer than anyone else has gotten before and I can tell she feels pretty proud of herself. She spins around, her dress twirling around her legs, and a huge grin crosses her face. The crowd goes wild. In that very moment, with her back turned, the vamps are able to reach her.

She screams as the younger of the three is able to grab her hair and yank her closer to the cage. The other two dig their claws into her skin while she screams out for help. The crowd screams and a few even rush on stage to help her. I cover my mouth with my hands and stare at the horrific event. It's already too late for that girl to have any chance at surviving.

Guns are drawn and a few bullets whiz through the air hitting the flesh of the vamps. One hits the arm of the older man and I watch him growl at the man who shot him. He lets go of the red head, blood dripping from his fingers and mouth. He slams himself into the bars of the cage and it shakes much more ferociously. He does this again and again.

Dad grabs my arm and says, "We need to get out of here."

I nod and turn to Sherry. Her family is one step ahead of us and already on their way to the exit. A few others in the crowd are rushing to get out as well. I hear another gunshot, followed by a sound even worse. The crowd gets quiet and I turn my head to the stage. The older vamp was able to use all of his strength to bust through the metal door on the cage. It flew off its hinges and crashed to the floor.

The red head is already dead or will be soon. She has turned pale and they let her fall to the floor in order to make their way out of the cage. I see Henry take off through a flap in the tent, leaving the other men to shoot at the vamps. Their shouting doesn't help much. The female vamp screams and jumps five feet in the air landing on top of one of them, biting into him the second she touches him. The other two jump into the crowd and it's at that second I reach behind for my gun. I grip it tight in my fingers and prepare myself for whatever happens.

Dad keeps my arm in his grasp and we try to get to the exit. Even more of the townspeople are pushing and shoving their way to get out. They bump into whoever is in their way, knocking people off balance and letting them fall to the floor. Their screams burn my ears as I listen.

"We need to get back to the hotel!" dad shouts over the screaming crowd.

I don't reply. It's no use to try to say anything when everyone is yelling around you. There are more gunshots and I turn my head one last time toward the commotion. The younger vamp is jumping through the crowd, knocking over anyone in his path. I can't tell if he is trying to get out or trying to find the perfect person for his meal. Either way, I want no part of it.

We are able to make it to the opening, but there are still plenty of people shoving each other on the outside. I try to stay close to dad, even when dozens of people shove by me and he loses his grip on my arm. I am forced to move with the crowd, not knowing if dad is right behind me or not.

Out in the open, everyone is running back to their homes for safety away from those monsters. I move out into the middle of the street, then turn around to face the tent. My eyes scan the faces of the people still piling outside, hoping one of those faces will belong to dad.

My heart pounds. I jump with every gunshot I hear. I don't see him in any direction I turn. The screaming grows louder and more intense and I keep my eyes glued to the opening in the tent. The crowd of people running outside is growing thin and there's still no sign of my dad.

"Dad!" I scream and my voice blends in with the other shrieks around me.

Two older women, holding each other rush outside

and the way is empty for a brief moment. There are three more gunshots and the air around me changes to an eerie silence. Others around me notice and stand in the street as well. I see a shadow moving behind the fabric of the white tent and pray to whatever god in the sky there is that my dad will be the one walking outside. I can't take any more of my heavy breathing or the sound of my gun shaking in my hand. This has already been too much for one night.

The thing responsible for the shadow comes strolling outside, blood seeping out of his mouth. Bullet wounds in his legs and stomach and still he stands as though he isn't hurt. It's the younger of the three vamps and I'm hoping the only one still alive. A few of the people around me stop waiting for their loved ones and run to wherever they think they'll be safe. The fear of leaving my dad behind, not knowing if he's still alive, is one thing holding me back. Another thing, is just the straight up fear of that damn vampire.

It takes a few steps toward me, tilting his head to the side as our eyes meet. He seems too young to be so violent and bloodthirsty. Yet, he slowly moves closer to me and has the ability to frighten me much more than the zombies. The way his grey eyes burn a hole straight through to my soul. The way he saunters toward me with a bloodlust look on his face. That's enough to scare the hell out of even the toughest guy on the planet.

Don't get me wrong, I am more than capable of killing him. My aim is pretty damn good, but being this close to something like him, I'm completely frozen. Fear is causing the gun to weigh my arm down and not shoot this thing in his heart. My mind is screaming at me to do it, but my body can't comprehend the message.

"Brave?" his growly voice speaks to me, then he takes in a big whiff of air through his nose. "I smell...fear. Not brave."

His words are choppy but he gets the message out. The next few steps he takes toward me are quicker and filled with hunger. The look in his pale eyes should be enough to get my hand to raise my gun. It should be enough to get my legs to move so I can run away. I'm just so frozen in place and await whatever fate is about to come.

It's too late to run now, he'd catch me in a matter of seconds. His footsteps get louder and I hold my breath. I shut my eyes tight and wait for my life to flash in the darkness behind them. Then I hear something that allows me to breathe again. A single gunshot echoes around me and when I open my eyes, the young vamp has fallen to the ground. I look down at him and see a gaping hole in his back where the bullet entered and struck his heart. My eyes move back up and I let a few tears fall from them.

Dad stands at the opening of the tent, a rifle in his hands. I keep my distance away from the vamp on the ground and run to my dad. He drops the gun and wraps his arms around me, squeezing me in a tight bear hug.

"I told you we needed to get to the hotel. You idiot, you should have gone." He says.

"I'm sorry. I couldn't leave you." I cry into his shoulder.

"It's okay." He replies as he strokes my hair to calm me, "The other two are dead. A couple guys inside got them, so we'll be okay for now."

He pulls away from me and stares into my eyes. I stare back and wipe the tears from my face. It's a horrible thing to think you lost the only person left in the world who truly cares about you. But, it's a far better feeling to see them right after you thought they were gone forever.

"Let's get back to the hotel. Once the sun comes up, we're leaving and never looking back." Dad says and I nod in agreement.

***

Dad doesn't say much on the walk back to the hotel. We get to our rooms and he kisses me on the forehead and closes the door to the guys' room. I go to the room across the hall and quietly shut the door as well. Sherry is sitting on the edge of the bed, rocking back and forth. Her mother sits next to her with her arm around her shoulder, an ill attempt to comfort her. The second I close the door, both of them turn their eyes to me and Sherry jumps off the bed and rushes across the room. She wraps her arms around me and squeezes. Hug number two for the evening.

"I am so glad you're okay," she says then backs away, "After we got separated, I was so worried that you got caught up with the vampires or something. I didn't see you or your dad."

"We got out okay, almost okay anyway." I reply.

"Did you have a daring escape?" she asks, sounding intrigued.

"I guess you could call it that."

She smiles a bit, "I love hearing about these things. You have to tell me everything."

We wait until her mother and her cousin are asleep before we talk about what happened earlier in the evening. I glance at my watch and it's almost one in the morning. We have a tall candle burning on the nightstand next to the bed we're sitting on. Both of us have kicked our shoes off and sit with our legs crossed in front of us, Indian style.

I keep quiet as I tell her what happened at the tent when we got separated. The horrible shrieks coming from the people who were being attacked. How it was hard to get out of that place without being trampled. I told her how I lost my father and didn't want to come back to the hotel without him. She hung onto my every word when I told her about the young vamp standing outside with me. The one thing I left out was how scared I was to kill it when I had the perfect chance.

"I can't believe it was that close to you." She says when I finish telling my story.

I've never had anyone to tell these crazy things to before. Other than my dad, of course, but he was normally involved in it with me. Having Sherry here to talk to about all this, makes things a lot better.

"You know, I'm not gonna lie, but that younger vamp was actually pretty cute. If he wasn't all veiny and crap." Sherry smiles as she speaks.

I giggle, "He did have that sort of hot, bad boy look going on."

"And he talked to you? I didn't think either the vamps or the zombies were able to do that." She states.

"I could tell he had to really force the words to come out, but I have heard them speak before running into this last one. The zombies can't articulate anything even if they wanted to. I think there's something that gets shut off in their brain when they turn into one of those things."

"A lot gets shut off when either monster comes to life. I sometimes wonder if the people left inside even know what they're doing while they're doing it. Like if they're in there somewhere trying to stop themselves from eating people or sucking the blood out of them." Sherry says.

"I've thought about that too. I've had this feeling that the vamps sort of do, but the zombies, I always figured were too far gone to realize anything. But the other day, we ran into three of them and two were the normal zombies, but the third one was kinda different. She hesitated, almost like she was weighing the options on attacking me." I explain.

She cocks her head to the side and says, "Weird. I can

see the vamps doing that, but definitely not the zombies."

I nod, but don't say anything. I turn my head toward the candle, wax is dripping on the wooden table. The flame's shadow dances on the wall and flickers a bit. Living in this new world with monsters makes me feel wild, much like the flame on that candle. In one quick second, the candle stick could fall over and that small flame would have the choice to take the entire hotel out or dissipate the second it hits the ground. There would be nothing to stop it. I might not be as destructive as a fire, but sometimes, when I'm faced with those horrible things, I can feel that destructive fire burning in my heart and I can't wait to take those monsters out. Maybe it's because I have seen them do horrible things to the human population. Maybe it's because I've seen both the zombies and the vampires destroy my family and I couldn't do anything to stop it. I'd have to go with that second thought over the first.

I look back at Sherry, she's scratching at her scalp where her braids have been pulled too tight. I haven't told her that my dad and I are leaving in the morning. I know it will be a hard thing to do, which is odd because we've only just met. It just feels like we would be great friends, the kind that grow old together and always stay in touch. Every friend I've had in the past is gone now and having Sherry around brings a part of them back. I'm not ready to lose that. I know my dad will never go for hanging around too long. We tend to not stay in a town or city for more than a day or two.

"Sherry, which way are you guys headed?" I ask.

Her eyes snap up and meet with mine, "West to California. Why?"

I lower my head, my hopes shot through the roof and are gone in an instant, "We're still headed North. I was hoping you would be going the same way."

She nods, "Yeah, that would be nice. My dad knows a few people out west and they found a safe place. That's what he believes anyway. We can still hang out here for a while though. We aren't leaving for a couple days."

"My dad and I are leaving when the sun comes up. After what happened with those vamps at the tent, he doesn't think we'll be safe here for very long." I reply.

A sad look crosses her face, "That sucks. I don't want you to leave yet. I want to keep hanging out. I want us to travel together."

I nod, "Me too. You're the first real friend I've had in a long time. I don't want to lose that."

A smile forms on her lips, "I'm your friend?"

"Well yeah. Unless you don't want to be."

"I do, it's just," she begins, "this might seem hard to believe, but before all this happened, I only had my one friend. The one who killed herself. I wasn't a very popular person in school or anything and I got made fun of a lot because I tend to talk too much. People don't really like that, I guess."

"That's because they're stupid. I like that you talk a lot. It gives me the chance to hear about someone else's life other than my own. I don't care that you didn't have a lot of friends back then, it doesn't matter now." I say.

"You are right on that one. Did you have a lot of friends?"

"Eh, I tried to be friendly to everyone. It didn't matter to me if they were poor or rich or weird or anything. As long as they were nice to me, I considered them my friend. So, yeah I was kinda popular in school and whatnot. Not the preppy annoying kind or anything. The normal kind." I joke.

The more we speak, the harder I know it is going to be to leave in the morning. Learning things about each other and getting to know that neither of us want the other to leave, makes this life harder to live. It's bad enough trying to survive each day without getting eaten or sucked dry. Knowing there is another person out there in the world that you care about or have cared about, makes things worse. You'll never know if they're okay. You'll never know if you're ever going to see them again. And you'll never know if they are thinking about you like you are thinking about them. I'd like to hope that Sherry will be one of those people who will think about me from time to time. The crazy, brave friend she once had who stood up to two zombies and a vamp in the two short days we spent together. She'll always be my somewhat annoying friend who always talked way too much for her own good. Not a complaint.

***

Eventually we fell asleep next to one another on the bed. Neither of us wanted to, but our eyes couldn't take it anymore and we had to give in. I didn't dream or anything, at least I don't remember it if I did. Normally I dream about my mom or my sister and brother. Most of the time it ends in a nightmare about how they died and I wake up with tears in my eyes and dad there to console me. This time, I wake up to the sun shining through the cracks of the boarded up window on the wall. Birds are chirping outside and I sit up on the bed to stretch.

I put my feet on the floor and reach down for my boots. I must have shaken the bed a little because Sherry starts moving around as well. I turn my head and see her raising her arms over her head with a yawn. I try to smile when our eyes meet, but inside I don't want to. I know I'll be leaving shortly and there's a good chance I'll never see her again. I turn back to my boots and zip them up once they are over my feet and calves.

"I can't believe it's morning already." She says.

"I know." I stand from the bed and walk over to where my bag is sitting.

We hear a slight tapping on the door and I turn my head. Sherry is the one who gets up and walks across the room to answer it. She pulls the door open and forces a smile at my dad. He's all ready to go with his bag on his back. He's even wearing a nice looking leather jacket. Not sure why. It's actually pretty warm outside.

He steps into the room and looks at me, "You ready to go?"

"Already? I figured we would eat breakfast first." I reply.

He shakes his head, "We'll eat on the road. We need to get going, Bridget."

I fling my bag over my shoulders and say, "I guess."

"Wait for me to get my shoes on. I at least want to walk with you outside." Sherry insists.

"Totally." I say with a smile.

She has them on in no time and the three of us head out of the hotel room. We follow my dad through the short hallway and down the flight of stairs to the lobby. The place seems to be empty and the girl who was sitting behind the desk isn't there this morning. Either it's too early for her to be working or something else is going on entirely.

Dad pulls the door open and allows us to step outside first. We are greeted with the morning sun and a small crowd of people walking together down the middle of the street. They are all headed to where the tent was setup last night.

"What do you think is going on?" I ask when dad joins us.

He shrugs, "I don't know. I guess we'll find out on our way out of town."

"I'll come with you." Sherry adds.

She sticks by my side as we follow the people down

the street. We get to the empty lot where the tent is in the process of being taken down. A few young men and boys are busy folding up the sheets and taking posts out of the ground. They pay no attention to the people scattering around the area. I happen to catch a glimpse of something lying on the ground. It's covered up with a white sheet, a few blood stains seeping through the fabric. After I notice the first body, I see a few more spread out on the grass. Each covered with a light colored sheet or blanket.

Women are crying as they kneel next to their loved ones lying dead on the ground. Their sobs are quiet, but loud enough for everyone to hear. I count at least twelve bodies and I'm sure three of those are the vamps who did all of this. A few people are gathered around the stage setup in the grass. The cage is still lying on its side and blood stains the wood around it. I'm used to seeing this much blood and gore in one place, just not in a place that should have been safe from things like this. Those vamps never should have been brought here, they never should have been captured.

On the stage, everyone is glaring at the one and only Henry Johnson. He is forced to stand in front of the crowd and I assume apologize for the mistake he made by bringing those monsters here. Instead, he keeps his mouth shut and watches as a bigger man approaches him. His hair and beard are red and his biceps bulge out of the sleeves of his black t-shirt. The expression on his face is that of despair and rage. I'm glad I'm not the one who's going to be on the brute end of his force.

"I hope you're happy with what you did here last night, Henry. I told you from the very beginning, capturing those things was a bad idea. You should have known something bad was going to happen." The red haired man says.

"Look, I said I was sorry," Henry raises his hands in protest, "but you have to understand, everyone was in love with the idea just as much as I was. As far as I can tell, you were the only one against it, Tom."

The one he called Tom lowers his head, "Nine of our people were killed last night by those damn things you brought here. One of those people killed was my daughter, Becky." He motions toward one of the bodies lying on stage, her red hair sticking out from under the sheets.

"I know I can't take back what happened. I wish I could, but you'll just have to give me another chance. I can prove to you that I can put this town on the map. I can make this place famous." Henry says.

Tom shakes his head, "We don't care about any of that. We were fine before you got here and we'll be find when you're gone."

"You're kicking me out of town just like that?" Henry questions.

"No, we're not kicking you out of town. That will just give you the opportunity to ruin someone else's home." Tom replies.

"I see," Henry takes a deep breath, "then what does the future hold for me?"

"This." Tom raises a gun and doesn't bother making his aim perfect.

The shot echoes through the air around us and Henry's body falls limp to the stage. I jump a little and Sherry lets out a slight gasp. I've never seen one human murder another. Killing zombies and vamps doesn't count as murder when they are trying to kill you as well. This is different. This is what shouldn't happen at all. Humans need to survive.

"Let's get out of here, Bridge." Dad says.

I follow him away from the massacre and we walk back to the street. He's headed the way we need to go and I stagger behind. It's time to say goodbye. We get to the edge of the small town and I stop walking entirely. Dad keeps going, but makes sure he stays within my sight. I turn to Sherry and can already feel the tears building in my eyes.

"I know we only just met, but I'm really going to miss

you, Bridget." She says.

I nod, "Me too. I wish the world was different and we could be friends forever."

"Yeah, it kind of sucks right now. Maybe we'll run into each other again someday." She says, wiping her eyes.

"I hope so. Just make sure you keep yourself safe and try not to get eaten."

"I don't have to tell you to do the same. You're good at doing that already."

I shrug and glance down to my feet, "So, I guess this is good bye."

"I guess so."

I close my eyes and let a stray tear drift down my cheek. When I open them again, I reach out and wrap my arms around her and squeeze her in a bear hug for once. She hugs me back and all I can think of is not wanting to go. I love being with my dad, he's the best, but there comes a time in every girl's life where she needs more than just a dad to be around. I need a friend and I wish there was a way to talk my dad into going with them to California. It would be impossible to say the least, and I know we have to stick to our plan and keep going north. No matter what might be up there waiting for us. We have to risk going there in order to find safety so we can survive this world.

I peel myself away from Sherry and we both wipe our eyes. I take a few steps away from her and smile through my tears. She does the same and I keep walking.

"I really hope we see each other again someday." I say as I continue walking backwards.

"Me too." She replies.

I have to force myself to turn around and walk quickly in order to catch up with dad. I'll never forget the last two days I spent with another human being I am proud to call my friend. If I do ever see her again, I hope our friendship still remains and we can pick up where we left off here in this town. As for right now, it's just going to be me and my dad on the road again. Just the two of us trying to survive this crazy, hellish world.

***

We spent over half the day in silence. It was awkward. The only time I opened my mouth to speak was to ask for the water and to tell my dad I had to go to the bathroom. My mind is just so wrapped up around how I actually met someone I got along with greatly and I had to leave just like that. Sure, I could try talking my dad into turning back and joining Sherry's family on their journey to the west coast. That would be like asking for the winning lottery numbers right before the drawing.

It's just not going to happen.

So, I keep my mouth shut and wallow in the fact that I'll never have any friends so long as there are zombies and vampires ruling the world. A horrible truth to live with, but one most humans are stuck with. At least us travelers anyway.

We make it to an old rest stop in the middle of nowhere. An overturned semi takes up two parking spots and its trailer blocks the rest of the lot. A few cars are still parked with a layer of dust and grime covering them. Dad glances through the windows of a few, checking for keys or any kind of supplies that would be useful for us. As usual, he comes up empty handed. I walk to an old vending machine with the glass all busted and lying in fragments on the floor. Everything is cleaned out except for a few empty candy wrappers.

One of the things I miss most is chocolate. I could have ate chocolate for every meal of the day and still not get tired of it. I miss the taste, the texture, the way it melted in my mouth with every bite. And there, lying at the bottom of the vending machine is the empty remains of a chocolate bar that would have made this day *so* much better. The damn thing is taunting me. I'm sure if the candy was still in the machine it would probably be expired, but I think I would have eaten it anyway. That's just how much I love that stuff. It's kind of like a drug to me.

I take a deep breath then turn away from the machine. Dad comes up to me, sweat dripping off his brow and chin. He's still wearing his jacket while the sun beats down on us. Night will come soon and the air will get slightly cooler, but I would love to know why he insists on keeping the jacket on.

"What time is it?" he asks, wiping some of the sweat from his face.

I look at my watch, "Close enough to dinnertime that we can have it now."

He smiles, "Okay, let's go to a picnic table and eat. Then we'll scope the place out for anything useful."

I shrug and follow him to a green picnic table next to an old playground, "I doubt we find anything here. It's probably been cleaned out already."

He sits on one side and I sit on the other, "We need to check anyway. I want to be prepared for anything."

"Okay?" I say, half confused.

I take my bag off and set it on the ground next to the table. Dad does the same, then digs inside for whatever food he was able to get in Nash Tenn. A couple small loafs of homemade bread, a few oranges and apples, but no meat or anything sweet. Those were luxuries we couldn't afford to trade for. People normally wanted good things, like diamonds or jewelry for that, not whatever scraps we could find. Sometimes dad would hunt, but that rarely happens. You never know if the meat you'll be eating in the wild is tainted or not. It's best to just stick to the fruits and veggies.

He breaks a loaf of bread in half and hands one to me along with an orange. Then he sets the bottle of water on the table and we each begin taking small bites of our meal. He's taking much smaller bites than I am and I'm not sure why. He's not normally the one to savor food. He's normally the one who will finish your dinner for you if you get full.

"Are you okay, dad?" I ask.

He nods, "I'm fine," it seems like he's hiding something from me.

I take another bite, "You don't seem fine. You're sweating like crazy and you won't take your coat off. You're eating really small bites and I haven't seen you take a single drink of water all day. What's wrong? Are you sick?"

He shakes his head, "No, I'm fine. I promise you that everything is going to be alright. I'm more worried about you than myself right now."

I raise an eyebrow and ask, "Why are you worried about me?"

He runs his fingers through his hair and says, "I'm worried that you hate me for making you leave that girl back there. It made me happy to see that you made a friend in her and it killed me to force you to leave. I just hope you understand that we need to keep going. We can't afford to get caught up in other peoples' lives and have to worry about keeping them alive along with ourselves. It's hard enough to survive out here with just the two of us. You do understand that, right Bridge?"

I slowly nod my head, "I do. I wish it was different though."

"So do I. This is just a horrible place and the less people we have to worry about, the better it is for us."

"Yeah, but it was a good feeling having to protect them when we ran into those two zombies yesterday. Sherry made me feel like a badass after that." I say with a smile.

"You are really good at it. One thing I'll never have to worry about. You'll be able to keep yourself safe in tough situations, even without me." He says.

I stop myself before taking another bite of bread, "What do you mean by that?"

"Nothing," he shakes his head and shoves a big bite of an orange in his mouth, "just finish eating." He replies.

I wait a second before taking a bite. It still feels like he's keeping something from me. Something big. Something I want to get to the bottom of. He won't give it up easily, but I know he'll have to tell me eventually. It will drive me crazy until I figure out what is so important and I'll do my best not to pester him about it. It's just really hard being a teenager and not being told something. If it didn't already feel like the end of the world right now, it sure would with dad keeping a secret from me.

My eyes stay glued to him as he finishes with his bread and orange. His hands are slightly shaking and he looks paler than normal. My best guess is because he won't take his jacket off and he's overheating himself. With it being so close to summer, it's easy to do that out here in the middle of no-where, especially in the southern half of the country. But, he feels like he needs to wear it, so who am I to tell him otherwise.

When I'm finished with the dry bread, I wash it down with a gulp of water, then dad and I stand from the benches. Both of us grab our bags and head for the main building of the rest area. The metal door has been busted off its hinges and is lying on the floor in the doorway. Trash and leaves flutter in and out of the building with the slight breeze in the air. An old newspaper brushes against my foot and I glance at it.

I reach down and pick it up. It's dated August 28th, 2015, two weeks after I turned fifteen. The picture on the front page shows a crowd of people running in the streets, being chased by a mob of zombies. The caption under the picture states that it was taken in Chicago. It was worse in the bigger cities than in the smaller ones like my hometown. The headline above the picture simply states "The Human Race Has Begun". I guess whoever came up with that had a bit of a sense of humor. The people in the picture do look like they're racing, despite the fact that they are scared out of their minds and literally racing for their lives. Still, glad to know someone was able to hold onto their humility while trying to live in this world when it all began.

I don't bother reading anymore of the old article. I'm sure it will say the same thing our newspaper said the last day it was delivered to our house. How we need to prepare our-selves for the end and make sure to lock the doors and board the windows in order to keep safe. Not that it did any good for a majority of the people in the world. Zombies will do what they can to get in a house and vamps are strong enough to break the doors down. It's a losing situation regardless. People still do those things anyway thinking it will keep them safe. I hope they're right. We can't afford to lose any more of our kind.

Out of an undying habit, I toss the old paper in the trash can right outside the door as I follow dad inside. No point in doing that anymore, but no sense in adding to the waste covering the land outside. There's a musty smell to the air when we get in the building. The sound of dripping water comes from one of the bathrooms. The men's room is to the left and the women's is on the right. Directly in front of us is an old information station. Empty racks where maps used to be surround the walls next to a counter where someone would stand behind for assistance. A poster sized picture frame is on the wall next to the counter and is completely smashed. I assume there was at one point a map in that frame and someone needed it more than the wall did.

"You go right, I'll go left. Look for anything that might be of use for trading or a weapon." Dad says, then lets out a sigh. "Be careful, Bridge, I love you."

I smile and say, "Love you too, dad."

I turn to my right and walk away from him. I don't hear his footsteps at first, but after a few seconds, I can hear them. He must have been watching me or something. Maybe it has to do with the secret I think he's hiding. There's nothing I can do besides shrug it off and walk into the ladies' room.

The sound of dripping water gets louder when I walk into this room. A small amount of sunlight shines through the windows at the top of the walls and is enough for me to see without a flashlight. *Not like I have one of those anyway.* The leak is coming from an old pipe under one of the faucets. It's dripping into the expanding puddle on the tiled floor. Other than that noise, the place is quiet. Too quiet for me to be comfortable.

I take a few slow steps into the room and glance into the first stall. The door is hanging off one of the hinges and blocks part of the view. There's nothing to see in that stall anyway, so I go to the next one. The next two stalls are empty, other than graffiti covering the walls. Old phone numbers people put up in case someone wanted to have a good time. Seeing that makes me smile.

I keep moving and look inside the fourth stall, instantly wishing I hadn't. Somebody really missed the toilet and didn't bother to flush. It's like they painted the walls with their crap, *literally.* The brown nastiness is crusted all over the walls and on the rim of the toilet. That's almost as disgusting as looking a zombie in the face. I grimace and move on to the last stall before the showers. It's empty just like the others. I enter the shower room and stop right at the doorway. It's more devastating than what I saw in stall number four.

A family, complete with two young children lie dead in the corner on the shower floor. A single gun is at the fing-ertips of the father's outstretched hand, a bullet wound in his head. The same wound in the heads' of his family members.

They must have been here a while. The blood has turned brown and their bodies are starting to decompose. Not enough to mask the faces of the little boy and girl in the arms of their mother. I guess they couldn't take this world any longer and chose the only way out instead of risking their lives on the road.

I feel a bit relieved to know my dad didn't choose that way to find safety.

I look away from the wretched scene and notice one of their backpacks in the opposite corner of the room. I hate that I have to do this, but we need whatever supplies are in that bag more than that family. I walk over to it, keeping my distance away from them. There's not much weight to the bag when I pick it up. It still feels like there's something inside so I'll take it with me anyway.

I turn back toward the doorway and take a few steps away from the family. My mind goes to the gun lying on the floor next to them and I spin around to stare at it. I don't really want to take the thing they used to end whatever suffering they were going through. It's a horrid reminder of what they forced themselves to do in order to escape this world. Dad would tell me I'm being too sympathetic for those people. That I need to stop caring so much about people who were badly affected by this world. He'd be right, sympathy can get in the way of things. This family doesn't need that gun anymore and it might come in handy for those of us still with a beating heart.

I tiptoe close to the father, his head is turned my way adding to the already eerie feeling I'm getting just by being in the room with them. I know it looks like they are one hundred percent gone and onto whatever their next life shall be, but looks can be deceiving. Dead can come back to life, hearts can stop beating yet you can still stare into the eyes of the people you care about. A horrible thing to be thinking about when I'm alone in a not so big room with four dead people rotting in the corner. It's best if I just get with the program and get out of here.

With my left foot, I reach out and step on top of the gun and slide it away from the dead man. His fingers make a cracking sound as they release the gun. My eyes stay focused to his unmoving face. *It better stay that way.* I slowly kneel down and feel for the gun with my right hand. I lift it from the floor then stand up straight. My feet slide across the floor taking me back to the entryway. Before I leave the shower room, I scan over the family one last time.

"Sorry, you had to do this to yourselves." I say, feeling like something needs to be said for them. "I hope wherever you are now is a lot better than this place. Thank you for the gun and whatever I find useful in your pack."

I'm not the greatest when it comes to saying meaningful things to the actually deceased humans. At least I said something and that's all that counts. I turn away from them and walk back through the bathroom and out into the visitors' area.

Dad is waiting for me by the information desk, hands empty, but he smiles when he sees that I have found something, "There's no one here, might be a good place to stay for the night."

"There is a family in the girls' bathroom. They're dead though. I found this bag and a gun with them." I reply.

He nods, "We'll hole up here for the night, go through that bag and hopefully find something of use. In the morning, after you eat, we'll set out again."

"Okay." I agree, handing him the bag and gun I found.

***

We make camp behind the information counter inside the rest area. Dad barricades the main entrance with two of the old vending machines. He goes through the bag I found with the family in the bathroom, starting with their small, black handgun. There's only one bullet left inside, so he stows it in his own bag. There's no food, not that that's a surprise. That poor family probably finished whatever morsels they had left as a last meal. Dad finds a flashlight, but the batteries are missing, an old shirt with some football team's logo on it, and a bible. Nothing of much use. He keeps the flashlight, thinking we could use it to trade for something and tosses the bag to the corner of the room.

When the sun goes down and we both notice it's getting pretty late outside, dad makes up the sleeping bag for me against the wall He then decides he's going to let me sleep all night while he stays up to keep watch. I don't argue. I am much too tired for that, but I still find it odd. With him staying up the entire night, we'll have to make more stops to rest on our journey when we leave in the morning. He'll be too tired to go on without taking a break. I know, I've tried a few times before. But like I said, I don't argue and I curl up in the sleeping bag and close my eyes for the night.

I wake up early in the morning and instantly hear the pitter-patter of raindrops on the tin roof of the structure. I check the time on my watch, only seven in the morning. Five years ago, I'd be getting ready for school right now. It would almost be the end of the school year. I wouldn't be getting ready to walk across the country in hopes of finding sanctuary in Canada. Growing up sure is different nowadays.

I get up from my makeshift bed and roll up the sleeping bag right away. Dad takes it with a shaking hand and straps it to his backpack. I go about fixing my hair and put my hoodie on to keep dry in the rain. Before we leave the rest area, dad hands me a piece of the bread to eat for breakfast. He takes none for himself, not even a drink of water or anything. It's then when I notice how pale and sickly he looks. Even in the dim light, I can tell he doesn't look like himself anymore. There are purple bags under his glazed over eyes and even with his jacket on, I can see him shiver a bit. There's sweat beading on his cheeks and forehead and I know something isn't right.

"Dad, are you okay?" I ask, finishing my breakfast.

He nods, "I'm fine, just a little lightheaded. Let's get going."

He doesn't grant me any time to contest with him and instantly starts heading for the door. I lift my bag and put it on my shoulders. I follow him through the building and he slides the vending machines out of the doorway. Luckily there are no zombies lurking about when we get outside. Always a plus when we stay indoors somewhere. I put my hood over my head and follow dad out into the rain. It's not pouring, just a heavy sprinkle. Nothing that will stop us from walking anywhere.

We get back to the highway and head north again. Dozens of cars are scattered about just like on every other road we venture on. Some have crashed into the ditches or slid into the grassy median and are being overrun with weeds. In a few of them, I can see the remains of whoever was driving the car when they crashed and no one bothered to help them out before they died. We ignore them all and press onward. Much like the family back at the rest stop, there's no point in taking the time to feel sad for them. We barely took the time to mourn our own family members when they met their horrible end. Just a few minutes to say our goodbyes and then we hit the road again. Except for mom, that took a little longer to say goodbye to her.

I don't want to think about that right now.

We walk for about an hour and I notice dad is gradually slowing down. The rain has turned into a light mist and

I turn my eyes to my father. A pained look has crossed his face and every step seems to be a struggle. His feet are sliding across the concrete, making a shuffling sound, and he's not even looking at the road ahead of us. His breathing sounds labored and his hands are shaking ferociously.

"Dad?" I say, trying to get him to look at me.

His eyes stay focused at his feet. They are hazy and dull and the purple bags underneath them have gotten darker. He doesn't look my way at all. Every few seconds, he claws at the straps of his backpack like they are digging into his shoulders. He stumbles, tripping over his own feet, but catches himself quickly. I stare at him and a lump forms in my throat. He stumbles again and this time I'm there to catch him.

"I need...to sit." He says, out of breath.

I nod and immediately begin looking for someplace to sit down for a moment. There are trees to our left and they look awfully dark and I refuse to go there. To our right, is an old metal shack with a partially missing roof. I motion toward the shack and the two of us stagger across the highway to get there.

He takes the bag off his back and lets it fall to the ground. I help him sit down on the south side of the small building and he leans against it. I kneel on the ground next to him and take his hand in mine. It's icy cold and shaking. There's a horrible feeling in the pit of my stomach and I just know something bad is about to happen.

"Dad, please tell me what's wrong." I beg.

He takes a deep, croaky breath and looks at me, "I'm so...so sorry, Bridget."

"Please. What's wrong?"

He lets go of my hand and slowly peels his jacket off. Every movement he makes sends shockwaves of pain through his body and I can see it on his face. He lets the coat fall to the ground behind him, then turns his left arm to show me what has happen. My jaw drops as I stare at the black marks on his forearm. The blood has dried and around the bite mark is a pasty white color. The other night in that town with the vamps comes to my mind.

"What happened?" I whisper as tears build in my eyes.

"I tried to get away, Bridge, that...that boy got me first then he went for you." Dad says quietly. "I'm sorry I didn't...tell you before. I was afraid." He's starting to sound just like one of them as he speaks.

I blink my eyes, letting the first of many tears fall to my cheeks. The only person left in my family is about to leave me forever and there's absolutely nothing I can do to stop it. The only cure in the entire world for this disease will have him ending up as a zombie, a fate worse than death.

I don't want to accept this. I don't want to know that my dad is about to not be my dad anymore. My heart is breaking and the more I try to stop it, the more everything hurts.

I shake my head and say, "No, you can't leave me."

He blinks a few times, "I don't want to, but you know I...I have to."

"What am I going to do without you, dad?" I say, trying not to sound as upset as I feel.

He takes a breath and swallows hard, "You are going to survive. I know you can, Bridget, you...you are capable of anything."

I shake my head, "I can't do this without you. I can't do this alone."

"Yes...yes you can. I've seen you do amazing things to keep us safe...you can continue to do those things." He says, taking a breath between just about every word he says.

I sniffle and wipe the tears from my eyes, "But I can't do this, I can't kill..."

He stops me before I can finish my sentence, "Hand me my bag."

I nod and reach for it. He takes it and unzips the front pouch. He pulls out the small gun I found with the family last night at the rest stop. Then, he pushes his bag aside and holds the gun in his hand.

"I will do it...while there's still time. While I'm still...myself." He says.

I stare at the gun, then back at his face. The effects from that vamp's bite are starting to show even more now that I know what happened to him. The paleness of his skin, the dull hue to his eyes. He's starting to change and there isn't much time for him to stop the process. If he doesn't take his own life soon, the sun will take it for him. It will be a far more painful death if he waits for that.

He squeezes my hand and looks up into my eyes, "You will survive, Bridge. You promise me...that you will do whatever it takes to keep on living. It will be hard...I know you can do it. Promise me now."

The lump in my throat makes it hard for me to say anything, but I force myself to speak, "I promise, dad. I love you."

I wrap my arms around him and hold him for a few long seconds. I can feel his arms around my back as well and can hear him sobbing against my shoulder. There's no worse feeling in the world than knowing in a few minutes you will be completely alone. Without anyone else on the planet to care about you. Without someone else there to make sure you are on the right path and are going to make it through this terrible life on your own. In a few short minutes, my life will be over.

Dad takes his arms away from me and I force myself to let go. He looks into my eyes and I really try not to let everything out and burst into tear filled sobs. That's not how I want our last moment to go.

"Bridget?" he says.

"Yeah, dad?"

"Do you remember that silly little lullaby...your mother made up? The one she used to sing to you guys when you were kids?" he asks.

I nod, "Yeah, I remember it."

"Good. You need to sing it for me...one last time." He says. "I want you to get up and walk away...singing me that lullaby. I want it to be the last thing...I hear. Don't look back, Bridge, just keep going and keep singing me that song. Do you understand me?"

"Yeah." I say through tears.

"Then take my bag and go." he orders. "Just remember that I...I love you and I will always love you. I will always be with you...right by your side, just like the rest of the family. We will be right there with you."

I nod, "I know, dad. I promise I'll do my best to survive. I love you."

I grab his bag and stand up. I force myself to walk away from him and think of the song my mom made up when I was younger. She used to sing it to me, Charlie, and Maggie when we couldn't get to sleep. It will now be the last thing my father hears just before he pulls the trigger on his own life. I get to the other side of the little shack before I start to sing the lullaby.

I take a deep breath, "Everything is gonna be alright," the words shake as they come out of my mouth, "as long as you can get to sleep tonight." I sniffle and wipe my eyes, "Just lay your weary head in bed and you will sleep," I pause for a second and try swallowing the lump in my throat, "just like the dead."

I can't believe it has taken me until this very moment to realize how wrong that one line of the song is. With most of the dead walking amongst the living, there's no telling what they sleep like. I keep walking though, trying to sing the lullaby loud enough so my father can hear me. Any second now I know my world will be shattered.

I wipe more tears from my eyes and force myself to continue, "I know you don't wanna close your eyes, but listen to my simple lullaby," another sniffle, "and know that everything will be alright, because I love you," the gunshot echoes around me and I drop to my knees, "sweet dreams and goodnight." I finish the song.

Dad's bag falls from my hand when I hit the ground. The tears don't stop themselves and I don't try to stop them either. The lump in my throat expands and I cover my face with my hands. A few mournful cries escape my throat and I don't care if a million zombies or vamps are around to hear it. Let them come for me, let them take my life like they have taken the lives of everyone I care about. My entire family is dead because of them. I might as well join them.

***

I stayed in that spot for a couple hours. I took my backpack off and put it under my head and cried into it. The tears just won't stop coming. No matter how hard I try, how much I beg myself to stop and get to my feet, my heart refuses to let me. It's broken, most likely never to be fixed again, and there's a tremendous amount of pain I can feel inside. Losing my brother didn't hurt this much. When Maggie died, I was still able to move on and try to forget. Even when mom left us, I stayed strong. I still miss them and just thinking about them makes the tears come all the more. If there is a heaven up there somewhere, I really would like to think that dad is there with the rest of my family.

The rain has picked up again and I'm practically soaked. Not that it matters anymore. No one will be here to take care of me if I get sick. Dad was the only person I had left and he was forced to take his own life because of what that damn vamp did to him. At least I was able to be there and say goodbye to him before he went. I didn't get that chance with my mom and after what happened with dad, that horrible day plays over in my mind.

It's been a little over a year and I remember everything perfectly. I was sitting outside of my grandparents' house in Florida. Maggie had just died a few weeks earlier and we were all pretty upset about it. Dad ran to gather suplies. He wanted to get on the road and head north, thinking the sooner we get there, the better. I guess I should have been inside with mom that day, but I wanted to keep watch outside in case anything unexpected showed up. I knew there was something wrong with her and I still chose to stay outside.

My mom never got over Maggie's death. Her eyes were constantly red and we always found her crying to herself. I know that in every family with more than one kid, the parent always has a favorite but they never let it show. Mom was letting it show that Maggie was hers. She didn't cry as much over Charlie and she never really spent a whole lot of time with me. We had our moments, but I was more of a daddy's girl than anything. Maggie was the one who stayed in mom's heart the longest. She loved each of us kids with all her heart, but my sister would always hold a special place. I'm guessing it's because she was her first born child and there's always a special bond there.

It was such a nice sunny day outside. I was actually looking forward to getting on the road and heading somewhere new. It's amazing how a single gunshot can ruin even the best moments. Dad's last gunshot sounded much like my mom's. It echoed through the air around me just the same and broke my heart into a million pieces the same as well. I remember running back inside the house and calling for my mother who would never answer. I found her on the bed in my grandparents' room with the gun still in her hand. She would rather end her life than go on living with what was left of her family. Makes me wonder what was going through her mind when she pulled the trigger. If she was thinking of me and dad or not. I'd like to hope that she was, at least for a moment.

Thunder claps above my head and I snap back to reality. I hate thinking of that day. I know I'll hate thinking of this one even more. It's not that I didn't love my mom, I did with all my heart. Dad was all I had left and he's gone. I won't get to have any random conversations with him about what day it might be or have fun killing zombies and vamps with him. Whatever is left of my journey, will be spent utterly alone with only myself to talk to.

I have to stay strong. I have to keep on going and survive this world that dad left me in.

I sit up on the ground and wipe the tears from my face. I'm sure my eyes are bright red and tear stains are on my cheeks. I glance to the small shack. Dad is sitting on the other side, never to move again. I know he told me to go on. To never look back.

I can't do that.

I can't just leave him sitting there in the open. I've been to places where dozens of rotting corpses cover the streets and I wonder what kind of person they must have been to not deserve a burial. Most of them were probably zombies, but of the few that weren't, they deserved the small amount of respect to be given a decent funeral. Dad deserves that and I'll be damned if that's not what he gets.

My heart is still aching as I force myself to stand. I grab my bag along the way, then reach down for dad's as well. I saunter back toward the metal shack and toss the bags on the ground next to it. I can't risk leaving them out of sight in case someone decides to sneak up on me. I pause before turning the corner to where dad is sitting. It's the last thing I want to do in the world, seeing him lie dead in the mud. In order to give myself a few more minutes of not seeing him like that, I decide to check out the inside of the shack.

The door bangs against the wall when I push it open and it sounds like the thunder overhead. Luckily there are no living or nonliving things dwelling inside. My eyes scan the place, the few dismantled shelves hanging on the wall across from me. Rain water splashes on the tops of old paint cans and the wooden shelves. The ground is nothing other than mud and leaves and a few pieces of metal. I take a step inside and continue to look around. A garden hoe leans against the wall and on the ground next to it is something that almost makes me smile.

A shovel.

The handle is broken, but it should still get the job done. I walk over to it and lift it from the ground. I back up to the doorway and look around once more to make sure there's nothing else I could use. I'm positive I'll have no use for an old barrel or any of the cans of the presumably hardened paint. With my free hand, I wipe the rain and tears out of my eyes and turn around to leave the shack only to witness a horrible figure about twenty feet from me and closing in.

It growls at me as it drags itself toward me. Blood stains the once white shirt and blue jeans it's wearing. Holes in its jeans reveal bruised and cut open skin. A few fingers on its right hand are missing and a there's a decent sized gap at the top of its head with a piece of skin flapping around as it walks. It was at one point a man. It's too disfigured for me to distinguish an approximate age or anything. Soon it won't matter who it was at one point in time or how old it was.

I keep my eyes on the zombie lumbering toward me. My gun is tucked inside my backpack. I forgot to take it out after I walked away from dad. I still have the shovel in my hand though. I'm sure I can make that work.

The growl grows more intense with every step it takes. I remain still and wait for it to get close enough. The tiniest part of me wants my hand to let go of the shovel and let this beast end my life so I can be with my family again. It would be an incredibly painful way to go out and it wouldn't end quickly. A bigger part of me thinks of my dad and I know I have to do whatever it takes to live. He wouldn't want to see me give up on life so easily and so soon after his death. I don't want to be one of those people who disappoints their parents and I am going to do whatever I can to survive.

I clutch the shovel tightly in my hand and move away from the shack. The zombie groans even louder and moves slightly faster. I can smell the death on it and see the blackness of its eyes. Whoever that man was at one point in time I really hope he's not in there somewhere. I would hate for him to know what's about to come next.

I raise the shovel above my head and stand like a baseball player. When it gets to the right spot, I take a swing and smack it right in the head. It flies back a couple feet and lands on the ground. Its arms are swinging around and legs are kicking at the ground. The moans coming from its throat sound labored and I move closer to stand over it.

There's a burning sensation deep in my chest as I think of everything that's happened to my family ever since the cure came to be. Those scientists ruined my life the day they created their precious miracle cure. My own kind ruined the lives of millions of people on this planet with just one tiny prick of a needle. What's left of us, are doomed to pay for their mistakes.

With all the anger I can muster up, which is quite a bit, I raise the shovel above my head. I then let the anger of losing the people I love flow through my veins. The anger of having to go through the rest of my life without anyone flows out to my fingertips and into the shovel itself. I let out a grunt as my arms bring the shovel down on the zombies head with a loud bash. I can hear its skull breaking as I hit it again and again. Brown mush and bits of its brain fly through the air, landing on the ground and I take one last swing with the shovel. Whatever life was left in that man is gone now and his soul can finally have peace.

I stare down at what I've done. There isn't much left

of the zombies head. A broken pile of ooze and bits of skin and bone. A few tufts of hair stick out and I can see some stuck to the blade of the shovel. A little bit got on my boots, but I don't care anymore. There's no point in caring about material things. I let the shovel drag on the ground behind me as I walk away from the corpse.

The next thing I have to do, find a nice spot to dig a hole big enough to bury my father.

***

It took longer than I expected to dig a grave for my dad. The sky is growing dark as I finish with the hole. It's only a couple feet deep, but deep enough for a grave. I stab the earth with the shovel and stare at my hard work. I had to guess at how long to make it and used myself as a model. I made sure it was at least a foot taller than me because dad is a few inches taller. I found a shallow puddle where rain water has collected and wash my hands in it. With the small amount of daylight that's left, I need to get this finished.

The grave isn't far from the shack. I didn't want to have to drag my dad too far across the ground to get him there. I still haven't been able to bring myself to go to his body. Time is growing short and that's all I have left to do. I saunter to the shack and go around to the side where his body is leaning against the metal frame. I take a deep breath before stepping around the corner and see him sitting there.

He's slouched over a bit, the gun is in his hand resting

in his lap. He didn't shoot himself in the head, that wouldn't kill a vampire. He aimed the gun at his heart when he pulled the trigger. The blood is still wet on his grey shirt and I steady myself as I approach him. My hands are shaking and my heart is pounding uncontrollably in my chest. I stare down at my father, wishing he would wake up and this would all be a nightmare. That he would look up at me with a goofy smile on his face telling me it was all for fun. Sure I would hate him for a little while, but that hate would dwindle.

My dad isn't going to wake up though. This isn't the kind of nightmare I wish it was and I'm still going to be alone for god knows how long.

The lump comes back to my throat as I move closer to him. The only way to do this is to do it quickly and get it over with. I grab the gun from his hand and toss it away from me. I never want to see that horrible life ender ever again. It destroyed the lives of that family back at the rest stop and now it has taken my father from me too.

Next, I have to command myself to grab his arms and pull him away from the shack. I struggle, thanking whatever god *is* out there that my dad is not an overweight fellow. Being on the road meant we had to be in decent shape and he was pretty well built. It takes me a few seconds, but eventually his limp body falls away from the metal wall. I move my hands under his arms from behind him and dig my heels into the ground in order to drag him to the grave. With the rain that fell all day, the grass is slick therefore easy to drag a body across it. Still a struggle, still took a few minutes, but I got the job done and made it to the grave.

I lay his body inside and it's the perfect size for my dad. I walk back to the shack and pick up his old jacket lying where he left it. I carry it back to the grave and cover my dad up with it. I drape it over his chest, hiding the bullet wound, then I climb out of the grave. I go back to the shovel and pull it out of the ground.

I stare up at the sky. It's getting darker with every

passing second. Rain still falls and I'm completely soaked. My eyes move down to my father's body. This will be the last time I stare at his face. This will be the last image I have of him. His pale face and the purple bags under his eyes, his hair matted down by the rain. This isn't how I'll remember him though. I'll remember the good days we had when we were just goofing around on our travels. The times where we had absolutely nothing to say to each other but the day was still great because we were together and we kept each other alive.

I'll never forget any of the moments I shared with my father. Whatever memory I have with him will always be in my heart. From before the vamps and zombies took over the world. To just the other day when we were sitting around a campfire with our new friends eating a hearty meal of bread and old chicken. These are the memories I want to keep for-ever. These are the things I will have with me until the day I meet my end. He'll always be with me, in my heart, my mind, everywhere. He'll be here, watching out for me with the rest of my family to make sure I survive this world. It might feel like I'm completely alone, but I know they are going to be here with me in some way, shape, or form. They'll always be here.

I let a few tears fall from my eyes. No one would be able to tell I'm crying with all the rain dripping from my hair. I walk to the pile of dirt and mud from the hole and stick the shovel in it. I take one last, long look at my father before I begin piling the dirt on top of him.

"I promise you dad that I will do whatever it takes to make it through this life. I'm not going to let you down, ever." I say out loud, knowing he can't hear my words. "Everything is going to be alright, because I love you, sweet dreams and goodnight."

Part Two

I can't get used to the fact that I'm alone now. It feels like my dad is going to come waltzing around the next bend in the road and I won't have to be sad anymore. It hurts my heart and my head knowing that I'll never see him again. I'll never get to hear his voice or fake a laugh at his jokes. I know it will take a while for the hurt to go away, more than the few days it's already been, but I just wish it would go away sooner. I can't afford to be sad *all* the time.

That first night, I camped out in the shack under the part of the roof that was still there. The sleeping bag served as a sort of comfortable seat while I leaned against the wall. I didn't get more than a couple hours of sleep that night. Every time I closed my eyes, all I could see was my dad and it made things much worse. That morning, I packed my things, left the soaking wet sleeping bag, it would only slow me down, and went outside. I found a few old bricks and stacked them at the head of my dad's grave as a marker and said one final goodbye before heading out again.

I've only managed to get a few hours of sleep each night since I left my father's grave. I tried sleeping in the back of an abandoned pickup truck, but there wasn't enough room to stretch my legs and I couldn't sleep that well. What little sleep I got, my dreams were filled with images of my father and my family. The times we spent together when I was younger and our journey to Florida. I woke up with tears in my eyes every time.

The rain has finally stopped now and my clothes have dried out. I'm still walking on the highway heading north, keeping to my father's plan. There's no sign of any other human out on this road. The only signs of anything were the few zombies I shot and the two vamps I encountered at night. After that little spat, I had to reload my gun and realized I only have a few bullets left. I need to find more supplies before I have nothing left. At least I still have my dad's gun, but it's running low as well.

Clouds are scattered in the sky and the sun peaks out from behind them. A few cars and trucks are spread out all over the highway and I keep my distance from each one. It's pointless to check if they'll run or not. I'm not in any hurry to get to a place I'll probably never find or die in the process. Not that I really care too much about that anymore. When you have no family left, you run out of things to live for. The only thing I've got going for me now, is the promise I made to my dad. I'll do my very best to survive out here as long as I can, but if things look bleak, there's no use in trying anymore.

It's horrible that I think like that. Charlie would tell me to buck up or go with the flow. That's just the kind of guy he was. The kind that said screw the consequences and went for whatever he wanted. Maggie would be too afraid to let one of those things touch her if she were in my shoes. Death by zombie would definitely be the last thing on her mind.

I'm still carrying both of our bags, mine on my back and I carry my dad's with my left hand. I tuck my gun in my jeans behind my back and realize it's getting too hard to keep going with so much weight. It's time to go through my things and get rid of what I don't need. I just need to find a safe place to do so.

There's an off-ramp coming up to my right and I can see an old gas station not far from the exit. I might get lucky enough and have some time to go through what I have in the packs before running into trouble. Maybe I'll find something of use in that building as well. I head for the exit and walk a little faster to get there. As far as I can tell, there's no one around and the place seems dead. Not in the zombie or vamp sense, but in the no one's around sense.

A semi is parked off to the side of the station and a small sedan has crashed into one of the pumps. It must have exploded because it's charred and has been gutted by a fire. I steer clear of the car and semi and head for the glass door to the station. I take my gun out and nervously pull the door open. I let out a sigh of relief after finding out it's not locked.

Inside the convenience store is dark and dreary. The shelves are empty and a few have been pushed over. I scan the area, making sure I'm alone. I can't see anyone around or hear any signs of life at all. That doesn't take away the feeling like I'm being watched. I can practically feel the eyes staring at me. I step further into the store and check behind the counter for anything dead. It's clear, then I focus on the dark corners. The first appears empty, other than an old newspaper stand. Back by the refrigerators the store gets darker and much harder to see.

The perfect hangout for vamps.

I set dad's bag on the floor and lift the gun, pointing it straight ahead of me. I strain my ears to listen for movement or anything at all that might strike me as something that doesn't belong. I move my eyes and the gun along the back wall of the store. It's dark and an eerie feeling creeps up my spine. In the farthest corner of the gas station, I can barely make out the one thing in the place that doesn't belong there. A tall figure, black enough to blend in with the wall, is hiding in that corner. I can feel it staring at me, but I can't tell if it's living or one of two types of dead that roam around.

I keep my eyes glued to the corner and wait. It moves, very slightly, but enough for me to tell. I tilt my head to the side and it moves again, quicker than before and coming my way. Too quick to be a zombie and I have a feeling it's not human either. I glance back to the door a few feet away and know I could make it before things get out of hand. The clouds aren't enough to block out the sun's rays, so whatever is in the store with me won't last long unless it *is* a human.

I think back to the last time dad and I ran into a vamp during the day. It wasn't much different than this. We were rummaging through an old house and one of them popped out of a closet. Dad and I made sure it followed us outside and ignored its instincts to stay out of the sunlight. Sometimes these things get stupid hungry and would do anything for a taste of fresh blood.

I stare at this one, it moves ever closer to me. A smile comes to my lips as I see the ray of sunshine coming through the glass door. I lower my gun and take a deep breath.

Maybe it's time to play a game and get rid of some of this sadness.

"You're hungry, aren't you?" I ask.

I'm answered with more shuffling of feet. It's close enough now for me to see what it looks like. A young woman, no older than thirty. Her dark skin a pale shade of brown and her black hair has changed to a dull grey. Her eyes are white and lifeless, but I still see the hunger burning in them. I reach my hand out, offering her a taste of my blood. One bite from that vamp and my life will be over just like my father's. That's how their disease is spread from human to human. Whatever poison they carry gets transferred from their saliva and into our bloodstream, not unlike the zombies. Although, with either a bite or scratch from a zombie and in a matter of minutes you'll be lying on the ground in pain while your body dies and you transform into one of them.

I'm not ready to die either way just yet.

"Come on, I know you're hungry." I coax her to come closer.

She opens her mouth and lets out a raspy voice, "Blood," is all she asks for.

I nod and pass her a sly smile. She reaches out for my hand and I take a step back. She's mere inches from grabbing my wrist and pulling her mouth to my hand. Exactly where I want her to be. She reaches out again and this time, I grab one of her hands and yank her toward me. She lets out a squeal as her mouth reaches for my skin. With my gun, I jab it against her skull hearing a sharp crack and she stammers back a few paces. She lunges at me one more time and I know whatever is going on in her mind will not stop her from plunging into the daylight. I rush backwards and run to the glass door, forcing it open so the sun can enter the store.

Just as I thought, she still comes at me, a harsh anger to her howls. The instant the sun hits her skin, she falls to her knees with steam rising from her body. I step away and let the sun do the dirty work for me. The girl screams with all her might and slams her boiling fists into the concrete thinking that will take the pain away. She can't gather enough strength to go back inside the gas station and is in too much pain to come after me. Her dark skin is already bubbling with boils and a severe sunburn no amount of aloe lotion will soothe. Her hair is even starting to sear and smoke bellows out of her nostrils and mouth as she screams. She's in so much pain, there's literally smoke coming from her ears.

Her white eyes look my way and she curses me for bringing her such agony. I know it isn't her fault my father is dead, but he *was* bitten by a vamp much like her. There will forever be a strong hatred for vamps deep in my heart. The kind that will only go away by killing more of them. Because of them, my father is dead and I am left to wander the world alone. They deserve to suffer just like he had to.

The boils on her skin start to burst, sending droplets of

puss splattering against the cement and door leading into the station. Her screams could be heard for miles and I'm sure something close enough can hear them. I hope they take their sweet time getting here.

I watch her writhe in pain for another moment before a hint of mercy comes to my heart. Her pleading eyes are begging me to end this suffering. Whatever human part of her that's left, is trying to break free to get me to see that she's ready to die. That she can't stand living in this state any longer.

With a deep breath, I inch my way closer to the gory scene. Her fingers are now bloody stubs clawing at the ground. She doesn't even reach out for my feet when I stop within an arm's length away from her. I guess blood can't even soothe the amount of torture she's going through right now. I hold the gun out in front of me and aim for the middle of her back, right where her black heart will be. I squeeze my finger around the trigger and her screams go silent. The only sound now, is the rustle of leaves blowing in the wind.

***

After making sure the vamp is one hundred percent dead, I walk back into the store. Dad's bag is by the counter where I left it. Before I can go through anything, I need to make sure the rest of the place is empty. I'm not up for any more chances. Up by the counter is still clear so I walk back to the darker section by the coolers. I keep my eyes peeled for anything

I can eat or something that will come in handy.

Trash has collected in most corners on the floor and dust covers the shelves and floats in the air. I step over a fallen rack and hear a crinkle of a plastic bag under my foot. I look down and notice a pile of old magazines in shreds next to the bag. I move around it and keep moving forward.

I glance back to the entrance, only to make sure nothing else is standing there waiting for me. The sun is starting to shine a little more and is beginning to brighten up the place. It shines through the grime on the windows and I can see a little better back here. I pass by the coolers and peer inside each one of them. So far, I'm not coming up with anything at all and I can hear my stomach growling. I haven't eaten much in the last few days. Sadness sort of takes the point of eating anything out of your head entirely.

I keep walking through the store, kicking trash and debris out of my way. I see my reflection in the glass doors of the coolers and stop to stare at myself for a moment. I still look the same as I did a few days ago. My hair is a little frizzy at the moment and my pony tail needs to be fixed. I take a moment and decide to fix it. I pull the hair tie from my hair and run my fingers through the tangles to smooth it out. Once the frizz is gone, I tie it back into the same ponytail I've been wearing for the last few years.

I don't feel the same as I did the last time I saw my reflection. I feel older, more grown up. Maybe losing everyone in my family was the final ticket I needed to be completely grown up and mature. I have to take care of myself now and have no one to depend on. There's no one to take care of me when I get sick and no one to look out for me. I'm all I have and I'll never be okay with that.

I notice something else in the reflection, something on one of the shelves behind me. It's small and yellow and most likely expired, but I spin around on my heels to make sure it's actually there. I walk down the aisle, stepping over more trash in my way, and stare at the object of my desire. A small bag of potato chips sits in the middle of one of the shelves with a slight layer of dust on it. It's sealed and I lick my lips as I stare at it. It's been a very long time since I've had something like this to eat. Just the thought of having something from my past takes a enough of the sadness away for me to gain an appetite.

I reach out and take the chips from the shelf and blow the dust off the bag. There's not a doubt in my mind they are stale and not crunchy at all, but it is the only thing around and I need something to eat. I bring my prize to the front of the store and sit down next to dad's backpack. It isn't much of a lunch, but better than nothing.

I pop the bag open and the smell of salt fills my nose. My stomach growls and I reach in for a chip. I stare at it for a moment, taking in this wonderful thing. There's no saying when or if I'll ever get to eat something like this again and I want to enjoy this little moment of mine. I shove the chip in my mouth and close my eyes as I chew the food. It might not be crunchy and it might not taste as good as it did when it was fresh, but it's still the best thing I've had in a while.

As I enjoy my small meal, I slip my bag off my back and set it on the floor next to me. Then I reach for dad's and unzip it. His gun is the first thing I see and the first thing I set in the pile of things to keep. Next, are his spare change of clothes. A pair of jeans and an old t-shirt. Not something I need to keep, but it brings a lump to my throat as I set them off to the side and continue digging. I find a paperback book, *The Hobbit*, something we found on our way to Florida. He used to read it to us when we couldn't fall asleep or were stuck in the rain. I put that in the keep pile. A nice memory I can't throw away. The flashlight we found at the rest area, the one that doesn't work. I know I'll never run into any batteries and I doubt anyone will trade things for a broken flashlight. It goes in the trash pile.

I keep digging finding a few plastic bags, empty of course, at the bottom of the bag along with a pocket knife which I shove in my pants' pocket. I also find a box of ammo I didn't know he had. I take the box out and open it noticing that the bullets are for *my* gun. It makes my heart hurt knowing he had these stashed in his bag just for me. It was like he knew I would run out soon.

There isn't much else in his bag that I feel the need to keep. He didn't have anything sentimental from our home and never bothered to carry any photos. He always had his old wallet on him and it was in his pocket when I buried him. There are pictures of us kids and my mom in there and that's all he ever needed. I toss his old bag off to the side along with his clothes and the broken flashlight. Then I reach for my own pack and begin going through my things.

I keep my extra clothes, my hairbrush and the soap. I found two apples on my way here and keep them in a plastic bag. The water bottle is shoved in its own little compartment on the side of the bag and that's where it will stay. I have some old things from my childhood home and start to realize I don't need them anymore. I don't need to hang onto a music box that will never play again. I don't need makeup I'll never wear or the toys I kept because they remind me of home. I do, however, need our family photo album. I can't bring myself to open the book, but I'll never be able to throw it away.

I pack everything up in my bag, reloading my gun before stowing away the ammo. After it's zipped, I lean my head back against the wall and stare out into the empty gas station. I hold the gun in my hand, resting it on my lap and close my eyes for a few seconds. It's such a dreadful thought knowing I have such a long way to go and I have to go it alone. It makes things seem a million times worse when there's no one else around for me to talk to. Talking to myself is fine for a little while, but answering my own questions gets really old. If I knew for sure Sherry and her family would have still been in that town, I would have went back. I could have traveled with them and had someone to talk to. I'll never see them again and I have to find a way to accept that. The same way I have to accept that my family is dead.

The wind blows through the open door sending shivers up my spine and the horrible smell of burning flesh up my nose. I open my eyes and glare at the vampire corpse in the doorway. At least she's still lying there instead of running at me with a revengeful lust for blood in her eyes. I take a deep breath, trying not to breathe in the rancid smell, then force myself to get off the grimy floor. I grab my backpack and fling it over my shoulders. I head back for the door and step over the body and out into the sunlight.

The highway is a short walk to my left and an even longer walk to wherever it is I need to go. I look to my right and see a few buildings about a mile away. A small town, possibly abandoned like most of the small towns I've come across. A good majority of the people have chosen to leave their homes in hopes of finding sanctuary away from the monsters. I can't say I blame them when my own family did the same thing. Still, I decide I'm going to check it out. There might be food or something of use there.

My feet carry me away from the gas station and down the short stretch of road to the few buildings ahead. I pass by a few groupings of trees and peer through them. A deer runs away in the distance and a of couple birds fly through the branches. I wonder if they are afraid of the zombies and vamps. I wonder if they even know what has happened to the human population or just plain don't care. My guess would have to be that second thought.

I pass a red barn with a tractor parked outside of it. The body of an old man is lying on the gravel next to the machine. From what I can tell, it doesn't look like he's been lying there long. He isn't all decomposed yet and the blood on the white rocks underneath him is still red and glistens in the sunlight. I pause in the middle of the street and look around for a moment. I raise an eyebrow when I don't see anything lurking in the shadows and choose to go on.

This place isn't much of a town, a few houses and a

tall apartment building. A scorched bar is on the corner of a street, the smell of smoke looms in the air. I glance around at the few houses. The front door on a white house has been busted open and a splatter of blood stains the siding. What looks like a leg or an arm lies on the porch where the stain has drifted down the outer wall of the house.

That looks fresh as well and my heart is starting to race.

Something isn't right with this town and regret instantly floods my mind about coming this way instead of getting back on the highway. The feeling gets worse when I take a breath through my nose and smell what's coming toward me.

***

I stop walking and stare at the road straight ahead. Two of them stumble and moan, tripping over rocks and sticks in the street. My heart starts pounding and I take a few steps back wanting to turn and run away. I hear a noise to my right and my head quickly turns in that direction. Three more pile out of an open garage, blood dripping from their mouths and tattered clothes. The second they see me, fresh meat, their moaning gets louder and their movements faster.

"Shit." I say, under my breath.

Glass breaks from one of the windows of the apartment building and a few more fall onto the sidewalk. A total of nine zombies are coming for me. I've never been face to face with that many by myself before. Dad has always been right by my side and I never had to worry about a thing. He always had my back and I had his. I'm alone now and I'm the only one to have my back. I could try running away, I might be successful at it but they would still chase me. They would follow me until I run out of energy and give up. That's when they would take their time to devour my body and soul.

Giving up and running away isn't an option. Dad wants me to survive and that's exactly what I'm going to do. I slip my bag off my shoulders, I can move faster without it, and toss it on the ground next to a black minivan. I stare at the faces of the zombies as they close in on me. All of them are old enough to be parents or grandparents, save for one. A small boy, maybe seven years old, lumbers toward me with his arms outstretched, a childlike moan coming from his throat. It's going to break my heart a little, but I have to do what has to be done.

I take a slow, deep breath and raise my gun. My feet move a few steps closer to the few that came from the garage. I aim for the first one and pull the trigger. Brown blood squirts from his head and he falls to the cement like a sack of potatoes. His death doesn't bother any of the others and I aim for the next one. The bullet enters her shoulder and she stumbles back. I fire again and don't miss her head this time.

I look around, the others from the apartment building are getting much too close for comfort. I take aim for them and fire three times only hitting one of them in the head. Three down, six to go and I'm running out of ammo with no time to reload. I back away from the approaching zombies and shoot again hitting one in the gut. Nervousness really affects my aim.

"Shit." I say again and start looking around for something to use as a weapon.

There's no time to sift through my bag for dad's gun. They would be on top of me before I could get the damn thing unzipped. The one I shot in the gut lets out a loud moan and charges for me. I move backward and shoot the gun one more time at him. He finally falls to the ground, but the others are getting awfully close. I keep looking around for anything I can use. A thick branch lies in the middle of a yard, too big for me to even try to lift. Behind that, I see a garden hoe leaning against the house. That could come in handy.

I inch my way toward it, pulling the trigger two more times, another zombie falls dead. The barrel is empty and I toss the gun to the ground. I think they can tell when I have no other options. The zombies start moving faster once the gun hits the ground and their horrible moaning gets louder. It's like they're singing to one another in a tune no musician could ever hope to repeat.

I quit walking backwards and start running to the house. Their footsteps are right on my tail and I jump over the thick tree branch. I reach for the hoe and can feel that one is right behind me. I swing my new weapon through the air as I spin around. The blade connects with the zombie's neck and blood sprays out of the gash I created. I yank my weapon out of its flesh and swing it at the monster again. The crack of its skull sounds through the air and it topples on the grass.

Three more to go.

I hold the garden tool tight in my fist as the final three come after me. The little boy stands amongst them and his eyes are just as black as the others. I stare at their faces. A big hulking black man has a gnarly gash across his bare chest. Black blood oozes out of the wound and I can see his bones poking through the skin. His eyes are screaming at me with hunger and of the three of them, he's the one who scares me the most.

He moves in closer, I take a few steps back. A terrible moan comes from his throat and he reaches out for me. I swing the hoe at him and miss him by mere inches. He lunges at me and I allow myself to fall backward to the ground in order to keep him from touching me. A single scratch alone and I'd be just like him in minutes. I raise the hoe above my head and chop it through the air coming down on the man's shoulder. It doesn't even phase him.

He still comes after me, the garden hoe stuck in his shoulder. I crabwalk away and finally scramble to my feet. I dart my eyes back and forth, desperately searching for something else I could use as a weapon. There's nothing around me. No shovel, no axe, *nothing*. Then I remember the knife in my pocket. It isn't much, but all I have to do is get close enough to stab the creature in the head.

Much easier said than done.

I pull the knife out and keep moving backwards. He lunges at me one more time and I let out a sharp scream and stab at him with the knife. I can feel its thick blood running down my finger tips and I'm afraid to look at my hand. His moaning stops and he falls forward leaving me no choice but to let go of the knife. I got lucky and stabbed him in the right temple on his forehead. My hand covered in his blood.

I let out a much needed sigh of relief and stare at the final two zombies. There's still a decent chance of dying here today, but the thought that I single-handedly took out seven of those bastards makes everything worth it. A good sense of pride flows through me as I stare at the last two standing a few feet away. A woman, old enough to be my grandmother, stands with the little boy. Her clothes are drenched with blood and her grey hair is matted. Her black eyes glare at me, but she also glances at her dead friend lying on the grass in a pool of his own murky blood. Maybe she will stay distracted with him long enough for me to finish this so I can go on with my life.

The little boy next to her growls at me, but remains frozen in his place. I can see the looks of contemplation on their dead faces. Much like the look on that female zombie I killed a few days back. That seems like ages ago now, but her face still burns in my mind. She weighed the options of coming after me much like these two are doing right now. Like they are deciding whether I'm worth it or not. The little boy obviously thinks I am.

He lets out a childish grunt and sprints toward me. I react quickly and yank the hoe out of the dead zombie's shoulder, thanking god it came out easily. The boy ran up faster than I expected and I swung my weapon smacking him in the head. His skull cracks open and he lets out a loud shriek then falls to the ground on top of the other. It saddens me to know children are capable of turning into flesh eating zombies. I still kill the few I come across. There's no point in sparing them just because they're kids. They might appear innocent, but if you look past how young they are and stare into those black, evil eyes, you can get past the innocence long enough to shoot them in the head.

I let go of the garden tool and my breathing quickens. My eyes glare at the old woman standing at the other edge of the lawn. The only monster I have left to face, then I'm out of this hellhole. She doesn't seem like she wants to move.

"Aren't you hungry too? Don't you want a piece of me?" I shout at her, feeling *extremely* tough.

She stands and acts like she's considering her options. Anger has filled my heart completely and I storm across the yard, heading for my backpack. Who cares if she doesn't charge after me like the others. She deserves the same treatment as them just for being what she is. Zombies and vampires do not deserve to be ahead of us humans on the food chain. If I let one of them live then a hundred more humans could die because of me. Not a chance in hell am I going to let that happen because one zombie *chooses* not to attack me.

I rip open my bag and grab dad's gun from inside. The old woman has taken a few steps into the street, slowly get-ing further away from me. She must have decided I'm not worth the risk. My feet carry me across the street, closing the gap between us. The look in her blackened eyes almost pleads with me to not pull the trigger. Whatever human is left inside of her must be controlling that part of her mind right now because no zombie would ever plead for their life. No zombie would refuse a meal like she is doing and I'm even more confused by it than ever. Maybe one day I'll take the time to figure things out, but right now I have one more of those damn things to kill and I'm not going anywhere till it's done.

A final groan escapes her throat right as I pull the trigger letting a few bullets enter her brain. Blood sprays out of her head and she falls back to the cement. I listen to the crack of her skull as her head hits the ground, then I lower the gun and walk away. I grab my gun from the ground and toss it in my bag then zip it back up. I fling it over my shoulders and hold dad's gun tight as I walk away from the gruesome scene.

I don't even care to look through the houses in this damn place anymore. Getting out of here has become my number one priority.

"Hey wait!" that thought changes a bit.

I freeze in my tracks and my heart starts racing again.

***

I hear the footsteps running up behind me and I slowly turn around. I half expect to see another zombie running after me, one that is far more advanced than the others and can speak to us. That would be a good way for them to blend in with the living. Instead, I see a boy, my age, running away from the apartment building toward me. His black shirt torn at his neck and his jeans are ripped at one of the knees. A light blue satchel hangs over his shoulder at his side. His brown hair blows in the breeze as he makes his way to me. It's been a few days since I have seen another human being. I am a little speechless when I see this pretty good looking man coming up to me.

He stops running a few feet away, then looks back at my handy work. A smile crosses his face and he nods at me.

"That was pretty awesome." He says.

I take a breath, "Yeah, I know."

"I've never seen anyone take out so many of them alone before." He comments, "Who are you?"

"Bridget. Who are you?"

"Ryder." He replies. "Are you on the road by yourself?"

I nod, not sure if I should be telling him any of this.

"Me too. I came this way about a week ago and found a place to stay for a few nights. Those zombies showed up and I barricaded myself in a bathroom for two days. They killed everyone here and trapped me in that room until you showed up. I thought for sure I was dead until I heard all the commotion outside. I watched you from a small window and you took out *nine* of them. You saved my life." Ryder states.

"Well, you're welcome. In case you think you owe me anything, you don't. I didn't even know you were here." I say.

"I wasn't thinking that, but I do want to thank you."

"Anytime. I've been told I'm a bit of a badass when it comes to zombie killing so if you're ever in a bind, feel free to look me up." I say a bit sarcastically, but I say it with a smile.

"You're hard to get along with, aren't you?" he asks.

I shake my head, "Not really. I'm normally a delight, but when you lose everything worth living for and run into a horde of zombies, it can bring out a side of anyone that isn't very pleasant."

"I can see that." He says.

"Okay, well, I'm wanting to put as much distance between me and this place as possible, so good luck." I say, then turn around to leave.

I hear him rush up behind me and say, "Wait."

I turn back around and face him, "What?"

"Look, we're both alone, why don't we travel together?" he suggests.

I raise an eyebrow, "I'm sorry, but I don't know you at all. What makes you think traveling together would be a smart thing to do?"

Ryder shrugs, "I don't know. This wasn't part of my plan. I've been on my own for over a year now and I've come to realize that being with someone else has its benefits. We can look out for each other until we get where we need to be, then we can go our own way. Which way are you headed?"

"North." I reply.

"Same here. There's a city I'm trying to get to. What do you say?"

I stare into his amazing hazel eyes and think things over for a moment. He makes a good point. Having another person with me has always proven to be a good thing in the past. Dad was always there for me when he was alive and it was a blast traveling with Sherry's family. We did help them out when they needed it, maybe Ryder can help me out.

"What city are you trying to find?" I ask before giving him a direct answer.

"Des Moines. I've heard rumors that it's walled off and relatively safe. They let humans come in as long as they aren't infected." He says.

"That's in Iowa right?" I ask.

He nods, "So, is that a 'yes', because you know I don't really need your permission. With this being the end of the world and all, I can do just about whatever I want."

"Yeah, that makes me want to travel with you even more." I say, rolling my eyes.

I turn around and start walking back toward the highway. I can hear him rushing up behind me and soon he's right by my side. I can't tell if he's purposely trying to be annoying or if he really hasn't been around humans for a while and doesn't quite know how to act around them anymore. I'm sure I get a little weird around others. After going so long with just my dad, I know I say the wrong thing or do the wrong thing and they probably want nothing to do with me. I got lucky and Sherry is just as strange as I am. I just don't get why this Ryder fellow doesn't want to leave me alone. He wears this goofy smile on his face and he talks more than any other guy I've met out here.

"I take it you don't care if walk with you?" he asks after a few seconds of following me.

I let out a deep breath and say, "Only if you tell me that you don't just want to go with me because I saved your life. Don't think I'm going to keep protecting you forever. If we go north together, it's an equal opportunity journey."

"Totally. I'm pretty good at keeping myself safe as well as anyone around me." He replies.

I stare at him, then glance back toward the apartment building he said he was trapped in, "I can see that."

"I am, honestly." He protests. "You just caught me on an off day."

I smile and shake my head, "Whatever you say, buddy."

I guess it won't be so bad to have a guy my age to travel with. It beats talking to myself all the time and having no one there to answer my ridiculous questions. It doesn't hurt that he's *really* hot too. His hair is the perfect amount of shagginess and his smile makes him even more attractive. He's a few inches taller than me and has the right amount of muscle, not too bulky and not too scrawny. Just perfect.

I think I could get used to being around him.

***

We don't say much the first hour or so of walking together. It's actually a bit awkward walking right next to him without saying a single word. I'm still a bit shaken up about running into that many zombies on my own. I never thought I was going to die more than during those few minutes of trying not to be eaten by them. It makes me feel somewhat good about myself that during the whole process of killing things that should already be dead, I was able to save the life of someone. A very handsome someone.

I love the way his hazel eyes light up in the sunlight. How is shaggy, brown hair blows in the wind. I can't help but glance over at him every so often. Maybe I'm checking him out. Maybe I'm trying to see if he's staring back at me. No matter what, this could be the start of a good thing.

"So," he says to break the silence between us, "I have to ask, why north?"

I shrug, "I don't know. My dad always thought we would be safer up there. Like the cold weather would keep the zombies and vamps at bay."

He shakes his head, "I hate to tell you, but he's wrong. Zombies might be scarce that way, they freeze in the cold, but the vamps are everywhere. The nights are longer up north, which means they have more time to hunt and eat. Whatever humans are there, are really lucky to still be alive."

Well there goes everything my dad thought to be true. He always said going north would be a good thing. We would find civilization there and survive with the other humans. Not end up being a juice box to even more vamps.

"How do you know all this?" I ask.

"I'm from Minnesota, a few miles away from the border of Canada." He replies. "The last time I was there, those were the rumors that were being spread as people were trying to make their way south."

I take a deep breath, "Well, that sucks."

Ryder nods, "I'm sorry if I just ruined everything for you. I'd hate to see you go through all the trouble to get there only to find out it's no better off than anywhere else on the planet."

I shrug, "That's okay. Better to find out now then when it's too late."

This just freed up the rest of my presumably short life. If I don't continue north, going on with dad's plan, I have absolutely no idea what I'm going to do. For the last five years of my life, I have grown to believe that these things weren't able to survive in the extreme cold. That was always the reason for dad wanting to go there. I've always had my doubts about finding safety there, but there was a small part of me that wanted to believe that's exactly what we would find. I am a little glad that dad isn't around to hear this. I have a feeling he would still want to stick with his plan and keep going until we made it to Canada. Who knows how long we would have survived if we made it.

"So, where are you from?" Ryder asks, thankfully taking my mind off things.

"West Virginia." I reply.

"And where's your family?"

I shake my head, "Gone."

"Sorry."

"It's okay." I say forcing the lump in my throat to go away. "What about yours?"

He lets out a slight chuckle then says, "I didn't have much of a family. When I was five my parents were killed in a car accident and my grandparents didn't want me so I became a ward of the state going from foster home to foster home. The last one I lived with were horrible people. They only did it for the money and treated us kids like shit. I threw myself into school and after school activities to stay away from the house."

"That's terrible. Makes me feel bad thinking of how great my childhood was." I say.

"That's okay. Not every moment was a bad one." Ryder adds.

"So, how old are you?" I ask, again wanting to change the subject.

He takes a deep breath, "Twenty, I think. It depends what time of year it is. My birthday is in the winter and I was fifteen when this happened and just went through the fifth winter so I must be twenty now. What about you?"

"Nineteen. My birthday is in the summer." I reply.

He smiles and laughs a bit. I raise an eyebrow trying to figure out what's so funny about how old I am.

"Why are you laughing? Did I miss something?" I ask.

"You're only nineteen, yet you destroyed those zombies back there like they were nothing. I've never seen anyone do that before, let alone a girl like you." He chuckles.

Not too sure if I should be insulted by that. No one has ever said anything like that to me before and I'm not positive how I want to take it.

"What do you mean by that?" I ask trying not to sound too snooty.

"Nothing bad, Bridget, you're just young and hot and don't seem like the kind of chick to be a badass zombie killer. I hope you're that good when it comes to the vamps too." He explains.

A smile comes to my face. Not for the zombie killing comment or the being young comment. He called me hot and only one other person on this planet has called me that before. Sherry's just not the kind of person I could go for. Not that I have anything against that, it's just not my thing. I guess there's a part of me that's pretty vain when it comes to hearing how good I look. It's not every day I get to hear it.

We keep walking, passing another exit that would take us to some town probably infested with the undead. Definitely not something I want to deal with again. Nine zombies and one vamp in a single day is plenty for me. There's a few cars crashed on the side of the road. A few with black burn marks on the hood and the tires appear to have melted off the rims. Right about now, dad would be making some snide remark about how he thinks the accident happened. He always tried to come up with the weirdest solutions, like the kids in the back of the soccer-mom van turned into bloodsucking vampires and decided they didn't need mommy dearest anymore. Something like that very well could have happened, probably has, but whatever actually happened shouldn't have. All of those people who died in those accidents, should still be here going on with their lives.

The "cure" took that away from them.

"So, Bridge," Ryder says, using my father's nickname for me, "what were you doing when all the bad things started to go down? You know, when the *awesome cure* for everything came out?"

I shake my head, "I wasn't really doing anything. I was at home with my brother and parents. My sister came home from college because she was scared. We tried to stick it out and stayed with the few neighbors that were left. We made it about a year, then headed for Florida to meet up with my grandparents whom we found dead when we got to their beach house." I sniffle as I think of those horrible memories. "What about you?"

"Well, being an honor student, I was granted the privilege of going on a field trip to the capital in Washington. We were going to meet the president and everything. We got stuck there. It was when all the planes were grounded and we had no way to get home. Then vamps started showing up in the hotel and zombies started roaming the streets. A big city like that was the worst place to be." He replies.

"So, what'd you do?"

"I stayed with the few friends I had on that trip. We were there for a few months before we found a ride home. That wound up being a terrible thing. The driver failed to mention he was injected with the cure to get rid of his cancer. Five hours into the road trip and he was sucking the life out of the guy in the passenger seat. Two others and myself were able to get away, but the other three weren't so lucky. At least the driver got what he deserved for it and burst into flames when the sun came out." He says. "Not a pretty sight."

I shake my head and recall the image of that woman burning in the sun this morning. It makes me wonder what happened to their bodies to make them reject the sunlight like that. Obviously it has something to do with whatever ingredients were in the cure so many people thought they needed. What I don't get, is why vampires can't be in the sunlight, but zombies, which are a direct result of trying to cure the vamps, the sunlight has no effect on them. Must have something to do with the different types of cure the amazing scientists tried to use. They should have just left well enough alone and let the world go on as it was.

"You think a lot, don't you?" Ryder asks, breaking my train of thought.

I shrug, "A little bit. I guess being in a world like this for so long makes me wonder about things. Probably the same things you wonder about too."

"I don't know. I stopped trying to wonder about why things are the way they are a while ago." He replies.

"Why? Don't you ever want to know why the cure had that effect on people?"

He shakes his head, "No. It's better not knowing why this happened and why those monsters do what they do."

I stare at him for a moment. Trying to read the expression on his face. He seems sort of sad about whatever is going on in his mind. Maybe I got him thinking about something that happened to him and he hates reliving that. Not a very good first impression on my part. I should just stick to killing zombies and never open my mouth. People seem to enjoy watching me work and I'm not left feeling like I've said the wrong thing.

***

After the sun disappears over the horizon, we find a nice place under an oak tree right off the highway to make camp for the night. I can tell someone else has used this spot for a place to stay. Blackened sticks are still piled in the middle with two large logs on either side for a place to sit. There are initials carved into the tree with a heart drawn around them. Whoever TF and BJ are, I hope they're still alive out there somewhere and this heart isn't the last piece of their lives together.

Listen to me being all sentimental again. I've really got to quit that.

Ryder builds a small fire for warmth in the cool night air while I take the small amount of food I have in my bag out for our dinner. He doesn't have anything to contribute. Whatever food he had, he ate while being trapped in the bathroom at that apartment building where I came to save the day. So, he is more than grateful when I toss him a green apple.

After we eat, I reload my small handgun with the bullets dad left for me. It's a much easier gun to use in my opinion. I'm not much for the automatic ones. My aiming is off more with that one compared to my 9mm. The only weapon

Ryder has in his satchel, is a knife and not a very sharp one. I felt a little bad for him, but still too wary to offer him one of mine. There's no saying what he would do with it once it's in his hands. I'm not willing to risk my life for that just yet.

We eat our small, not very appetizing meal without saying more than two words to each other. Sure it's awkward. Sure we could be having nice dinnertime chat, but who needs that? A family surrounding a dining room table in a beautiful house, that's who.

I watch Ryder wipe his hands on his jeans and toss me a small smile, "I've got a weird question for you." he says to break the silence.

I raise an eyebrow and say, "Okay."

"Have you ever wondered what would happen if a zombie bit a vampire or vice versa?"

He obviously doesn't know the definition of what a weird question is nowadays.

I nod and say, "Yeah, a few times. My dad and I used to come up with something for them to change into and each time it was something horrible."

"Me too. I don't think the world could handle a mixture of the two monsters." He says.

"It would be bad."

Another few seconds of silence before he breaks it again, "Are you ever nervous about being out in the open at night?" Ryder asks, poking at the fire with a long stick.

I nod, "All the time. I know those vamps hide in the trees during the day and come out at night when we're asleep and the zombies can pop up anywhere."

"Yeah," he says, "I wish I could go one day without being nervous or afraid to look over my shoulder. That's the price you pay when you're out here alone, though."

"I used to have someone to look over my shoulder with me, so I haven't been completely alone for very long." I reply.

"How long?"

"A few days."

"What happened?"

I think back to a few nights ago. Being in that tent with my dad and Sherry and everyone else in that town. That Henry Johnson guy, the biggest idiot I've ever come across. There's no reason for anyone to want to capture zombies or vamps just for show. Anyone else who does should know something horrible will come out of it.

"Bridge? You okay?" Ryder asks.

I nod with a lump forming in my throat as I think of my dad, "I lost my dad a few days ago. He was the only family I had left and because of a stupid mistake made by somebody else, he's dead."

"Sorry that happened to you."

"It's okay. This was something that really shouldn't have happened. I mean, we were fine and everything was okay. Then we stopped at this stupid town and went to this stupid event thing where these stupid people actually get off on capturing those things and locking them in a cage. They didn't realize that vampires are stronger than they look." I say, fighting the tears building in my eyes.

"That is a lot of stupid." He says.

That's the only thing he has to say. It doesn't really make me feel better about my situation. Having someone to talk with, to vent my issues to, is all that really matters right now and that alone makes me feel slightly better.

"Is that what happened to the rest of your family too? They were taken by the zombies and vamps?"

I slowly nod my head and wipe my eyes, "Yeah. My brother was first, then my sister. My mom killed herself because she couldn't live in a world like this anymore. Then it was just me and dad and now he's gone as well. It's a shitty feeling knowing you have no one else in the world who cares about you."

He nods, "It's not all bad though. I've been through some really bad things during all this. No matter how bad the situation gets, as long as you can force yourself to survive, things will get better. Trust me on this one."

"You really believe that?" I ask.

"I do, because for the last two days I locked myself in a disgusting bathroom and thought I was a goner. That still wasn't enough for me to give up and I never let them win. Then you showed up and things instantly got better. That's why I wanted to go with you." He says.

"Not because you think I'm hot." I say, mockingly.

He smiles and continues poking at the fire. The cracking of the flames fills the air and I glance up at the starry sky. I recognize a few of the constellations. The two dippers, Orion and his belt, and a few I've made up for myself. Like this cluster of stars looks strangely similar to a very obese man riding one of those motorized scooters. It's amazing what our minds can create when we have nothing else to entertain us. *I really miss TV.*

It's so wonderful staring up at the night's sky, seeing the millions of tiny lights watching over this planet. I wonder if there are other planets out there like ours. One that isn't filled with half dead humanoids who basically destroyed the food chain. Maybe one day they'll come here and save what's left of us.

I turn my head back to the fire. The shadow of the flames dance around the ground at my feet. Things seem really quiet all of a sudden. The wind has died down and the crickets have stopped chirping. I have a really bad feeling in the pit of my stomach that we aren't alone anymore.

I glance to Ryder. I think he can sense something is off as well. His eyes are alert and he stopped poking at the fire. I reach for my gun sitting on top of my bag, keeping my eyes peeled for anything. If zombies were around, we'd hear their moaning and grunting by now. They aren't the quietest creatures when it comes to sneaking up on their food source. Vamps are the things I'm worried about the most. They are quiet and have no smell to them at all. If you weren't on high alert, you wouldn't even have time to react if one was right on top of you.

"Did you hear that?" Ryder whispers, the very second a stick breaks not far from us.

I nod, "I don't think we're alone out here."

I stand from the log I'm sitting on and look around. The moon isn't doing much to illuminate the area and the stars aren't as bright as I would love them to be right now. I peer into the darkness, hoping I catch sight of whatever made that noise. It comes again and I hold my breath for a second. The sound was closer than before and my heart's beating much faster. I can see something not far away, a set of eyes glimmering in the firelight. It's too short to be a person and the eyes are too round. It comes closer to our camp and I let my breath out.

Ryder chuckles behind me as the two of us stare at the small deer walking through the weeds, "Too bad we don't have the tools to gut that thing. Meat would be a great meal right about now." He says.

I smile and turn to face him, "You do have a very dull knife."

He fingers the blade and lets out a sigh, "Probably get tetanus after using this thing though. I found it by a lake."

I go back to my seat and sit down on the log. The second I'm completely seated, a terrified look crosses Ryder's face. I don't have any time to turn around to see what he's staring at. He stands quickly and flings his dull knife. The blade rushes right above my head, ripping through the air. I hear a grunt coming from behind me followed by a thud as something hits the ground. My heart practically stops for a second and I watch Ryder walk by me. I turn around and see the body he's approaching.

The knife is sticking out of the chest of the person it hit. I can't tell who or what it is, but it isn't moving anymore and that's probably a good thing. Ryder kneels down next to the body and pushes the knife deeper into its chest. A final moan comes from the person's throat and Ryder pulls the knife out of the wound.

He turns his head and looks at me, "Vampire," he says, "I guess this makes us even now."

He stands and walks back to his seat on the ground, "I killed nine zombies and saved your ass. One vampire hardly makes us even." I retort.

"Yeah, but you didn't know you were saving me and I did. Therefore, this makes us even." He says as he wipes the bloody knife on the ground to clean it.

I don't know what it is about this boy, but he sure is getting under my skin. In a very good way.

***

We sleep in shifts, keeping an eye out for each other. A good system that has yet to fail me. Even now after being on the road with a guy I've only just met. I think he's the kind of guy I can trust. Maybe more than trust. I like the way he smiles at me and the way he jokes around to bring a smile to my own face. He sort of takes the sadness away. A girl could get used to being around a good looking guy like him.

Morning comes along and not a very bright and shiny one either. The sky is cloudy and it looks like it could rain at some point during the day. It's been a very wet year already. I know I said the weather should match the emotion of the planet, but *come on*. Enough is enough. I'm tired of being soaked one day and drying off the next only to get soaked by the rain on the third day. The clouds can hang around all they want, but send the rain somewhere else for once.

We hit the road again, leaving behind the dead vampire to cook in the clouded sunlight. The only thing we have to eat is my last piece of bread which we split in half. Hopefully we'll come across a place for food soon or else we'll starve. I'm hoping a town comes up so the choice of starvation doesn't cross our minds.

Noon comes and goes and the sky continues to threaten us with a storm. I can hear both of our stomachs growling and each of us search for a town or someplace we can look for food. Every car we pass, we take a look inside for anything we could eat. Some moldy candy bars and empty bottles of soda. Nothing edible so we keep moving forward.

"You know what I could go for right about now," Ryder says, "an extra-large pizza with everything on top. Peppers, olives, sausage, the works."

"Don't forget the mountain of cheese on top of all that." I add.

"It's making my mouth water." He says.

I look down at my feet, missing the things of my past, "We probably shouldn't reminisce about stuff we'll never have again."

"Why not? What else do we have to live for other than to remember the things we used to have?" he comments. "If we don't remember, we might as well be a zombie like the rest of the world."

He does makes a good point. I've spent the last few years trying not to think about the things I'll never have again because it makes me upset. I'll never have that computer I begged my parents for or the I-pad I left little hints around the house at Christmastime. I will have the memories of everything and those are something to never forget. It sucks thinking about it from time to time, which is why I avoid doing so. Like Ryder so elegantly put, if we don't remember what life was like, we might as well turn ourselves into zombies and forget absolutely everything.

I smile and take in his advice, "You know what I would rather have instead of pizza? Chocolate. I don't care how it's made or what it covers, chocolate is the best flavor in the entire world."

He laughs, "Definitely won't argue with you on that one. I could devour an entire pack of Oreos in one sitting. Double stuffed, with a full glass of milk to drink with them."

"My thing was the marshmallow and chocolate ice cream. My brother and I would go through an entire gallon of that stuff in one night. Chocolate syrup always made it better too." I add.

He sighs, "We're just talking about this stuff and I can actually taste it."

"I wish we *were* actually tasting it."

We come across a part of the highway overrun with cars. Accident upon accident and it's almost impossible to get through the carnage without climbing over something. Ryder climbs on the hood of a small pickup truck and helps me climb up with him. He takes my hand and I can feel the butterflies churning in my stomach the second our skin touches. He hops down to the other side and turns to help me. He puts his hands on my waist and I jump off the truck with his help. Our eyes meet at that moment and it's more than butterflies I feel in my stomach. There's something more going on inside me and I can only hope he's feeling it too. Maybe what they say is true. You know that whole love at first sight thing. It seems old fashioned to me, but maybe those old geezers were on to something.

Ryder nervously takes his hands away and runs his fingers through his hair. A shade of pink comes to his cheeks and I can feel my face blushing as well. I bite my bottom lip as I follow him through the rest of the wrecked vehicles. I never thought I would meet someone who could make me feel this way. Especially not with the way the world is at the moment. I just can't shake the feeling coming over me. It's like nothing I've ever felt before.

We make our way out of the heap of cars and the highway is clear up ahead. Grass has grown through the cracks in the cement and a few tree branches are scattered around. I stay close to Ryder, feeling his warmth on my arm.

"Can I ask you something, Bridget?" he says, keeping his eyes on the road.

I nod, "I guess."

"It's just something completely stupid, but I guess I was just wondering if maybe," he takes a deep breath, "when we get to that city I was talking about, if it's even there, if you would consider staying? You know, not go off wandering to someplace that is probably covered in vampires and zombies."

I shrug, "I don't know. I haven't thought about it. Getting to Canada was the only plan my dad ever made for my family. If there's nothing there like you said, I don't really have any other plan on where to go. I do want to find a safe place to live. Someplace where I'm not constantly fighting off the undead. I'll miss that, don't get me wrong. But I want to be in a place where someone else is there to keep me safe instead of only having myself to rely on."

"And if we find that in Des Moines, you'll stay?" he asks.

"Probably." I reply. "Why do you want to know?"

He glances down at his feet, "I don't know. You're just the first nice person I've come across out here in the last year and a half. The only person who didn't push me away, who seems to trust me a little. It's only been a day since we met, but that's long enough for me to consider you as a friend. Unless you don't want that."

I let out a sarcastic sigh, "I don't know. I have *so* many friends as it is, I might not have room for one more."

He chuckles, "I'll just take that as a maybe."

I stare at him for a moment. Even with the smile on his face, he still appears to be troubled. Whatever caused him to be alone for so long has really taken a toll on him. It makes me feel bad about having at least one person in my life to depend on almost every day since things went downhill. I always forget that not everyone was as lucky as me.

"I'm sorry you don't have anyone, Ryder. Losing my family was the worst thing I could have gone through, but I can't imagine never having someone in the first place." I state.

He gives me a half smile, "It's okay. I should be used to it, but there are times when you just need someone there to talk to, to lean on. Like you said, you want to have someone to keep you safe instead of no one there at all. It makes me glad that you didn't just walk away from me back there after I asked to go with you."

"Me too. Although, I don't think I would have gotten very far on my own. You made that very clear last night when that vamp came up from behind me. I guess I should say 'thank you' for that."

He shrugs, "I'd do it again and I know you'd do the same."

I nod, "Yeah, someone has to help the human race win this thing."

***

Another day down and an eternity left to spend trying to find safety. We spent the night in the back of an old minivan, each taking turns sleeping while the other kept watch. You know, the same old routine just on a different night. It was much better than sleeping in the grass or on the hard cement, despite the fact that the van smelled like death. At least there weren't any rotting corpses to keep us company.

We got moving soon after the sun came up, still heading north in hopes of finding some place with actual living people. We have nothing to eat for breakfast and only half a bottle of water left. The rain never came and neither of us wanted to look for a nearby lake in the woods by the highway, so we have no way to refill the bottle. Our stomachs growl at us, our legs beg us to stop moving and sit for a while. The longer we sit, the longer it will take us to find a safe place and the longer we'll go without eating. Sorry to say, but our legs won't win this battle.

"What time is it?" Ryder asks, running his fingers through his messy hair.

I glance at my watch, "One o'clock."

"We have to find food soon or we won't make it very far. My stomach's growling and I can hear yours as well. We have to be coming close to a town or a house with food in it or something. This highway can't seriously be empty." Ryder says.

"It seems like it is, though."

He shakes his head, "It just can't be. There *has* to be something close."

"We could try catching a squirrel or hunting a deer. If we don't find a town anytime soon, we'll have to do that." I say.

He smiles but doesn't say anything. Both of us keep our eyes peeled for anything we could use for food. There's really nothing out here, besides trees and grass. Maybe when I was a little kid a grass and leaf pie would sound amazing, but that doesn't even sound the least bit appetizing right now.

I've gone a couple days without eating much of anything before and it's not a very easy thing to do. Your mind sort of slips into a state of insanity for a few minutes. You start freaking out, thinking you're going to die at any second. I remember feeling like my stomach was going to implode on itself and I would just vanish into thin air because my body was so hungry it ate itself. Not something I am looking forward to going through again.

We come across a green landmark sign. Ryder glances at it, but keeps moving. I stop and stare at it for a moment. It seems very familiar to me and I have a feeling of what it might mean. The names of the cities are scratched out with black spray paint, much like the one my dad and I came across days ago. My feet quickly move so I can see the back of the sign and a smile crosses my face.

Ryder finally stops walking and gives me a funny look, "What are you so happy about?"

I point to what's painted on the back of the sign, "You see that? S 10 N. It means in ten miles north of here, we will find a safe place."

He squints his eyes in confusion, "How you do know that?"

"My dad taught it to me about a week ago when we were trying to find a town. It's how traveler's communicate with each other, I guess." I reply.

"So, you're telling me that in just a few miles we will find a town or something?"

I smile and nod.

"Then there's a good chance we'll find food and a place to stay tonight?"

Again I smile and nod, "Damn right."

Finally, a smile comes to his lips, "Then let's get moving, Bridge."

He grabs my hand and pulls me away from the sign. I let out a small laugh as I walk quickly beside him. We might be stuck living in hell towards the bottom of the food chain, but being with Ryder somehow makes things better. I miss my dad and my family, I'll never stop missing them. But I can't dwell on them forever and Ryder is doing a good job at taking my mind off them.

We keep moving as fast as our legs can carry us without breaking into a run. I don't think either of us has enough energy for that right now. The sun shines through a break in the clouds and lights up the world a little bit. A slight breeze blows through the trees and I take in a deep breath through my nose. My heart skips a beat as that familiar scent of death enters my nostrils.

That's enough to ruin *any* day.

"Ryder, I think there's something bad up ahead." I say.

"What are you talking about?" he asks, still pulling me along with him.

"Don't you smell it? The death in the air?"

He takes a second to sniff the air, then shakes his head, "I don't smell anything."

"I do and it has never failed me before."

We stop walking and he looks me dead in the eye, "So, what are you saying?"

"I'm saying there is most likely something dead on the road ahead of us. Not the actual dead kind of thing either." I reply.

He glances to the road ahead. I do the same. If we turn back to find a safer route, we risk starving ourselves for even longer. Our only choice is to keep going straight.

"We should keep going. Whatever it is, we can fight them off." He says, hiding the fear in his voice. "With your badassedness and my strong will to live, I think we can do it."

"You *think* we can do it? I know we can." I walk away from him, a sense of pride on my shoulders. "Remember, killing zombies is one of my strong points."

Ryder rushes to my side and pulls my dad's gun out of his satchel. I loaned it to him over night in case something popped out of nowhere. Mine is safely tucked behind my back, but I quickly pull it out and turn the safety off. The smell grows stronger and I can tell we're getting close. So close in fact, we can hear their quiet moaning. We walk by a few more cars and come across them. There's two of them standing alone, but that isn't what catches our eyes.

A group of men, each wearing green pants and shirts and combat boots, carrying large guns, are fighting off the two zombies. I notice even more dead monsters lying in pools of their brown blood on the ground. Not a single one of the men fires a shot at the zombies. Instead, we watch as they jab them in the head a few times before they fall to the ground with their friends. That's when one of the guys pulls out a machete and stabs each of them in the brain thus ending their pathetic excuse for a life. A gurgled moan is the last thing to escape their throats.

I turn the safety back on my gun and hold it down at my side. Ryder and I keep walking toward the group of men. It doesn't take much for one of them to notice us and start walking our way. He aims his rifle and we stop in our tracks.

"You humans?" he shouts.

Both of us nod and say, "yes," at the same time.

He lowers the gun and smiles, "You must be looking for Hatfeld. We're headed there right now."

"Is that the safe zone not far ahead?" Ryder asks.

He nods, "Yeah, just a few more miles down the highway."

"And there's food there?" Ryder asks again.

"Yeah, there's plenty of food. You two are welcome to join us seeing as how we are headed in the same direction." The man says then moves a little closer to us. "My name is Nick. The others and I are in charge of keeping those zombie bastards away from the fence surrounding the city."

"I'm Ryder and this is Bridget. We are just trying to find a safe place for a little while."

"Then you're going to the right place. We welcome any and all travelers. Just follow us." Nick says with a smile, then turns away.

Ryder and I follow him and the others, stepping over

the bodies along the way. I can't believe I missed an opportunity to kill a few zombies. I'm sure I'll have other chances to shed a few bullets on the undead, but I still hate the times when I miss it. At least going to a city for food and a bed to sleep in tonight will make up for that slightly.

Only slightly.

***

It takes twenty minutes to walk to the gates of Hatfeld, an old city people are trying to make new again. There's a ten foot high fence with barbed wire at the top which surrounds the entire place. According to Nick, it keeps the zombies at bay. I've never seen a chain link fence stand in the way of a flesh hungry zombie before. They are pretty strong and can take down a really big guy when they're given the chance. Then Nick pointed out the guard towers spread thirty feet apart along the perimeter of the fence. There's never a time when any of the towers are empty. That makes me feel a little better about being here.

We wait a few seconds for the gate to be pushed open. Then we're greeted by even more smiling men in dark green outfits with guns. Each offers us a handshake and welcomes us to Hatfeld. It's a little weird seeing all the big guys happy that we chose their city to come to. I'm not the only one who isn't used to this sort of thing. Ryder is more on edge than I am. He's holding my hand and I can feel it shaking. I guess the bravery he felt when we were about to fight off some zombies has faded.

Nick leads us away from the gate and away from the rest of their little army. We follow him into a small metal building with a desk on the inside. On the walls, are photos of different people with a sad face drawn on each of them.

"What's with the pictures?" I ask, not fighting my curiosity at all.

Nick looks around the room as he makes his way behind the desk, "Oh, those are loved ones of some of the people who live here. We keep them on the wall so we know what we're fighting for every time we go out looking for zombies. They give us hope."

I nod, "I see. What about the ones the vamps get?"

He snaps his head my way and answers, "They don't come this way."

I raise an eyebrow. That's the first time I've ever heard of a vampire staying away from a town for no good reason. I wonder if I'll find out why that is while I'm here.

Nick sits on a swiveling chair and stares up at us with a smile, "Again, I want to welcome you both to Hatfeld. We have limited electricity throughout the city. We were able to tie into some old power lines and reconfigure them to work. Just in the important buildings like our hospital and school and the armory. Every other place has more than enough candles and is equipped with flashlights and glow sticks.

"Like I said earlier, we have plenty of food to go around. A farm just on the other side of town is responsible for our meat supply and fresh fruits and veggies. There's a few wells throughout the city to provide us with drinking water, but the plumbing is scarce. We are still working on getting that going again, but it does work in some buildings. The toilets where you'll be staying work well. Also, there are shops all over town and everybody is incredibly nice. We love newcomers. It means humans are able to survive out there."

"Yeah, we aren't the only ones either." I say.

"And we are more than grateful for that." Nick says then leans forward again.

He pulls open a drawer from the desk and reaches inside. He comes back with a small black bag and tosses it on top of the wooden desk.

"Take that. Explore the city. Get yourselves some food and clean clothes to change into. There's a hotel on Fifth Street, the Renaissance. I'll meet you there after dinner, say seven o'clock tonight." Nick says.

"What's at the hotel?" I ask.

"A place for both of you to stay for a while." the smile never leaves his face, "Just take that little bag and enjoy yourselves. Our city is your city now."

Ryder's hands are still shaking, so I hesitantly reach for the small bag. I hold it open in the palm of my hand and peer inside. A handful of small, colorful jewels are all I see. My mouth drops and I let Ryder look at them. I've never seen precious stones like this before.

"Are these real?" I ask, shocked.

Nick nods, "Yeah, it's our form of currency here. A welcome present for travelers."

Ryder takes the velvety bag out of my hand and smiles, "Thank you."

"You are very welcome. You two kids enjoy the rest of the day."

Ryder pulls me along with him and we walk out of the small building. He closes the bag and puts it in his jean's pocket for safekeeping. I can't stop thinking of how weird this place seems so far. Nick couldn't stop smiling at us the *entire* time he was talking. Even the other guys in his little group of fighters all had creepy smiles on their faces as they welcomed us. Whatever is going on here, I hope it's all just in my head. I don't want this place to not be what I want it to be.

I want it to be safe.

We walk further in the city. Tall buildings line each side of the street and people scurry about on the sidewalks below them. They all seem to be in a hurry to get somewhere. I glance through one of the big picture windows on a building. A diner is setup inside with a few people sitting down for a nice meal. Above that diner, are apartments. I look up and see clothes hanging from wires over the street to dry. There's an older couple sitting out on their balcony enjoying the day with mugs of whatever they're drinking in their hands. A young woman is shaking out a brown rug out on her balcony and a couple of kids are playing a board game at her feet.

Ryder turns onto another street. Our hands are still entwined so I am forced to go along with him. More buildings with various stores and cafés are setup on the main floor with living space above. It's like they took the busiest part of whatever city this used to be and changed it into something else. Something warm and cozy and way too welcoming to make me feel comfortable.

We turn onto another street and are greeted by an aroma so wonderful, I can feel the drool building in my mouth. Whatever is baking, sends a rage of hunger in both of our stomachs. They growl and ache as we walk toward the origin of the scent. It leads us to a small bakery in a building all of its own. Tables are setup outside and only two other people are there enjoying a slice of pie. My mouth waters at the very sight of something so wonderful.

"I think we found our first meal here." Ryder says with a smile.

I nod and rush to the bakery with him. He pulls the door open and the smell is even more wonderful inside. Apples, blueberries, even the smell of cooked bananas fill our noses and we take in the amazing scent as though we will never experience it again.

The old woman standing behind the counter smiles at us, "I haven't seen you two around here before. Are you traveling?"

I nod, "Yeah, we are headed north."

"Well, we just love when travelers stop in for a spell.

Why don't you two find a table and I'll bring you a couple slices of my famous blueberry pie along with a glass of fresh milk." She offers.

"That sounds amazing." Ryder replies.

He lets go of my hand and we choose a table right next to the window looking out at the street. The two people sitting outside smile and wave when they notice our stares. We wave back and wait patiently for our meal to be brought out to us.

"This place is wonderful." Ryder exclaims.

I nod, "Yeah, seems too wonderful though. Everyone is being super nice and they don't even know us."

"Yeah, I noticed that. It makes me a little nervous, but that's just how these people are I guess. Maybe they don't judge as quickly as others." He says.

I shrug, "I hope you're right."

The old woman brings out a tray with two glasses of milk and two plates, each with a decent sized piece of pie. She smiles again, sets a couple forks on the table as well, then walks away. My eyes widen and I lift the fork from the table. It's been so long since I've had something this fantastic to eat. I've probably forgotten just how great it tastes. Ryder has already dug into his pie and shoved the first bite in his mouth. I take my time and savor the moment.

I stab the pie with my fork, making sure I get some of the blueberries with it, then bring it up to my nose and take in its luxurious scent. I close my eyes and, finally, put the bite in my mouth. My taste buds come alive in a frenzy as the sweet taste covers my tongue.

"Oh my god, this is great stuff." I say with my mouth full, then go for another bite.

Ryder smiles with a mouth full of food and nods his head.

***

City life is so much different than being on the road. Especially in this city. There are so many people and each one of them smiles at us as we walk by. Every other safe town I've been too, I've never been more welcomed. Like the people here are super excited about strange travelers coming into their city, taking some of their food, and sleeping in a place their own people should be sleeping. I'm not an expert when it comes to being around a bunch of people, but I really don't think most cities are this friendly or happy when two strange kids walk into their home.

Other than the weird smiles we get from everybody on the street, the city isn't so bad. There's plenty of things to see and places to go. There's a different kind of shop on about every corner. They even have a place where people go to pay taxes right next to a clothing store. One Ryder and I happily ventured into. We each found a new pair of jeans, a couple shirts, and other things we couldn't go too long without having. After that, we explored a little more.

There's a public bath house right next to their little hospital building. Since the hospital has running water, it was easier for them to build a place for people to get clean right next door. Not a place I want to visit anytime soon. I'd rather not have a group of random nice people see me naked. Even though the showers are all inside and blocked off with curtains, it wouldn't stop an old, creepy guy to walk in on a helpless young girl like me. I'll take my chances elsewhere.

The school is a few blocks down from the hospital. It was at one point a community college, but now it's home to the few hundred kids who need to learn things. It is important to have a place for everyone to learn what this world used to be like at one point in time. There's no saying how long we'll have to live with zombies and vampires constantly on our tail so it's good to keep our history going. The future generations need to know what life used to be like without those creatures wandering around.

There are countless apartment buildings made out of old offices above some of the stores. We don't see many houses or anything like that. I guess these people want to stick close together. I see people staring down from their apartments as we walk along the street. The ones looking through their windows don't seem as happy as the ones we pass on the street. From what I can see of their faces, they seem distraught, like they know something we don't. I have no intention of staying here long enough to find out the secrets of the city, no matter how much I kind of want to. As soon as Ryder and I have everything we need to go on with our trip, we'll be out of here. I'm really hoping that's sooner rather than later. This big city life isn't meant for a traveler like me.

After getting directions from a lovely young lady selling flowers, we make our way to that hotel Nick told us about earlier. It's a little before seven, but we stand outside and wait for him to show up. A woman with a little poodle walks by, her smile not as sincere as most, like she feels sorry for us. I follow her with my eyes and happen to catch sight of something familiar in the arms of a little boy. His back is to me, so I can't tell who he is, but the teddy bear in his arms has me wondering.

"What are you staring at, Bridge?" Ryder asks, staring right along with me.

"I think I know that little boy over there." I point toward the teddy bear.

I keep my eyes on the boy. He's standing with an older man who's in the process of buying some bread from an old couple on the corner. He seems familiar as well and I start walking in their direction. Ryder follows me as we cross the street. The man pays for their food then turns around and I am finally able to see his face. A face I thought I would never see again.

"Bridget? Is that you?" Sherry's father asks with a look of confusion on his face when he sees me walking their way.

I smile and nod, "Yeah, it's me."

"What are you doing here?" he asks.

"We needed some food and this city was on our path." I reply. "Is Sherry here too?"

He nods, "Yeah, she's right behind you."

I quickly turn around and lock eyes with Sherry. A huge grin comes to her face and she lets out a little squeal before running up and wrapping her arms around me. I hug her back, trying to figure out what her family is doing here. They were headed west the last time I saw them and this city is north of where we were days ago. Sherry pulls away from me after a few seconds and still smiles.

"Oh my god, I thought I'd never see you again. What are you doing here, Bridget?" she asks.

"We came here for food and a place to stay a while." I reply. "What are you guys doing here?"

The smile disappears from her face and she looks down at her feet, "Something horrible happened after we left that town with the vampires. We were heading to California, but we ran into some zombies and things got really bad really fast. They got my uncles while dad tried to protect us. Then we ran away and mom fell behind. It was too late when we realized it." I can see tears building in her eyes. "We got lost when and wound up finding this place yesterday. They gave us food and water and fresh clothes to change into. Even a nice room in that big hotel across the street."

"Same here. We're meeting that guy, Nick, in a few minutes so he can show us to our room." I say.

Sherry looks around me, finding the other person I'm with, "Where's your dad?"

I shrug and shake my head, "He's gone."

She lets out a sigh, "This whole world just sucks for both of us right now."

I nod, "Yeah, but it's not all bad. I met Ryder a couple days ago and decided to travel north together."

He steps up to my side and smiles. Sherry smiles back then gives me a thumbs up. I'm guessing that's her way of saying he's hot. I totally agree with her on that, if that is what she's thinking.

"I think that Nick guy is over there waiting for us." Ryder says quietly.

I glance across the street and see the big guy standing at the entrance to the hotel waiting for us. He sees us and smiles, waving a friendly hello. Ryder waves back, but I stay still. I see the look on Sherry's face and I find myself wondering what she's thinking as she stares at the man across the street. In a way, she seems almost frightened and, at the very least, she seems worried.

"I guess I gotta go see where we're going to stay for the night." I say, hoping it changes her expression.

It doesn't and she turns her eyes my way.

"I have to tell you something important, Bridget." She says so quiet only I can hear her.

"Okay. What is it?" I ask.

"It's something about this place. Something that will make you wish you never came here." She says.

"Just tell me what it is already." I press.

"That guy over there. He's not who you think he is. He's something worse and will try to ta..." she gets cut off by Nick shouting at us to hurry along.

I smile at her and say, "Tell me later?"

She closes her lips and nods. I smile then join Ryder and walk across the street. I look over my shoulder. Sherry and her father watch as we walk away from them. Both of them seem worried and it's giving me a worried feeling as well. Maybe I should have let her finish her sentence before cutting her off.

"So glad you two made it here okay." Nick says as we step onto the sidewalk. "Sorry to be in such a hurry, but I need to get back to the fence. Zombies like to hang around when it's the rainy season. It's like they think the rain will give them an edge on getting through the gate."

We follow him through the glass doors of the hotel and walk into a luxurious lobby. Everything is clean and polished. It looks like this place has never even seen the effects of the cure. It smells so fresh and feels exactly like a hotel should feel like. A home away from home.

"Again, sorry but there isn't electricity here. One of the fallbacks of trying to preserve the important things. The only plumbing is a water pipe we have running to each floor of the hotel for a drinking fountain and another for the toilets. We're very slowly getting the plumbing going throughout the city. I've set up a room for you on the fifth floor. You'll have a fireplace and even a balcony to look out at the city. It is a beautiful view when the sun is shining, but with the storm rolling in, it's not much to look at." Nick states.

He shows us the way to the stairs and we follow him up each one. We're out of breath by the time we make it to the fifth floor and are more than ready to plop down on the bed as soon as we have the chance. Our room is at the very end of the hallway with an old pop machine right across the hall from the door. The number on the door is 27E in big, gold digits. Nick opens the door for us and I smile when I see inside.

The bed is massive, at least a king size, and the sheets and pillows look so soft and comfortable. The fireplace has already been lit and a few candles have been placed around the room to lighten it up a bit. The sliding French doors leading to the balcony are open, letting the breeze flow through the room. The bathroom is right behind the door, but only the toilet works as Nick so simply stated.

Ryder and I walk into the room and he sets his satchel on the floor next to the bed. I take my backpack off and do the same.

"Well, I'll leave you two to get comfy for the night. I've been told it's going to rain pretty good in a few hours so if you go back out into the city, be careful." Nick says with a smile then closes the door to our room.

***

Ryder and I didn't bother going back outside to venture the city. Neither of us wanted to be around anymore super nice people and I can always catch up with Sherry when I see her again. She is staying in the same hotel as we are and I'm sure I'll bump into her eventually. As for right now, I just want to lay on the bed, listen to the rain hitting the glass of the sliding doors, and be with Ryder.

All we've been doing since Nick left is talking. He told me what life was like for him being an orphan. I tried not to make my life seem a lot better with my stories of a normal childhood and an actual family. He hated every foster family he had to live with which is why he chose to force himself to love school. He threw himself into extracurricular activities just to get away and became quite the smart student. I, on the other hand, was not a big fan of school and I really don't miss it, other than the whole journalism thing. I wasn't the brightest crayon in the box, but I got good enough grades to pass my classes.

"So," Ryder says, "what do you think you would be doing right this moment if there weren't any zombies and vampires out there?"

I sit across from him on the bed, both of us sitting with our legs crossed, "I don't know. I guess I'd be at some college somewhere studying to be a journalist. Not the sit behind the desk writing nonsense for a newspaper type. I wanted to be the one who went out to get the stories first hand. To be right there when the action happens."

He smiles, "That fits you."

"What about you?"

He shrugs, "I never really had a plan on what I wanted to be. I just wanted to turn eighteen and stop being in a foster family. I like to hope that I wouldn't be living on the streets right now if things were different. I guess I do live on the streets right now, but it just seems worse when you take the zombies and vamps out of the picture for some reason."

"I think I get what you mean. Being homeless without the monsters and knowing you could have a home but you're still forced to live on the streets, does seem a bit worse than living in this world. At least we know we will never have a home again." I say. "Really sucks ass either way you look at it, though."

He smiles, "Yeah it does."

"You know, you never really told me how you ended up alone. You told me about that group you were with when you were on your way home after this all happened, but you never said why you're alone now. I've told you my shitty reason, what's yours?" I ask.

The smile goes away and he runs his fingers through his messy hair. Whatever happened to him had to be something terrible. He looks upset and confused and sad all balled into one expression on his face. I know the story about my life is pretty sad and messed up, but the way he looks right now, his seems like it could be worse.

Ryder takes a deep breath as he opens his mouth to speak, "If I tell you something, will you promise not to freak out and run away?"

I raise an eyebrow, "I think I can do that."

"Thank you," he says, "It's just...I think I really like you, Bridget, and I don't want what happened in my life to ruin that. I know we just met and all, but you're the only person I've met out here that makes me feel nervous and relieved at the same time. I don't want to lose that."

Glad to know he feels the same way I do, "I understand. I really like you too."

He smiles, then moves his hands down to the bottom of his shirt. I watch as he lifts it off his body and over his head, my eyes ogling his perfect stomach as he does so. Another feature about him to fall in love with. He has a great personality, sense of humor, and it makes things even better seeing how amazing he looks without a shirt on. I feel like a tween making googly eyes at the latest poster boy to hit the scene.

He tosses his shirt to the floor and rubs his right shoulder. My eyes move across his chest to where his hand is massaging and my jaw drops. The perfectly shaped scar on his shoulder makes my heart race and I start to rethink everything. Maybe he's been lying to me this whole time and isn't what he looks like. That bite mark on his shoulder is enough to make anyone on the planet freak out, especially in a world where one bite mark can ruin your life forever.

"Please tell me that's not what it looks like?" I plead.

He shakes his head, "It's meant to."

"Why?"

He swallows hard and takes another deep, calming breath, "It happened over a year ago. I was with this group in New York City holed up in an old house in the suburbs. I went out one day to get food and when I came back, they were gone. They took everything, my clothes and supplies, everything. I was left alone, so I walked into the city hoping to find a different group I could be with. A week went by and no one wanted to help a poor boy like me. New York is a horrible place to be alone in. It's big and everyone there is mean and hateful. So, I figured if nobody wanted me around, I would just wait in an alley somewhere for death to find me. Something else happened and I thought everything was going to be okay.

"These two men offered me food and shelter and a place to sleep. I went with them and they lured me into a part of an old subway tunnel. I think it was a maintenance room or something. They gave me all the food I could eat and plenty of water. I thought I was going to be okay."

"You weren't, were you?" I ask, noticing his eyes turning red.

He shakes his head, "I should have taken a better look at them and listened to how they spoke before going with them. Once they lit a torch in that room, I noticed their pale skin and realized when they spoke, they weren't human. They talked slower and really had to force some of the words out. By the time I tried to leave, they knocked me out with something and when I woke up, I was chained to a wall with my shirt off." He looks away from me and sighs. "I thought they were going to bite me. I thought that's how they did it to turn regular humans into vamps like them. I was very wrong.

"The vamps in that city are different. They're smart and know how to act more human than most, like they adapted. They knew the human supply would run low eventually and knew they needed to find a way to savor the fresh blood supply. They took a knife and cut this into my skin." His fingers glide over his scar again. "They made it look like a bite mark in case I tried to escape. That way it looked like I was one of them so humans would want to kill me. Those vamps cut me like this every day for months, letting out just enough blood so they could survive."

"That's horrible. I never knew vampires were capable of tricking us like that or even smart enough to not kill us and steal our blood a different way." I say.

"I don't think anybody does. Most of the time they just attack, but these never did." He continues.

"How did you get out?" I ask, trying not to be too interruptive.

"They kept me down there for months, I think. Then one day, they took too much blood and I passed out. I guess they thought I was dead and threw me out into the tunnel. I woke up and realized I was free so I found my way outside and luckily it was daylight. That's when people started trying to kill me. The second they saw the mark on my shoulder, they thought I was one of them. Either a zombie or a vampire. I've been shot at, knives have been thrown at me numerous times. Every time I find a group who will allow me to travel with them, they end up seeing the scar and the attempts of murder start all over again. I can't tell you how many times I've had my ass kicked over this damn thing.

"That's why I was alone when you found me. Why I thought I would always be alone. No one understood this and no one wanted to give me a chance to explain. Then I saw you outside killing those zombies in the street. All I thought, was maybe she's different. She could be the one person who won't judge me because of this. I'm really hoping I was right about that."

I glance from his eyes to his shoulder again. It's remarkable how much it looks like a bite mark from one of those creatures out there. Even more remarkable that vampires are able to come up with a plan as devious as that. Tricking humans to follow them to their secret hideout and stealing their blood without killing them. That is sheer brilliance on their part. Makes me wonder what else they are capable of.

I move my eyes back to his and see the tears building up. I know he's waiting for me to say something. The pained look in his eyes gives that away. He went through something I could never imagine. Being a prisoner of a monster, not knowing if they'll ever kill him or just leave him chained to that wall forever. I can't be the one person to judge him based on something bad that happened to him over a year ago.

"I'm glad you told me that. That couldn't have been easy." I say.

"It wasn't."

"People are idiots. They don't realize that you're not something bad and assume you're a monster based on a scar. I know it looks like something a zombie or a vamp would do to you, but even if you never told me that story, I'd always know that you aren't one of them. You're a good guy." I say.

He smiles, "Thanks, you don't know how much that means to me. Especially hearing it come from you."

Here comes the butterflies again. That nervous feeling in the pit of my stomach is starting to surface and my lips are quivering. Is this one of those moments when I realize I could fall in love with this boy? Is this when I realize I care about someone else with a horrible past like mine? Someone I met a couple days ago and don't want to go anywhere on this planet without him next to me? There's a good chance this is one of those moments.

Ryder leans forward and brushes my bangs behind my ear. He stares into my eyes and my breathing quickens. Without saying a thing, he closes the small gap between us and presses his lips onto mine.

He's kissing me.

My first kiss.

Better yet, I'm kissing him back.

This will be that moment I'll remember for the rest of my life as the only time I'm ever grateful for those damned scientists who developed the cure five years ago. This moment wouldn't have happened without them.

***

The storm outside is getting worse, but the feeling I'm getting when I look at Ryder is getting even better. When he pulled away from me, breaking our kiss, those feelings only got more real. I feel like I can't let anything bad happen to him ever. I can't let him leave me and I don't ever want to leave him. From the very instant our lips touched the second time, my mind was made up about what my plan is going to be when we make it to Des Moines. Even if I hate it there, I'll never find it hard to stay as long as I'm with him.

We're still sitting on the bed, staring at each other. Neither of us have said a word since our last kiss came to an end. I can still feel his lips against my own and I never want that feeling to go away. The rain pounds against the window and I glance toward it. The sun has set and I'm sure most of the city is safe in their homes for the night.

As I watch the rain hitting the glass of the sliding doors, an idea pops into my head. This hotel doesn't have too much running water and it's been a while since I've taken a shower of some sort. The rain might not be the best choice, but it seems like a fun thing to do.

I slide off the bed and pull the hair tie from my hair letting it fall on my shoulders. Next, I lift my shirt over my head and toss it on the floor with my boots, then begin un-buttoning my jeans. I slide them down over my legs and pull my socks off along with them. I lose my balance a little bit, but keep my cool and laugh at myself. I can feel Ryder's eyes staring at me. I'm wearing nothing besides blue panties and a pink colored bra. I admit, I feel extremely naked in front of him, but it's the most I plan on letting him see of me, for the moment.

"What are you doing?" he asks.

I face him and shrug, "Can't you tell when a girl wants to take a shower?"

"How are you planning on doing that when this place doesn't have water?"

I point to the balcony, "I'll compromise."

I walk to my bag and reach inside for the bottles of soap. I carry them to the French doors and slide them open. The cool air feels good against my skin and rain splashes on the carpet hitting my toes.

I smile at Ryder and say, "You can join me, ya know. I have plenty of this stuff."

"Are you saying I stink?"

I shrug, "Maybe. Maybe not."

I back out onto the balcony and set the bottles on one of the white, plastic chairs sitting outside. The rain water is slightly cold, but not enough to ruin anything. I let it fall over my body, soaking my underwear. It feels good to wash everything away. The pain I feel over missing my father, the sadness I felt for Ryder after he told me his story, but the good feelings remain. Those are never allowed to leave.

Inside our room, Ryder slowly pulls himself from the bed. He's still shirtless, so he steps out of his pants and leaves them in a pile on the floor. His red boxer shorts are all that's left as he comes waltzing outside to join me. He shakes his head and smiles when the cool water caresses his skin.

"You're a little crazy, Bridget." He says.

I shrug, "I know. You can blame my dad for that one. He taught me everything I know."

He laughs, "It has been a while since I've felt clean, even though this rain water can't be too great."

I reach for the bottle of shampoo and squeeze a little in my hand. Ryder holds out his and I give him some as well. I set the bottle back down, then scrub my hair with the oceany-smelling shampoo. Ryder does the same and I watch the bubbles run down his body. They flow against every curve of the muscles on his chest, right down to his feet. Another feeling is starting to take over as I watch him wash his body. A yearning feeling. His hands move over his chest and stomach, then down to his legs. I bite my bottom lip and realize my hands have stopped moving. Every inch of him is beckoning me in ways I've never felt before.

"You okay over there, Bridge?" he asks.

I quickly nod my head and go back to work on cleaning my own body. I can see his eyes staring back at me, watching my hands move through my hair. They drift down the entirety of my body and he moves closer to me. The way his wet hair covers his forehead, I can't seem to take my eyes off him. His gorgeous hazel eyes and unforgettable smile. The muscles of his tan chest and stomach. All the way down to his bare feet as they stop a few inches away from me. My breathing quickens and I look up into his eyes. That feeling I'm getting is growing and I'm finding it very hard not to touch him. It's really hard not to grab onto him and force his lips against my own. I guess he can't find the strength to control himself either. He reaches out and puts his hands on my waist, moving them up and down my stomach and back, massaging the sudsy bubbles into my skin.

"I've never met anyone like you before." He says as he stares into my eyes. "I know it's only been a few days, but I can really see myself falling in love with you."

I give into whatever this feeling is. I put a hand on the back of his neck and pull his face to mine. I press my lips against his and close my eyes tight. He kisses me back, holding me tight in his arms. The rain falling on our heads is just a mere annoyance as we hold each other. His hands run up and down my spine. I wrap my arms around him, no part of me wanting this moment to end. A million zombies and vampires could show up and they still wouldn't be enough to break us apart.

Nothing could.

I can't shake this out of my head. Whatever this is, it's different than anything else I've ever experienced before. I've never wanted to be with someone more than I want to be with Ryder. Not in whatever way my body is wanting to be with him.

Things are really getting heated between us. We can't keep our hands off each other. Our kiss is getting stronger, the French kind, with our tongues massaging one another's. Whatever this feeling is inside me has changed into a sort of ache to be even closer to him. Something I can't control and he's totally feeling the same thing. We move back into the hotel room, out of the rain. We don't even make it to the bed. He trips over something on the floor and both of us topple over with me on top of him. Our lips remained locked together and the warmth of his body sends playful shivers up my spine. Ryder holds me tight as he takes control and rolls over to be above me.

I realize things are going from just a simple make-out session, to something I know will be more complex. I've never done anything like this before and my mind has no idea where to even start. My body is craving him, wanting him in a way I never thought I'd ever want a man before. It's a really good feeling, but my mind is still nervous.

I force myself to stop the kiss and he stares down at me thinking something's wrong, "Are you okay?"

I nod and swallow my nervousness, "I'm good, it's just," I sigh, "it's just that I've never done this before."

He smiles, "Neither have I, but I know that I want this more than anything. I'm glad it's going to happen with you."

"Me too."

"Good, now stop talking and kiss me again." He orders.

***

We fell asleep in each other's arms. All I could dream about were those intense, sensual moments between us. Everything was perfect. He was so gentle and amazing, I never wanted that time to end and neither did he. Then he held me in his arms as we lie on the floor. I've never felt safer with another human being. Don't get me wrong, my dad was always there for me and always made sure I stayed alive, but there's something more to Ryder. Something that makes the sadness in my life go away for more than just a few seconds. He's the kind of person who could make it go away forever.

He smiles at me when I open my eyes in the morning. The rain has stopped and I can hear birds chirping outside on the balcony. I can still smell the rain from last night on his skin and in his hair. I smile back at him and tuck my arm under the white pillow. He kisses my forehead and strokes my hair. My heart flutters when his hand touches my shoulder.

"Good morning." He says.

"Yes it is." I say with a smirk.

He props his head up with his arm, "I never thought I could be this happy. Even when the world outside is hell, you make things better."

I shrug, "So do you. You make this place a little more bearable. You make me almost forget about the monsters out there. I never thought it would be possible to ever feel like that."

"Me neither," he says, "so, again, thank you for saving my life even though you didn't know you were saving anyone besides yourself."

"I'd do it again." I say, then lean forward and kiss his lips.

I close my eyes and a flash from last night comes to my mind. The feel of his naked body against my own, the taste of his kiss on my mouth. I could spend the rest of my life with him.

I open my eyes and pull myself away from him. I yawn then sit up in bed. The white blanket is still draped over me. I look to the window by the balcony. The sun is shining as rain water drips from the eave and splashes on the white patio chairs. The sliding glass doors were left open and I can smell the fresh air blowing in from outside. I run my fingers through my hair and feel my stomach growling. A nice breakfast would do us both good, then we can plan our next move. To anyone else on the planet, this city would be the perfect place to settle down and be safe forever. I don't know if that's what I really want to do just yet. I plan on staying with Ryder no matter what our decision will be. If we choose to stay, I know it won't be long for me to miss life on the road. I'd miss the thrill of killing zombies and vamps. And, yes, I'd even miss the constant threat of death looming over my head.

I know, I'm a *little* crazy.

I turn my head to Ryder and smile, "We should probably get dressed and get something to eat."

He nods as he sits up next to me, "Sounds good to me. A nice meal of anything would be great right now."

I slide to the edge of the bed and reach for my bag sitting on the floor. My new set of clothes is packed neatly inside and my boots are sitting on the floor next to it. Ryder's is right next to mine so I pick it up and toss it to him. I grab the clothes from my bag and start getting dressed. I found a nice pair of dark blue, skinny jeans that fit just perfectly. Not too tight and easy to run in. The shirt I found is a plain blue V-neck that looks great over this white tank top I got as well. It feels nice to be wearing new, clean clothes for once. After I put on a new pair of socks, I slip my boots on and zip them up. Then I grab my brush from the bag and get to work on detangling the mess of hair on my head.

I walk into the old bathroom so I can see myself in the mirror. There's just enough light shining in from the window for me to see. There's something different about my reflection this time. I look the same, with the same cut, bruises, and scars. The same freckles flow across my nose and the same brown eyes look back at me. What's different this time, is that I don't look sad anymore. I may have lost everyone I care about and I miss them more than anything else in the world. My heart aches with how much I miss them sometimes. As I look at myself in the mirror, it would appear like I haven't lost anybody. That my life isn't shot all to hell because of the zombies and vampires.

I look happy and relieved.

I *feel* happy and relieved.

I guess I have Ryder to thank for all of these feelings. He's the only thing I have in my life right now and the only person having any effect on what goes on in it. I need to stop gushing over him and the way he makes me feel. I'm sure there's at least a hundred other people with the same feelings about someone they are in love with. I can't possibly be the only one.

I let out a sigh, then take the brush to my hair. Since I was able to wash it last night, it really isn't that much of a pain to brush. It isn't that frizzy either. Wavy and a little wild looking, yes, messy and out of control, not so much. Still, I take the hair tie off my wrist and go about pulling it back into the infamous ponytail.

"Don't do that." Ryder says as he walks into the bathroom.

I turn my head toward him and ask, "Why? I've always worn my hair back."

"It looks really good down." He replies. "I mean, you look good either way, but I like how it looks now. You should keep it down."

I leer at him for a second then let my hair drop back to my shoulders. I look at myself in the mirror one more time and realize he's right. It does look really good today. I wrap the hair tie around the base of the brush and carry it out of the bathroom. I toss it in my bag then look around the room.

Our old, dinghy clothes are still strewn about on the floor. The carpet is a little wet from the French doors being left open during the rain storm. Just another reminder of how awesome everything was last night. I run my fingers through my hair, then start picking up my clothes. I fold my jeans neatly and set them on the bed. Ryder throws my shirt at me and I fold that as well. I stuff everything in my bag, including the soap we left on the balcony all night. Then I zip it up and set it on the bed.

Ryder finishes packing his things as well, then looks around the rest of the room, "Not gonna lie, I will miss this place when we leave."

"Me too." I say.

"When should we leave? Should we stay a few more days or should we get going again and keep heading north?" he asks.

I shrug, "I don't know. My dad and I have only ever stayed in a town or city for one night, then gathered whatever we needed and kept going."

"Yeah, but what if we choose to stay for more than a day?" he asks.

"It doesn't matter to me if we stay or leave. This is the cheesiest thing I'm ever going to say, but I want to be wherever you are." I say and instantly feel my cheeks blush.

"Not too cheesy. I'm thinking the same thing." He says. "Let's just get some breakfast. We'll figure out what we want to do after that."

"Great idea." I say.

We hide our bags in a tight spot under the bed, then head for the door. With any luck, no one will go in that room and take what little belongings we have. I do bring my gun with me, tucking it safely in my jeans and hiding it with my shirt. Even though my shirt is pretty tight, so there really is no hiding it. Hopefully that isn't a problem.

We walk out into the hallway and head for the stairs. We pass a few other rooms along the way, each door is wide open. Last night they were closed. I peer inside as we walk by and see no one. Each one is just as empty as the last room I peer into. This hotel must only be meant for traveler's.

My feet carry me down the five flights of stairs and both of us are out of breath when we get to the bottom. There's a familiar face sitting on a chair in the lobby and she lights up when she sees us.

"Bridget, I've been waiting for you all morning." Sherry rushes over to us.

"Really, why?" I ask.

"I told you, I have to tell you something. It's really important." She says.

I smile, "I have something to tell you too."

"Believe me, my news is far more important than anything you..." she pauses and her eyes dart back and forth between me and Ryder, "Wait a minute, did you two do something last night? Something naughty?"

I shrug and Ryder shakes his head. He starts walking away from us, heading for the exit. He's obviously not the gossiping type of guy. Sherry and I follow him outside, staying close behind.

"You have to tell me everything that happened, Bridget." Sherry says as we walk through the doors. "Was it as amazing as I tried telling you or did you cry like a big baby? I know some girls do that because it hurts or some other dumb excuse like that."

I shake my head, "No, it was pretty amazing. But it wasn't just that. Something else happened and I know this might sound weird, seeing as how Ryder and I just met, but I think I might really like him. Like really, *really* like him."

Sherry smiles and her eyes grow big, "Like you're in love with him? He is pretty hot, I'd go for that."

I shrug, "I don't know. Haven't you ever met someone you just don't want to live without? Like even after one day, you can't imagine what life would be like without them?"

Sherry thinks for a moment, then quickly shakes her head, "No, never felt like that before. I'm more of the love and run away type of girl."

The two of us laugh as we follow Ryder down the street.

***

I notice something strange after we ate breakfast at a little restaurant a few blocks from the hotel. First off, the people who served our food weren't very friendly. They didn't care how long it took for our meal to get to us and they didn't care that it was burnt. Of course, we didn't mind the eggs being slightly over cooked, but it's the principle of the matter. We paid them more than the food was worth and they treated us like garbage. Sherry seemed like she knew what was going on. It probably has something to do with whatever she keeps trying to tell me.

Even after we left the restaurant, what were extremely happy people yesterday, suddenly transformed into not so nice people today. Snarls and horrible glares were tossed our way everywhere we went. I could hear them whispering about us as we walked through the city. A few even shouted terrible names as we passed them. The warm welcome we got must have expired because I feel all but welcome.

Sherry couldn't go all morning without checking in with her father, so Ryder and I are left alone to wander the city again. We have been trying to keep our distance from as many people as we can, but every now and then, we can't help but cross the path of someone. Like this older man got really mad when Ryder stepped out in front of him. He even went so far as to push Ryder out of his way and curse all the way down the street.

"I don't think I want to stay too much longer." Ryder says, holding my hand as we turn the corner away from the tall buildings.

"I'm feeling that way too. It doesn't seem like anyone wants us here anymore." I agree. "It's just so weird. When we got here yesterday, everyone was all happy and excited. Now it's like they hate us and want us to leave."

"Maybe that's what they do. They embrace visitors for a day, then go about hating them the next. Pretty drastic mood change for a city this big though." Ryder says.

"That's for sure."

The street we're on is pretty much empty. We pass a young girl roller skating who is nice enough to smile as we walk by. The buildings are getting smaller, going from office type buildings to houses and apartments. They look a little less occupied and a lot more run down. Most of the windows have been broken out and the doors are off the hinges. All of them are dark and give off an eerie sensation. They remind me a lot of that burnt town my dad and I found. These houses might not have caught fire, but they are just as dead as the ones in that town.

We keep going, getting further away from the populated part of the city. Even the trees are pretty much dead in this neighborhood. My eyes dart from house to house, half expecting to see a horde of zombies bursting outside one of them. That would definitely add quite a bit of excitement to this already weird day.

All of the houses are big, two-story homes complete with an attached garage. They look like they would be the perfect place to raise a family and spend the rest of your life. The perfect kind of life with the perfect kind of family. The two kids who always listen to their parents and the big golden retriever running lose in the backyard. The husband who works all day and spends every night at home with his family. The wife who takes excellent care of the home while selling makeup on the side so she feels like she contributes something. The kind of life girls only dream about having nowadays. I'm glad to say that I'm not one of those girls with that kind of dream.

I'd rather not have any kids with the way things are today. They would be just another thing in your life to worry about getting killed. As for the house and the dog, well, I'm not much for dogs and I don't really mind living on the road walking day in and day out. It's definitely more exciting. Plus, I always feel like I contribute to something without finding a meaningless part time job while my husband brings home the cheese. I never want that kind of life.

I stop walking and stare at one of the houses. This one's a white, one-story home with a red front door hanging wide open. The garage door is busted down and sitting in a metal heap in the driveway. The garden by the front porch is filled with dead flowers and sticks poking up from the ground. The grass isn't green anymore and is stained a familiar shade of red in a few places. I'm sure this was that perfect house for that perfect family most girls will never have.

"What are you doing?" Ryder asks as he spots me staring up at the house.

"Don't you ever wonder who used to live in some of the houses we see?" I ask.

He shrugs, "I guess I do sometimes. If you really wanna know, why don't we just go inside and check it out?"

I start walking toward the front door of the house and say, "Okay."

He goes along with me and we hop up the two stairs leading to the concrete porch. The last time I went wandering off in some random house, I got cornered by a vampire and dad had to come to my rescue. There's always the chance of those damn things hiding in the dark corners of the house, but we are willing to take that risk. This life wouldn't be much fun if we just hid away from everything and didn't explore every once in a while.

Ryder walks inside the house first and I follow close behind. The air is musty and smells of mold. I can see the black grime growing on the walls in the corner of the foyer. The brown carpet has been stained with either mud or blood, it's too dark and old for me to tell. We walk into the living room first and take in the scene. Everything is exactly where this family left it. The TV is still hanging on the wall with the entertainment stand underneath. Grey dust covers everything and a cloud of it fills the air when Ryder smacks his hand against the white couch. An even bigger brown stain has ruined that and this one was most likely made from blood.

There are photos hanging on the wall above the fireplace. Pictures of the family that used to live here. A mom and dad with one child, a baby boy. The mom and her long blonde hair and bright red lips. The dad with his combed over brown hair that has too much product in it and the baby who is much too innocent with that adorable, toothless smile on his face. They all look so happy and carefree. They are probably all dead right now or worse, they could still be wandering the world as mindless monsters trying to eat everyone who crosses their path. My mind can be so morbid sometimes.

I keep moving, away from the fireplace. The dining room is next with a small round table in the middle. Two chairs on either end and a highchair on a side by itself. This family must have just begun when the cure was developed.

They probably didn't even see it coming when bad things started to happen here.

"Hey, come look at this!" Ryder shouts from the kitchen.

I turn away from the dining room and enter the kitchen. Everything is dirty and dust covered. There are old fingerprints covering the stainless steel appliances and the sink is overrun with moldy dishes. I see Ryder standing by the refrigerator with a smile on his face as he blocks my view of what's inside.

"What did you find?" I ask.

"Something amazing. Something neither of us thought we would ever see again." He takes what he found out of the refrigerator and my jaw drops when I see the familiar packaging. "It was stuffed inside a bag with moldy bread. It's expired, but I'm pretty sure chocolate is one of those things that doesn't taste too horrible no matter how old it is." Ryder says with a smile.

I snatch the Hershey's bar out of his hand and my mouth waters at the mere sight of it. I find the expiration date on the back. It's been bad for about two years now so there's a decent chance it's okay to eat. As long as there's no mold or nastiness on the wrapper, which still looks brand new, then we should be okay. I think I'd tear into the package regardless what it looks like.

That's just how much I love chocolate.

"It's seems like it's been forever since I've had this." I say.

"Me too," Ryder says, then snatches it back, "that's why we're going to share it. Also, if it is bad, we'll both be sick."

I smile and watch him tear the package open. He carefully pulls one side of it off and the dark colored food of my dreams is revealed. It looks just as good as the last time I had a chocolate bar. He tosses the wrapper on the floor and breaks the candy in half so we each have an equal share.

He hands my half to me and, before taking a bite, I inhale the beautiful aroma. I let the scent of that simple treat fill my nose. This is one of those foods that is absolutely impossible to describe the taste of because it is that damn good. It's like every amazing taste all balled up into one amazing treat. Before everything went to hell, I couldn't get enough of it. I'm surprised I didn't end up overweight with how many candy bars I used to get from the gas station down the street from my house.

"I know I should savor this, but I can't help it." Ryder says, then takes a decent sized bite from his half.

I take a smaller bite and really take in the miraculous taste as it hits my tongue. Something I thought I would never have again, and I probably never will after this, and it still tastes just as amazing as I remember. There might be a bit of an old chocolate taste to it, but that doesn't stop either of us from enjoying it.

It takes us a few minutes to completely finish the last great thing we remember from our childhood. I walk back to the fridge and pull the door open hoping to find another treasure like the candy bar. There's a gallon of milk, half-empty and disgusting, the moldy loaf of bread in the plastic bag, and a few other things that are too old to be any use to us. Before I close the door, we hear a noise coming from one of the back rooms. Out of instinct, I grab my gun and prepare myself for anything.

Ryder goes to the second doorway of the kitchen and pokes his head around the corner. He looks back at me and shakes his head. Then we hear the noise again, a loud bumping sound. My heart starts pounding and the two of us step into the hallway. There are three closed doors down this way and the sound came from behind one of them.

Ryder goes to the first door on the left and presses his ear to it. He shrugs, then turns the knob and pushes it open. Both of us glance inside and see a grimy old bathroom. The walls are stained yellow and the bathtub is black with mold.

He closes that door and we move to the next one. We can definitely hear something moving around behind this door. It sounds like shuffling and quiet, high-pitched moans. I hold the gun up and let Ryder open the door.

The baby's room is empty, other than a crib and a few toys strewn on the floor. I can still hear the shuffling sounds coming from somewhere in this room. I take a few steps into the dimly lit area and look around. The closet door is wide open and there's nothing hiding inside. I glance under the crib and see nothing but empty space. Same with the toy box. I turn back to Ryder and shrug.

"Maybe we should just get out of here then. This place is starting to get a little creepy." He suggests.

I nod, "Sounds good to me."

I take another long look around this room. It seems like this little baby was going to have a great life with great parents. They didn't spare any expense to buy him the good toys and a really nice looking crib. Too bad all of that was stolen away from him before he even knew what happened. Good thing he was too young to realize anything.

I keep my eyes on Ryder and notice something happening behind him. The third bedroom door, the one we haven't checked yet, is slowly being pulled open. There's no wind in this house and it's not on a slope to where the door would open and close on its own. Something is causing it to move and it makes my heart pound harder as I stare at it.

It doesn't take long for Ryder to notice the horrified look on my face. He spins around, then backs into the baby's room with me. The door opens the rest of the way and we are standing a few feet away from a six foot tall vampire. Blood stains the corners of his pale lips and down the front of his green shirt. The room behind him is completely dark, the perfect hiding place for a vamp. He steps into the hall, getting closer to us. My hand is shaking and I find it hard to lift the gun to aim.

The vamp sniffs the air and opens his mouth to speak,

"Fresh...blood. It's been...awhile." it seems like he has to force the words to come out.

I guess this thing doesn't bother leaving the house at night. He's skinny and frail and his hands shake as he moves. Not sure why he wouldn't leave the house at night when he has a whole town to devour right in front of him. But, I'm not a vampire and I really don't care how they think.

He takes another step closer.

"Shoot the damn thing, Bridget." Ryder says quietly.

My hand is still shaking and my eyes are glued to the vamp. It's just like that night at the tent with dad. That young vamp coming after me and I was too afraid to raise the gun to shoot it. I was alone that night. Ryder's here with me this time and I feel his hand gripping my free one. He holds it tight and the fear begins to fade. My shaking hand raises the gun and aims for the vamp's heart. He stops walking and cocks his head to the side.

"Kill me." He says. "You humans...still die."

Ryder squeezes my hand, "Don't listen. Just shoot."

Excellent advise. I perfect my aim and pull the trigger. The vamp lets out a deep grunt, stares at the gaping hole in his chest, then falls limp to the floor. His black blood spews from the wound and I lower the gun.

"I think we should head back." I say.

Ryder nods, "I was just thinking the same thing."

"Something doesn't feel right about this city anymore and I think the sooner we get out of here, the better." I say.

***

We get back to our room at the hotel and dig our bags out from under the bed. Luckily no one decided to "borrow" our things. That could have been bad considering as how my father's gun is still in Ryder's bag. We are going to need as much firepower we can get in order to make the long trek to the next city. I can only hope Des Moines will feel much safer than this place.

We rush down the stairs and are out of breath by the time we make it to the lobby. Sherry's father, Jim, and her cousin, Dillon are leaning against the wall next to the door. I don't see Sherry anywhere and it doesn't appear they do either. I don't want to leave the city without them coming with us. They are trying to find a safe place just as much as we are and it would make more sense if we all traveled together. I'd going against my father's rule of always keeping our group small. Despite what he thought, more people means more protection for everyone.

I approach Jim and he forces a smile to his face, "Where's Sherry?" I ask.

He shrugs, "She should be on her way here. We were going to meet up and get supplies. We plan on leaving in the morning." His eyes catch my bag, "What are you doing?"

"I think we should leave now. Something seems off about this place." I say.

"I think I know what you mean." He says. "Their little army only worries about the zombies, never the vamps. It's like they're hiding something and I think Sherry might have found out what."

I raise an eyebrow and realize I never gave her the chance to tell me what she had to say. I either interrupted her with my own thing or she became too distracted with everything else.

"I think she did too. She was trying to tell me something, but I never let her." I say.

I turn to Ryder and grab his arm and pull him away from Jim and Dillon.

"What's wrong?" he asks.

"I don't want to leave without them, without Sherry. I know it sounds silly, but other than you, she's the only friend I've ever been able to make since the cure failed five years ago." I say.

He shakes his head, "It doesn't sound silly. If I had a friend like you have with her, I wouldn't want to leave without them either."

I glance back to Jim, his eyes glued to the glass door leading outside. He's nervous and keeps a tight grip on Dillon. I move my eyes around the rest of the lobby and realize we are the only few people in the entire room. Come to think of it, I haven't seen another soul come into this place, other than Nick when he showed us to our room. There are plenty of rooms available for people to live in or rest for a few days. Why would they just sit empty like the houses across town? Why wouldn't the city help people survive and offer them a home?

"Do you find it odd that we haven't seen any other person come in or out of this place since we got here?" I ask.

Ryder nods, "A little bit. I expected to see other travelers like us, but there's no one."

"Makes you wonder why, doesn't it?"

Another nod, "Maybe whatever your friend found out and needed to tell you has something to do with it. Maybe she found out this place's secret."

I run my fingers through my hair and really start to hate myself for not letting her tell me what she knew. It could have been something horrible about this place and I'll never know unless she walks through those doors right now. And, of course, that doesn't happen. In the movies, nothing ever happens when you want it to and it seems that way in real life as well. At least those people got that part of life right.

"What should we do?" I ask Ryder. "I don't want to

stay here, but I don't want to leave without Sherry and her family."

He shrugs, "I don't know. I guess we just wait."

"But, what if she never comes back? What if something bad happened to her? What if that same bad thing is the reason why we are in this hotel alone?"

He puts his hands on my shoulders in an attempt to calm my nervous heart. I stare into his eyes and can feel tears coming to my own.

"Hey," he says, "nothing bad is going to happen to us. Nothing bad is going to happen to you. I won't let anything like that happen. We will wait one more night and if she's not here in the morning and if her family can't find her, we'll figure out what to do then. I know you don't want to leave without your friend, but if something bad has happened to her and if that same thing could come upon us, then it isn't safe for us to be here. We'll have to leave if that time comes. I know you understand that."

I nod, "Unfortunately I do."

He leans closer to me and kisses my forehead, then says, "So, why don't we go get some food and whatever we'll need so we can leave soon. Then we'll go back to the room and play the most annoying game in the world."

"What game is that?"

He smiles, "The waiting game."

***

We spent an hour going through the town getting things we'll need. Food, a small case of bullets for my gun and my dad's, a sharper knife for Ryder, and a few other things that might come in handy. No one is friendly or nice to us at all and a few shops even turned us away. The ones that were nice enough to let us get some things, seemed strange to me. They were friendly and nice, yet appeared to be distraught and upset at the same time. It's like the second they knew we were travelers and plan on leaving soon, they felt bad and a real solemn look came across many of their faces. Maybe it has something to do with the secret Sherry found out.

Jim and Dillon are still waiting in the lobby when we get back to the hotel, still no sign of Sherry. Jim said they are going to wait all night if they have to. He's exactly like my dad. He won't give up until he knows his daughter is safe and sound or at least when he finds out what's happened to her.

We go back to our room and set our bags on the floor next to the bed. Ryder locks the door and makes sure the balcony door is locked as well. Not that someone couldn't break the glass if they wanted to, but the lock still gives us a small peace of mind.

He got us a pack of playing cards so we have something to pass the time a little more quickly. Unfortunately, the only card game I've ever known how to play is Go Fish. Ryder, on the other hand, spent a lot of time with kids after school who really enjoyed this kind of thing. He knows poker, gin, 21, and a lot of others I've never heard of. A good majority of the evening flew by with him trying to teach me how to play different card games. The game of war seemed to stick in my mind and that was the one that seemed to take the longest.

"Doesn't this game ever end?" I ask.

Ryder smiles and places another card down, "It does when someone has all the cards. It just takes a really long time to get there."

I sigh, "Well, it's boring and you keep stealing all of

my cards."

"Yeah, that's the point of the game." He says.

I roll my eyes and listen to his laughter. I glance out the window, the sun has already set and the sky is dark. At least it's not raining and the stars seem to be shining for once. It's a relief to know that if we need to make a quick getaway tonight, we won't get soaked in the process.

"Hey, what time is it?" Ryder asks.

I set another card down and look at my watch, "Almost ten. Why? Do you have a hot date tonight?"

He smiles, "I think you're the hottest date I could ever have."

"Awe, so corny." I reply.

He places another card on top of mine and takes them both away since his was higher than mine. He's been doing that all night and just when I think I'm getting a break, it goes right back to him winning again. This game serves *absolutely* no purpose and goes on forever. I only have a few cards left, like four of them in my hand, and I've reached my limit of doing something so boring. I toss the cards on the bed and let out an annoyed sigh.

"Okay, you win. Can we please do something else now?" I beg.

He laughs as he gathers the cards and stacks them together, "Fine. What do you want to do?"

"Anything other than play another boring card game."

"What did you do when you were a kid if you didn't play cards? Don't tell me you were one of those computer, gaming types?" he asks.

I scrunch up my nose and shake my head, "Hell no. I hated video games and the only time I was ever on the computer was when I needed to do research or write a paper for school. I spent a lot of my time outside. My brother was trying to get a baseball scholarship so we were always in the backyard for him to practice. I had pretty good aim with a baseball, so Charlie let me pitch sometimes."

"That must be why you are so good at killing zombies." He says.

"Yeah, pretty much."

"The vamps you still need to work on though." He says, mockingly.

"Hey, I still killed the one in that house earlier. I might've hesitated for a moment, but the job got done." I argue.

"How many *have* you killed?"

"Compared to zombies, not a whole lot. My dad normally took care of them." I say. "What about you?"

He smirks, "A few, but I try to avoid those things whenever I can."

"Then it's a good thing you met me. To have someone to cover your ass when you need it."

He nods his head in agreement, "That's not the only good thing about us meeting."

He leans across the bed and puts his hand on the back of my neck. His lips press against mine and I reach my hands up, caressing his face. I run my fingers through his hair and close my eyes letting this fantastic moment flood my mind. This evening went from boring to amazing in about a second.

Crazy what love does to the human mind.

Ryder moves his hands up and down my spine, sending shivers throughout my body. I can feel his fingers gradually go under my shirt. I wonder if he can feel the goose bumps on my skin. He grabs the hem of my shirt and pulls it up over my back. He breaks our kiss only so he can take my shirt completely off. I do the same with his, then we fall back on the bed with our lips locked together.

This might not be the ideal time for making love, or whatever people are calling it nowadays. My friend is still out there somewhere, either in danger or hiding in a safe place. But, being with Ryder makes things better. He makes the bad things disappear from my head and I'm able to forget what I'm supposed to be doing with my life. I can forget all about waiting for Sherry and hoping she's okay. I can forget that our lives could very well be in danger and I can forget that this world has gone to hell and will probably never come back.

Amazing how one young man is capable of making someone forget so many bad things for a small amount of time.

I'm not going to make him stop kissing me just so we can go on with worrying about everything else out there. I don't want him to stop kissing me. I want to feel his fingertips on my body. Feel his heart beating against my own. I love feeling the warmth of his skin as I run my hands down the length of his torso. It's the one, true thing that lets me know he's alive and that he's all mine.

I pull my lips away from his for a few seconds and look into his eyes. They are smiling at me and I know the feelings I have for him are more than sincere.

"You know how you said the other day you think you could fall in love with me." I say.

He nods, "I remember."

I swallow hard, feeling the nerves rise in my heart, "I think I could see myself falling in love with you too. I think I really want that."

He smiles, "So do I."

"Is it weird that after only a few days of knowing each other for us to feel this way?"

He shakes his head, "It's only weird when those feelings aren't real. I know that whatever we have going on between us is one hundred percent real. I can feel it in my heart every time I touch you or hold your hand. Every time I look at you, I can feel it."

"Then never stop looking at me." I say, then steal another long kiss from him.

He puts his hand on the small of my back and pulls me closer. The desire radiates between us. I never want it to stop. I can't believe I've gone so long and wasted so much time in my life never knowing how amazing this whole love feeling is. Not the kind of love you have for you family, but the kind meant only for your perfect other half. Deep in my heart, I know Ryder is my perfect other half.

***

Sometime after our intense moments, we found a way to fall asleep. Ryder wrapped his arms around me and I closed my eyes. I love feeling his warm body against my back. I love knowing how safe I feel with him right here next to me. It's wonderful knowing I'm capable of loving a someone like him. Ryder has one hundred percent stolen my heart and I am beginning to find it very hard to imagine going on any road in this world without him. I want him by my side every time we come across a horde of zombies or vampires. I want him there with me, holding my hand during the moments when we're so close to death we can taste it and find a way to cheat death one more time. I never want to go without him.

Knowing there's a part of my heart that could fall in love with Ryder, really brings out the mushy-gushy girl part of me. I remind myself of my sister. She was always into those wonderful romantic moments. The kind of love where the man sweeps the girl off her feet and they ride off into the sunset together. This might not be the kind of love story Maggie was dreaming about all her life. I hope she's up there smiling down at me for getting as close to romance as possible. If there is a heaven up there somewhere, I hope they are all smiling down at me for finding a way to move on and do the one thing that was stolen from them.

Living.

I feel Ryder moving around in the bed and it stirs me awake. My eyes are still closed and heavy, but I'm conscious enough to know he's awake. He holds me tighter against him as he leans over to plant a kiss on my cheek. A smile crosses my face after that.

"I'll be right back." He says.

"Where are you going?" I say with a yawn.

"The water bottle is empty and I'm parched. Just gonna go refill it." He slides out of bed and I can hear him stepping into his jeans and putting his shoes on.

"Don't take too long." I say, then hug my pillow tighter.

"It'll just be a couple minutes. I promise." He says.

I hear him walking across the room and I open my eyes a sliver just as he reaches the door. *I wonder if he knows how good he looks without a shirt on?* He closes the door, quietly and I hear his footsteps gradually getting quieter as he walks down the hall. I squeeze the pillow and stretch my legs along the bed. The cotton of the sheets is smooth against my bare skin, almost like silk. I close my eyes and try to fall asleep again.

I don't know if it's the fact that I'm alone in this room or that Ryder isn't lying next to me anymore as to why I'm finding it really hard to drift off into dreamland again. There have been plenty of times during my life when I couldn't fall back to sleep after waking up in the middle of the night. Normally I have a legitimate reason. There are monsters coming after me or a storm is right outside the spot we chose to spend the night. This time, there aren't any monsters or bad guys chasing after me. The only thing keeping me awake is the thought that I can't wait for Ryder to come back and hold me again. I roll onto my back and open my eyes wide, staring up at the dull ceiling. We left two candles lit giving off just enough light so we can see our way around the room.

I rub my eyes and smooth the hair out of my face. I'm tired. I can feel my eyes wanting to stay shut, but my mind is refusing to let them. It's like something is going on in my head that has completely turned off my ability to sleep without Ryder by my side.

"What is going on with me?" I think out loud.

I sit up in the bed, holding onto the sheets to cover myself. I glance at my watch, just past midnight. I move to the edge of the bed and put my feet on the floor. My clothes are folded neatly on top of my backpack and I reach for my bra and panties so I can put on at least something for now. I set the rest of my clothes on the bed next to me and grab my bag. I unzip the main part and start sifting through the contents. It's the same few things I've had with me for a while now. Nothing new to report. My hand hits the photo album and I stop for a moment. I haven't opened that book since the day my brother died. I found it too hard and painful to look at the pictures of him and refused to touch the book sometimes. No one else could bear to look at it either, but as I've said before, I could never bring myself to toss it in the fire with everything else.

I pull the album out of my bag and place it on my lap. The black leather is cracked and worn, even a little damaged from rain water. After going five years of traveling in a backpack, I think I'd be a little worn out as well. It still held together, though, like my family tried to do.

My fingers grip the bottom of the cover and I close my eyes as they lift it open. I know exactly what the picture is on the first page. It was my mother's favorite, which is why it's the first one you see when you open the book. I take a deep breath and let it out as I open my eyes and stare down at the photo.

All five of us are standing outside of an old amusement park. I think I was six or seven when the picture was taken and I can't remember which park we were at. I can see the huge Ferris Wheel in the background and a roller coaster peaks in on the edge of the picture. Mom and dad stand behind us three kids and we all have the biggest, cheesiest grins on our faces. I'm standing next to my brother and his hand is resting on my head. Maggie stands in front of mom, ducked down a bit because they were the same height. We looked ridiculous, but it's because of that ridiculousness why mom loved this picture the most.

I swallow the lump in my throat and turn the page. Old school pictures of Charlie, Maggie, and myself are placed neatly on the next few pages. Mom organized them starting from when we were in Kindergarten all the way up to the last year we had school pictures taken. Mine stopped my sophomore year of high school while Maggie and Charlie's stopped when they were wearing their cap and gown at graduation. They were super happy when they walked across the stage to get their diploma and I couldn't wait to get mine. To have that feeling of accomplishment, knowing my whole family is proud of me.

I'll never get that now. The cure took it all away from me. The cure took a lot away from me.

I flip through some more pages, each one forcing the lump to expand in my throat. I can feel my eyes starting to swell with tears and one even falls on a picture of my mom and dad at their wedding. They were dancing, hiding the fact that she was three months pregnant with my sister. They knew they were destined to be together forever and had to be married before their first child was born. They kind of jumped the gun on that one.

I turn the page and discover a few of our baby pictures. I smile when I get to the one after I was born. Mom was still in her hospital gown while dad, Maggie, and Charlie crowded in around her. Charlie was four at the time and had to climb on her lap in order to be in the picture. This one is my favorite family photo. It marks the moment where my little family became whole. I'm glad there will never be a photo to remember the moment when my family died.

A few more heartbreaking pages. My eyes letting more tears drift onto the memories of the only part of my family I have left. The great times we spent together are forever saved in this little book. All of our family reunions, seeing people I can't remember anymore. Cousins, aunts and uncles, my grandparents. All of them are gone now. I get to the last page of the book and see a picture that wasn't there the last time I looked through it. It's just a small wallet sized photo of us three kids. It was taken right before Maggie went away to college, two years before the cure came along. The corners of the photo are worn and tattered and the picture itself has faded.

I pull back the sticky plastic holding the picture in place and lift it from the page. The way it feels in my hand, I can tell it's been looked at a lot. It's wrinkly and feels old. I flip it over and instantly recognize my dad's handwriting on the back of it. It's a small note to me.

"Everything is going to be alright, Bridge. I know you'll survive this world and find a safe place to live for the whole family. Just know how much I love you, how much we all love you."

If that doesn't break my heart a little more, then I don't know what will.

I wipe the tears from my eyes and read his note one more time. Why does it hurt so much to know that he thought of me right before he died? Why does it kill me inside every time I think of him and the rest of the family? Why does love have to be so painful when you know you're never going to see the people you love ever again? I wish I had the answers to these questions, but I don't think anybody on this planet does.

I carefully put the picture back in place and close the album. I hug it against my chest, imaging my entire family hugging me back through those pages. I wish their arms were around me, holding me tight and giving me the strength I need to keep moving forward. I force myself to put the book back in my bag and zip it up. I run my fingers through my hair and wipe the tears under my eyes. My heart still hurts and the lump in my throat has made a home there.

I spend a few minutes taking calm, deep breaths in an attempt to take the sadness away. I hold my head in my hands and stare at the floor under my feet. The stained carpet is in desperate need of a cleaning it will never see. Dirt has been caked into the fibers from the years of strange people stomping on it.

Speaking of stomping around, I haven't heard Ryder's footsteps in a while. I haven't heard anything outside the room for a while. I lift my head and glance at my watch. A good twenty minutes passed since he left to get water. There is a pump right down the hall where an old water fountain used to be. He should have filled it up there and been back by now.

I look to the door and stare at it for a few seconds. My mind keeps telling it to open and for Ryder to walk in the room with a goofy smile on his face. The door just isn't doing what I want it to do and it's making me really nervous.

I stand from the bed and quickly start putting my clothes back on. I step into my pants and pull them over my legs. I put my shirt on then sit back down so I can put my boots on as well. As soon as they're zipped up, I reach for my hoodie draped over the side table and put it on as well. The nights can get a little chilly sometimes. My gun is on the table next to the bed and is the last thing I grab before heading for the door.

***

The hall is empty. I look both ways and no one is there. The only light is coming through the big window at the other end of the hallway and it's just enough for me to see as I make my way to the stairs. I pass by the water fountain and I happen to kick something lying on the floor. I reach down and feel around for whatever I kicked and my hands grab onto something familiar.

The water bottle. I lift it from the floor and stare at it for a second. It's still empty, but there are droplets of water around the rim from it trying to be filled.

"Ryder?" I call out in the darkness. "Ryder, where are you?"

The only answer I receive is the chilling silence this hotel is excellent at giving off. I let the bottle fall from my hand and I move a little faster to the stairs. I practically run down each and every step, my heart pounding as I descend. All I can think about is finding him and making sure he's okay.

I get to the last step and stare out into the lobby, "Ryder!" I shout again.

My eyes move to every dark corner of this massive room and come up empty. I run to the front desk and search behind it only to make sure he's not hiding somewhere. I run my fingers through my hair and continue searching for him. If he were to get taken by a vampire, I would have heard the commotion from our room upstairs. There would have been evidence of the struggle between him and the vamp. There was none of that. No trace amount of anything to point me in the right direction of where he might be.

My heart starts hurting again, this time at the thought of losing Ryder. Of allowing myself to fall in love so easily and care about someone so much only to have them taken out of my life so quickly. Just like everybody else I come in contact with. Such a cruel, unfair world to live in.

I hear footsteps racing down the stairs and I whip my head around to see who's coming. My mind and heart begging for the one and only person to run down those stairs and tell me everything's okay. I droop my head a bit when I see two people rushing to the lobby and neither of them are Ryder.

"Bridget?" Jim questions. "Is that you?"

I nod and meet him at the bottom of the stairs, "It's me. My friend is missing."

"What do you mean?" he asks.

I shake my head frantically and say, "I don't know. He went out for water and he never came back. Please tell me you've seen him."

"I haven't." Jim replies. "I haven't seen Sherry yet either. When I heard someone shouting, I thought it might've been her."

"I'm sorry to disappoint you." I say, then turn around and head for the exit.

"Where are you going?" he asks and starts following me.

"I'm going to find Ryder. I'm going to get to the bottom of whatever the hell is going on here. I'm not leaving this damn place until I do." I say.

"We're coming with you." Jim says and follows me outside with Dillon's hand in his.

The cool night air embraces my skin. This is why I grabbed my hoodie. I stand right outside the hotel door and turn my head in every direction. The full moon is doing a pretty good job illuminating the world. I can see all the way down each side of the street and see no one. The city feels like a ghost town. A place that was just full of life a few hours ago now seems dead. I don't hear any signs of struggle or any signs of life at all. I walk away from the door and head for the only direction where I think I might be able to find

Ryder.

Jim stays close by, Dillon practically running at his side with that teddy bear still tight in his grasp. I have to admit, I'm a little happy Jim chose to come with me. It makes me feel better knowing that whatever I find, I won't be alone to deal with it.

We turn the corner, passing a few closed shops. The windows are dark and the only sign of people is the constant feeling of being watched. I can feel eyes all over my body as we walk down the middle of the street. I look to every window in every building thinking I'll see someone staring back at me. I see the glass and my reflection in each one we walk by, but not a single person staring at me.

"It's so quiet out here." Jim whispers.

I nod, "That just means we're not alone."

The second those words leave my lips, we hear it. The sound of footsteps walking on the concrete. I hold the gun tight in my hand and search for the source of the sound. My mind thinking only one thing as the footsteps grow louder. Any second and we would be a nice meal for however many vamps are coming at us. I've prepared myself for the moment I meet my inevitable ending. How can one not when they are living in constant fear of it every day?

"What are you doing out here?" I hear a voice coming from behind us.

Slowly, I spin around on my heels and see five people standing a few yards away.

"You shouldn't be out here this late. It's not safe." The man is speaking clear enough for me to tell he's not a vamp.

"We're looking for someone." Jim answers.

The few men approach us and I am able to get a better look at them. All five of them are wearing tattered clothing, like they've been wearing it for too long. Their faces are dirty and in desperate need of a good shaving. Their hair is long and they remind me a lot of other travelers I've come in contact with. The one who spoke to us is taller than the others, giving off the leadership demeanor. His dark skin blends in with his jacket and the moonlight bounces off his bald head.

"You really shouldn't be out here. If they find you, your life is over." He says.

"If *who* finds us?" I ask.

"The bastards that run this place." He replies, taking a calm step forward.

"Who are you?" I ask, my hand still clenched on the gun.

He takes another step forward and says, "My name is Dwayne."

"And what exactly are you talking about, Dwayne?" I say.

Dwayne looks around, making sure the coast is clear, "Come with us. We can explain everything."

I turn to Jim and he shrugs. The man joins his friends and they begin walking back down the street. My feet start to follow them and soon Jim is right behind me. I hate that I'm allowing myself to follow them when I need to be looking for Ryder. He's the only thing that matters to me right now and he's the only person I have in this world I can care about.

Still, I follow these men to whatever place they are taking us to. Curiosity is the one thing that gets the best out of every human being. They turn down a dark alley, heading away from the hotel, and go to a door halfway down. One of the men knocks on the door. It sounds like a secret knock, one tap then a pause, followed by three more, heavier knocks, another pause, and finally two more light taps. The door opens a crack and I see an old man with a grey beard poking his head out. He looks us over, then opens the door the rest of the way.

Dwayne lets his men go inside first, then turns to us, "Please. I'll explain what we know inside."

I nod and walk through the door. Jim keeps Dillon close to his side and follows me. I barely make it through and

I find myself frozen in place. I stare at the faces in the room with a dumbstruck look on my face. There are so many of them and they all seem frightened and upset. Candles are spread all over the room and I spot a small group of women sobbing in the far corner. They all look dirty and their clothes are filled with holes. Some of them have found a way to keep their skin clean, but their clothes have not. Backpacks and tote bags are stacked together against a wall, each with a name written in white ink. All of their eyes stare at us.

"What is this place?" Jim asks.

The door gets shut and locked with a big bar going across it. Dwayne walks to our side and stares at the group of people.

"This is what's left of the travelers who come here. The ones who aren't taken away." Dwayne says.

"What do you mean?" Jim says.

"Why else do you think Nick and his army only worries about the zombies?" Dwayne asks. "Why do you think this place is overly friendly whenever a traveler comes here? They treat us like gods and give us whatever we need to be comfortable for a day or two. Then, when we're least expecting it, they snatch us up, one by one and take us into the woods late at night to meet the end."

I swallow the lump in my throat and open my mouth to speak, "Are you telling me," I have to pause, it's too unbelievable to even think, "they are trading human beings to the vamps? They are using them as bait?"

Dwayne slowly nods his head, "That's exactly what I'm saying. Most of us have been hiding down here for a while. Waiting for the perfect time to make our escape. When one of us thinks he can make it out, he gets caught and we never see him again."

My eyes scan the faces of the people in the room. A few kids are trying to get some sleep on a pile of blankets and pillows with a few older women standing by to keep an eye on them. Some of the men are grouped together, cleaning rifles and pistols, counting whatever ammo they have. I don't know for sure, but I'd say there's about fifty people hiding away in this room large enough for a few hundred. All of them huddled in little groups to keep safe. I don't know whether to feel sad for them or to be pissed off by their situation.

"When we saw you and your daughter come to the city a few days ago, we tried to warn you. Your daughter, Sherry, knows about this place and I told her to tell you about it. I'm assuming by her lack of presence, she wasn't able to pass along my message." Dwayne speaks directly to Jim.

Jim sadly shakes his head, "I haven't seen her since this morning when she left for breakfast."

"I'm sorry, but I have a bad feeling she's with Nick and his army." Dwayne turns his head to me. "I think that is where your friend is as well. It's best the three of you lie low down here for a while."

I refuse to look away from the people in the room. They have all been *lying low* for far too long. They shouldn't have to live like this. Being forced to hide themselves away like savages. They are innocent people trying to survive in a world that makes it an almost impossibility to do so. All of these people have been affected by this city's way of keeping it's people safe. All of these people have loved ones out there who are dead because they were trying to gather the things they needed to keep going on their journey.

Having someone tell me to lie low and not do anything, that's enough to piss me off a little bit more.

"Why haven't you fought back?" I ask.

"What did you say?" Dwayne says, sounding confused.

I turn to him, glaring into his dark eyes, "Why haven't you *fought* back?" anger growing in my heart. "Why haven't you taken a stand against this city in order to save the people you care about?"

He looks around the room, "In case you haven't noticed, girl, we don't necessarily have the resources to do that.

What limited ammo we have, we use in case someone finds this place."

I shake my head in protest, "No, you should be using it to take back what belongs to you. Just because we're all travelers doesn't give those assholes out there the right to take our lives away."

"I understand, but there really isn't much we can do. Once they get through that gate and take them into the woods, that's it. We can't stop them. They have fire power where we have our two hands. It's better to lose one person to than it is to lose our entire group." Dwayne retorts then motions to the people in the room. "This is what's left of us. The people here, some have lost their whole family because of this place. They can't risk losing what's left trying to get out."

I shake my head and walk away from him. The rage is boiling in my heart. Losing someone isn't a reason to hold back. It's the biggest reason in the world to keep going. To keep trying to find that one place where you'll be safe forever. I had to learn that the hard way and I'm still in the process of figuring it out.

I turn back to Dwayne and can't help but get angry with him, "You think losing family isn't reason enough to fight back? You think sitting in this room will make everything better and take those bad feelings away? I have lost my entire family because of this goddamn world. Because of those damn monsters out there, I am the only one left. Losing them hasn't stopped me from going onward with my life. It might've slowed me down a few times, but I still kept going. If anything, losing them has given me even more willpower to keep living, to keep fighting. Which is exactly what every abled body in here should be doing right now. They shouldn't just sit here and waste away like the people they've lost. They should be out there, doing something to get back the small piece of life they have left."

A lot of the crowd has turned their focus on me. They are standing, with their eyes glued to my every movement.

I've never spoken in front of a group like this before, but the anger and sadness in my heart drives me to keep going. To keep saying what I have to say.

"There are two people out there, the only two people left in this world that I care about. Who knows what's going to happen to them if I sit here and do nothing. I can't let myself lose anyone else. I won't let myself do that." I look at their focused faces. "All of you in here have the best reason in the world to go out that door and fight for what you've lost in order to keep what you have now. I know it's scary, but this is humans doing this to other humans. How can the human race win this thing if we keep letting our own kind destroy it? Someone needs to put a stop to this.

"Whether I'm going by myself or not, I'm going back out there and I'm going to do whatever I can to stop this city from doing this to anyone else." I turn toward the door and walk away from the group.

My heart is pounding harder than I've ever felt it pound before. It actually hurts a bit. I walk to the door, my mind focused on doing something I never thought I would have to do. I'll probably die in the process, but it'll be worth it. I'll go down with a fight knowing I did what I could to try to save my friend and the guy I'm in love with. This is the romantic love story Maggie should have been reading about all along.

I make it to the old man at the door and he moves away and takes the bar off the door to unlock it. I grip the handle and take a deep breath before turning the knob. Once I open this door, there's no turning back. There's not going to be any turning around and taking the coward's way out of this. I can't be the kind of person to hide in a basement for the rest of my life. I'd rather take the risk of dying in a world full of monsters than die in a pit of despair with dozens of other people who don't know how to fight for what is right. I grit my teeth and turn the knob, pulling the door open toward me. The cool air once again caresses my skin and I take an incredibly nervous step out into the city I've come to despise over the last few minutes.

***

You know how I know there isn't a God, because if there were one, I really think he *or* she would give me a god damn break for *once* in my life. I feel like I've gone through hell and back trying to survive in this world that people say God gave to us for a reason. If this is the vision he had for my life, then he really does have a sick sense of humor. He could at least let off the cruelness for a bit and send me a bone every once in a while. I could really use some kind of help with this whole trying to survive thing.

Especially right now.

I've got no one to help me. All of those people back in that basement they call a home, they're too stuck on whatever fear is holding them back in order to fight for something that's really important. Even if they've already lost most of the people they care about, fighting for the rest of the human population is reason enough to stop this city from destroying it. Why don't they get that? Why doesn't anyone else in the world see things the way I do? Why won't anyone help me?

More questions I'll never know the answers to add to my list.

I am *really* getting annoyed with those.

"Bridget!" I hear a quiet call from behind me.

My feet stop moving and I clench the gun in my hand.

The voice was too quiet for me to recognize and I don't want to take too many chances in this city in the middle of the night. Who's to say that when I turn around, there's not a vampire standing right behind me waiting to suck me dry. You never know what could be lurking around the shadows in a place like this.

I hear the footsteps getting closer. They're right behind me. I spin around on my heels, slowly raising my arm with the gun. I freeze when I catch eyes with Jim.

"What are you doing?" I ask, befuddled.

He tosses me a solemn look, "I promised Dillon I wouldn't come back without his favorite cousin. I'm going with you."

I force a smile to my face, "I honestly didn't think anyone would come after me, but I'm glad at least you did."

"I think your father would appreciate someone else looking after you while he's gone. I might not be the best person in the world with a gun, but I am good at looking after those I care about." He replies.

I raise an eyebrow, "You care about me?" a slight catch in my throat.

He nods, "After you and your dad left, you were all Sherry could talk about. She spoke about you like you were her own sister. She looks up to you as if you were." He smiles and chuckles a bit, "She even called you her hero. And if she cares that much about a girl she's only just met, then so do I."

"Thank you." I say. "I wish it was more than just the two of us right now, though. I don't think trying to save their lives is going to be an easy task."

"Yeah, that's why I'm not the only one who decided to come after you." Jim says, then steps out of the way revealing a small group of weapon wielding travelers.

Seven of the other people from the basement chose to fight with me and Jim, bringing my own little army from one to nine. Three of them are women, two my mother's age and one a few years older than me. Two of the men are older and one is a little younger, maybe fifteen. Very brave for a kid his age, I admire that. I recognized the dark skinned man standing in the middle of his group. The only one carrying a black rifle and a small handgun.

I let out a much needed sigh of relief and say, "What made you change your minds back there?"

Dwayne steps forward, "You made a lot of us realize that it was wrong of us to not do something about this. To not try to stop these assholes from taking our families or the lives of other humans. That's not how our race will survive this world."

"Good, glad to know you do care about the human race." I say.

"More than you think." Dwayne says.

"Well, thanks." I say with a small smile.

I spin around and start walking down the street again. Jim is right by my side and I can hear the others following close behind.

"How do you know where to go?" I hear someone asking from the group.

I shrug, "I don't. I just figured I'd start by checking out the gate first."

"Smart plan." Dwayne says, sarcastically.

"You got a better one?" I ask.

He shakes his head and keeps quiet. I don't really have a plan. I'm really just going with what I feel is right. That gate is the only way in and out of the city, unless there's some secret tunnel I don't know about. That's likely, but I don't have time to try to find out where it would be. Our best bet is to go to the gate. We'll ask the guards *very* nicely to let us out so we can save our friends from the bad things they're doing to them. Can't stop myself from smiling and laughing a bit at that thought. Those guys are probably just like Nick and are ready to destroy any attempt at getting through to the outside. They'll probably shoot us dead before we even get close enough. We are repulsive travelers after all.

We're not a very big group either. Nick's army has many more guns and weapons to choose from to keep us from stopping them. I'm sure most of the few people behind me aren't very coordinated when shooting a gun, but I'm praying that have good aim. If they've been cooped up in that basement for longer than I'd hope, then they haven't been getting the shooting practice they should have gotten. It's very important to make sure your aim stays almost perfect when you're a traveler. Practicing on zombies tends to work very well.

I'll ignore the thought that my group is nothing other nine random people. We've been thrown together because I can't keep my mouth shut about saving the person I care a lot about right now. I guess I have a way with words that I didn't even know I had. Anyway, it's great knowing this small number of people chose to help me instead of staying back there to rot away while the rest of the world falls apart. The world will still fall apart regardless what they choose to do with their lives, but what we're doing here tonight is enough to save a small part of it.

***

There's about fifteen guards surrounding the gate. All of them are wearing those ridiculous green outfits and combat boots with pretty big guns in their hands. Three of them stand together and laughing about god knows what. Two others are perched in those watch towers staring out to the other side of the gate. The rest are standing around, trying to make it look like they aren't bored. They're completely ignoring the fact that there's a small group of people hiding behind a building watching them.

Idiots.

I take a deep breath and lean against the building. A few of the others are making sure their guns are loaded and ready to go. One of the women is staring out to the guards with a nervous look on her face. They all look nervous and scared. I'm scared myself. You'd be a fool not to be when you're about to face a small army of actual soldiers with much bigger guns. I absolutely need to quit thinking about the bad things we're going up against. It makes this so much harder.

"Bridget?" Dwayne whispers in my ear, "You're the mastermind behind this little scheme. We can't just hide behind this building hoping those guys out there will disappear. What's the plan?"

I look into his dark eyes, then glance around the corner to the gate. The guards are out there pacing back and forth right next to it. I don't know what to do. Making plans for things like this isn't a strong point of mine. I normally try to go with the flow or, until recently, go with whatever my father said was right. He was the plan maker. I was the one who did as I was told. I haven't been able to prepare myself for something like this.

I'm not prepared for anything anymore. After losing my dad so unexpectedly and running into a guy I'm actually falling in love with, how can one be prepared for whatever happens next? This world is so random anymore and there's nothing we can do about it.

I keep my eyes focused on the guards. They have a plan and they are prepared for things. They're ready for a pack of zombies or a group of vamps to come knocking at the gate trying to come in. The rest of this city can sleep soundly knowing their army is well prepared for things like that to happen. If they're ready for those monsters out there, then I'm one hundred percent positive they'll be able to take on nine pathetic humans like us.

But, I might be able to confuse them a bit.

I take a deep breath and pull myself away from the building. I clench the gun in my hand and walk out into the street, heading for the gate. I can hear the others whispering to each other, wondering what the hell I'm doing. I don't bother turning around to explain to them what I *think* I'm doing. I'm not even positive on that yet. My feet keep moving down the street while my mind hopes beyond belief this night doesn't end badly.

The footsteps of the others comes next. All of them walking away from that building, following my every move. My eyes remain on the guards ahead of us. Most of them are still in tuned with their conversations and they don't notice the impending threat coming toward them. The ones in the towers aren't facing this way. There is, however, one young man, standing off to the side drinking from a canteen. He's the one who notices.

"Hey!" he shouts with a deep booming voice, "What are you doing out here?"

I keep going, even after a few other guards turn their eyes our way. I hear guns being raised behind me and we advance.

"Stop right there!" another guard shouts at us.

We keep going, my heart pounding in my chest. I keep my gun at my side with no intention on hurting any of these people here tonight. That's not part of my plan in life. The guards have their guns raised, but their aim is at our feet. I was hoping that would happen. Hoping they wouldn't be monsters just like the real ones out there and take aim at a bunch of humans who are just fighting to survive.

"I'm ordering you to stop!" the first guard shouts.

I get within a few feet of the guards and we have no choice but to cease our walking. My own little army stands around me with their weapons raised high.

"And I'm ordering you to open the gate." I say with a strong voice I don't recognize as my own.

One of the guards steps forward, closing the gap between he and I. He stands about a foot taller than me and his biceps are as big around as my head. If there's ever a time to be intimidated by someone, it's right now.

"I'm sure you can tell that ain't gonna happen tonight, little girl," his southern accent just as muscly as the rest of him, "Why don't you go back where you came from."

I shake my head and look up into his eyes, "Yeah, that's not gonna happen."

He tightens his grip on his gun and seethes, "Why the hell not?"

I take a deep breath and run my fingers through my hair, "You see, the place I came from, the place all of us came from, is on the other side of that fence." I point to the road leading away from here. "You might think you're not gonna open the gate for us, but I'm going to personally see that you do. There's someone out there who I really care about. I'm sick and tired of people and monsters like you taking those I care about away from me. So, like I said, you are going to open that goddamn gate so I can stop that asshole you call a boss from giving the person I care about to the vamps."

He lowers his gun and scrunches his face in confusion, "What are you talking about?"

"I think you know very damn well what I'm talking about." I say.

The big guy lowers his gun completely and shakes his head. The look of utter confusion has crossed his face and I'm beginning to notice that he really has no idea what I'm talking about. I glance around to a few of the other guards standing close by. The ones closest all have looks of befuddlement on their faces and they've lowered their weapons.

"You really don't know what I'm talking about, do you?" I ask, my plan of confusion might actually work.

Again, he shakes his head along with a few of the others. There is one of the guards who obviously knows exactly what I mean. He's the only one who's standing mere inches away from me with a gun pointed at the right side of my head.

"I do." He says with a quiet voice.

I can hear the people behind me shifting their weapons, aiming for the man with the gun to my head. If they could read my mind, they would hear me begging for them not to shoot him. All it would take is one wrong shot and I'd be dead. He wouldn't hesitate to pull the trigger sending that small piece of metal soaring into my brain, taking my life as though I were one of the zombies. That's not how I see my life ending. Especially not tonight.

"So, you know our little secret," he says. "You know the truth about what's keeping this city safe. I don't understand why you care so much. They're only travelers."

I shake my head, "We're people, just like you and we have a life until you help destroy it. Trading us to the vamps, because we *are* travelers, how the hell can you live with yourself?"

He shrugs, "Very well actually. The vampires get what they want and I get to sleep soundly each night. It is quite the pity that you had to find out. When I saw you come to town the other day, I was really hoping I'd get the chance to have you. Unfortunately, I'm gonna have to kill you and your little friends back there because none of them have a clear shot at taking me out."

"They might not," the big guy in front of me says, "but I sure do. Let her go."

The man doesn't budge, doesn't move an inch. Instead, he laughs and I can see his finger tightening around the trigger of his gun. I close my eyes and wait for this all to be over.

Funny. My life isn't flashing before my eyes like I've seen in the movies. My family isn't staring at me behind my closed eyes and I'm not face to face with whoever this *God* character truly is. There's nothing except the blackness in my head. I guess I've come close to this moment so many times over the past five years, my mind has gotten used to it and no longer recreates the memories of my past. Not like I want to stare into the eyes of my family as I break their promises of keeping myself alive in this hellish world. That alone is enough to break my heart and kill me a little inside without this guy pulling the trigger.

The gunshot sounds like a cannon going off less than a foot away from me.

It echoes in my ears and I can't hear anything else. I can't hear my heart beating nor can I feel it. I'm not sure if this is real. I can't tell if I'm actually dead. I've never had the chance to be dead before and I know if I keep my eyes closed, I'll never know if I'm alive or not. One good thing if I am dead, it was painless and I didn't have to suffer or anything. This still doesn't feel right.

I don't *feel* dead.

I feel like I'm alive and standing in the middle of the road.

Maybe it feels like that because I *am* still alive and standing in the middle of the road. I finally force my eyes to open and the man isn't right next to me anymore. He's lying on the ground at my feet with a hole in his head. There's a large puddle of the red blood mixed with a little bit of his brains pouring out of the wound.

"Thank you." I say with a sigh of relief over finding myself still alive.

The big guy lowers his gun and says, "You're welcome."

"I'm still gonna make you open the gate for us." I say.

He shakes his head, "You're not going to *make* me to do anything."

He turns around and heads for the gate. I follow him with my eyes, watching his every step as he gets closer to the metal fence. A few of the guards, whom I assume know all about Nick's idea of keeping the city safe, rush to block my new, giant friend from doing what he knows is right. They aim their guns at him, but he keeps moving. I clutch the gun in my hand and advance to the gate as well, hearing the footsteps of my group right behind me.

There are five guards trying to block us from opening the gate. A few of the others step off to the side to get out of the way and three join us with their guns pointed at members of their own team. These army guys are way outnumbered and they know it. Their hands are shaking. I can hear the metal of the guns clanking in their hands. These men, who should have way more experience in killing anything with or without a pulse, are scared for their lives as a bunch of random people approach them with guns of our own. Amazing how the tide can turn so quickly.

I take a step out farther than the big guy and point my small gun at the man closest to the latch, "Open it."

He keeps his hand on the gun and shakes his head.

I roll my eyes and take another step closer. He takes a staggering step backward, bumping into the fence.

"I'm not going to kill you," I say, "I just want you to open the damn gate. There's a decent chance that you'll never see any of us ever again once we step foot on the other side, so you might as well open it."

His eyes dart from my face to those of the people behind me. Just like those few zombies I've come across, he's weighing his options. He has to know there's no point in trying to keep us from doing what's right no matter how much he thinks we're wrong. There's no point in ending his life when all he has to do is move out of the way so we can get through to the other side.

"Just open it, man. This ain't worth it." I hear a whisper from one of the others standing against the fence.

This gets him to make a move and he lowers the gun. He slides out of the way and pulls a key from a pocket on his jacket. It goes to the giant padlock hanging from the gate and he takes his time to unlock it. The metal lock gives and the gate is free. The big guy rushes past me and quickly shoves it open.

"Thank you." I say, trying not to be as sarcastic as I want to.

I take the first, nervous step to the other side with my group and the few guards who chose to join behind me. The second all of us are outside the city, we hear the gate being closed and locked behind us. A few turn their heads in a panic thinking we're all going to die out here. There *is* a good chance of that happening, but I'm not going to be the one who ruins our evening by bringing it up. I keep my head up high, looking out at the street ahead of us.

"Where do we go now?" I hear one of the women ask.

"There's a trail up ahead, leading into the woods." One of the guards, a younger man, maybe a year or two older than me, speaks up.

"How do you know?" I ask.

He looks down at his feet, "I've gone with them once before. It killed me to watch them feed the vamps like that, but there was nothing I could do to stop them. In order to save my life, I kept my mouth shut and stayed as a night guard at the gate."

"It's okay. You're helping us now and that's all that matters." I say as the group starts walking along the highway. "What's your name?"

"Seth." He replies.

"I'm Bridget."

"I take it you know someone who was taken tonight?" he asks.

I nod, "A couple of people actually."

"I hope we find them in time." He says.

"We will." I say, not only to reassure him, but to reassure myself as well.

There's no such thing as too much reassurance in a

world that's slowly crumbling at your feet.

***

The trail isn't too far from the gate. Our new friend, Seth, lead us to a small, gravel path right off the highway. It will take us straight into the pitch blackness that makes up the woods and to what I can only assume will be our inevitable death.

A few of us hesitate. I'm right there with them. We all know what's waiting for us once we step foot on that trail and disappear amongst trees. It feels like suicide walking into a place we know is haunted by monsters that want our flesh and blood. Other's ignore their gut, pull out a flashlight and get right on the beaten path. After seeing the first person head down the path, I can't hesitate any longer. I clench a fist, feeling my finger nails poking into the palm of my hand, hold onto my gun and follow them.

The woods really aren't so bad. Despite the eerie sounds of the tree branches creaking every time the wind blows and the many dark shadows providing the ultimate hiding places for vampires. There's nothing to keep my mind from drifting to the thought of one of those creatures bursting out from behind a tree and sinking it's dull teeth into the skin of any one of us. We'd never see them coming. We'd hear the zombies moaning before they could get too close, but the vamps will never make a sound to let us know they're nearby.

My heart races as I attempt to lead this group down

the path. Dwayne and Jim are right beside me and Seth is close behind with the others. I can hear the hushed whispers coming from the few who want to turn back. The ones who are too afraid to go any further, but even more frightened of going back to the city alone. I'm scared as well, but I've been through worse things without the aid of others. I've fought off nine zombies all on my own. I've come face to face with death by vampire more times than I can count. I'm not going to let a little thing like walking through the woods in the middle of the night psyche me out so much that I'm going to give up on this mission. That's the last thing any of us could do.

Jim shines a flashlight on the trail at our feet and says, "Do you know what the plan is if we find them out here? I don't think they'll be as easy to persuade as those guards back there."

I shake my head, "Not gonna lie, I don't really have a plan right now. I'm just going with it for now."

"We can't just go with it, Bridget," Jim argues, "we *need* a plan."

"Sorry, but going with the flow of things is how this world works. When there are demons out there chasing us, we don't have time to stop to come up with a plan. We make snappy decisions when death is right on our tail and, most of the time, they seem to work." I retort.

"And what if we fail? I can't lose my daughter like this." Jim says loud enough to catch the attention of the others.

I stop walking and stare at him for a second. The group stops moving as well, waiting for me to say something. Waiting for me to make a great speech like I did back at the basement they called a home. I never thought I was any good at coming up with spirit lifting speeches that will get the heart pumping and make people want to do things. I know have to say something though. Their gloomy faces are starting to get to me.

"We're not going to fail." I say, making things up as I

go along seems to do the trick sometimes. "We're going to find them. We are going to set things right, for us and any other traveler who chooses to spend a few nights in Hatfeld. I've learned something over the last few days and I'm coming to realize it's true. No matter what lies ahead of us, whether we win this thing or not, things can always get worse. Take it however you want, but take it nonetheless."

A little advice I chose to borrow from Ryder. No idea if it's comforting or not, but it makes me feel a little better knowing I didn't choke on the little speech the people were waiting for. It makes me feel more grateful when no one runs back to the city. They nod their heads in agreement and wait for me to start leading the way again.

I turn on my heels and head through the woods. I let out a sigh and look up to the trees above my head. The branches are thick and covered with leaves. I can't see the stars in the sky. The moon is shining, just not out here where we need it. I glance over my shoulder and peer at the faces of my group one more time.

Things can always get worse, right? There's always something far scarier out there in the world, isn't there? I can't really think of what could be scarier than a vampire waiting to suck us dry or a pack of zombies devouring our twitching bodies.

So, my answer to those two questions would have to be a no.

At least I have an answer this time.

There isn't much worse than running into those monsters and that's exactly what we're headed into. I can't let the group behind me know I'm secretly hating the words that just came out of my mouth. I'm sure some of them know things can't get much worse than our current situation. Even death isn't so bad compared to this. But we have to hold our heads high and think of the one thing all of us need to do right now. That is surviving. It is the only thing my family wants me to do and I have to live up to that, while helping as many people do the same as I can. I keep going, trying not to think how easy this all seems to be so far. Trying not to wonder why there aren't any vampires or even some zombies wanting to attack us. It seems too quiet and makes me wonder if what we're walking into, we'll be able to walk back out of.

I have got to quit thinking like this. It could really harsh the buzz of the already nervous group on my heels and no one needs that. We need to ignore our gut feelings about wanting to run away to hide and go for gold to save the people we care about. That's what this mission is about and that's all I plan on doing.

I take a few more steps, trying not to break too many twigs or make too much noise. The element of surprise is all we have going for us and we can't do anything to screw that up. There's no saying what Nick and his goons will do to our friends if they see us coming before we want them to.

There's a faint glow coming into view not far ahead. It's coming from a couple flashlights and even a fire lit torch, I can see the flames flicker in the darkness. We must be getting close. I can see the shadows of the men floating on the trees as they walk by them. We're still too far off in order to see how many soldiers there are or how many prisoners they have with them. There still isn't a doubt in my mind Ryder is amongst that group.

"Is that them up ahead?" Dwayne asks, a nervous hitch to his whispering voice.

I nod, "I think so. I don't know who else would be out here in the middle of the forest when vamps roam this part of the world more than any other."

"Okay," he says, "so what's your plan now?"

My feet keep moving as my mind shoves his question out of the way. My eyes stay glued to the glow coming from our enemy's flashlights. They aren't moving as fast as I expected them to. We are actually catching up to them and we aren't moving so fast ourselves. The shadows coming from them are starting to take shape, forming into the outlines of six very large men. There are four others walking with them, each with a black bag over their head and their hands are somehow bound in front of them.

"Bridget?" Dwayne hurries to my side, "Do you even *have* a plan?"

"Not really." I say, still keeping my eyes focused in front of me.

There isn't a whole lot of planning that needs to go into something like this. At least I don't think there should be anyway. All we really need to do is go up to Nick and his men and force them to let a few innocent people go while the threat of vampires hangs over our shoulders.

Easy as pie, right?

"I really think we should pause for a moment and come up with a good idea for taking them down. I don't think rushing in there will do anything in our favor." Dwayne retorts. "If anything, that could worsen the situation."

"Yeah, those guys could end up killing the people they took from us before they give them to the vamps." I hear a concerned voice coming from behind me.

"Maybe we should have thought of something before coming out here to the middle of a vamp infested forest and risk getting ourselves killed." Another worried voice coming from an older woman.

The concerns coming from the group should be enough to stop my feet from moving. I should turn around and help them come up with the perfect way to make this night go smoothly and in our favor as Dwayne likes to put. I *should* do those things.

Something stronger is driving me onward.

Call it love. Call it the need to save the only person on this planet who I truly feel like I cannot live without. It might be weird to think that, after only a few days, I have found someone who can take the pain of everything away in a matter of seconds. With just one look of his face the bad things go away. Ryder is the only person who seems to make things better. He can make me shove aside what happened to my family and focus on the good things I can still find in this life. I can't waste my time trying to come up with the perfect solution on how to get him and the others back. The longer we wait, the less time they have at a chance of surviving.

"Bridget, we really need to think things through before we go on with this." Jim rushes to my side. "I can't just go with the flow of things and risk my daughter's life more than it already is."

There's just no getting through to these people. Zombies don't have a plan before they attack. Vampires might, but I highly doubt it. Why should humans be any different?

I stop walking and run my fingers through my hair. Leaving it down all day has led to a slight mess of tangles catching my fingers. I stare Jim in the eyes and see the look of concern written in the brown shade of them. I glance back to the others, all of them are waiting for my next words of brave wisdom.

I just don't have any this time.

"Bridget?" Jim asks.

I look back to him, then glance to the small group ahead of us. I can see them more clearly now and spot the shirtless prisoner that is Ryder. The lump in my throat is the drive telling me to do the one thing I know I must to do to get him back. It might be a little selfish or a little crazy even. This is something I have to do. I wasn't given the chance to save the last few people I cared about. I still have the chance right now and I'm going to take it.

"You guys stay and come up with a plan. I got one of my own." I say, then quickly turn away from my group.

I can hear them quietly calling my name, begging me to stop and come back. There's nothing to keep me from going through with the craziness my mind thinks is the right thing to do. Besides, things can always get worse.

Those words are just as crazy as what I'm doing.

***

I can hear their footsteps as I duck behind the trees, closing in on Nick's group. I can hear every twig snapping under their heavy boots and every piece of metal on their clothes clanking as they walk. Those are the only sounds breaking the eerie silence clouding the air around me. No one from my own group chose to follow and I refuse to turn back no matter how many of their voices I could hear calling for me to stop. I don't feel bad about leaving them. I know I should, but it's my own life I'm risking right now and they're better off staying back in the group. They'll come up with a plan of their own and I can only hope it will be a great one. Although, I can't say I'd blame them at all for turning around and heading back for the city.

Let's just hope that's not the case.

Nick's group stops moving and a few begin shining their flashlights through the trees in front of them. I stay off the trail, ducking between a few trees and bushes in order to get closer to them. I make sure to stay hidden in case they get the urge to shine their lights my way.

I can see them all more clearly now. Nick standing at the front of his group, staring into the dark woods. He looks proud of himself for doing something wrong and condemning himself to whatever hell exists. There are seven of his army men with him. Three surrounding the prisoners and the others are scanning the trees with their lights. Each one has a pretty big gun aimed out in front of them making mine look like a pea shooter.

Of the four prisoners tied up with bags over their heads, two are women and two are men. I can hear the quiet whimpers coming from the girls, one clearly belonging to Sherry. I could pick out her high pitched whine anywhere. The men are relatively quiet. The one wearing a black shirt keeps fighting with the ropes on his hands, trying not to be noticed by the guards. Ryder is standing at the end of the line with a gun pointed right at his back in case he or one of the others try to do something risky. I can see his body shaking in fear of what is awaiting him.

"Ryder." I whisper as I stare at him.

If only there was a way for me to send him comforting thoughts. To somehow let him know I'm close by and there's nothing to be afraid of. I'm going to try my damndest to get him out of this mess no matter what the consequences are. We all know what one of those consequences could be.

"Nick." I hear one of their deep voices and it causes me to jump. "Shouldn't they be here by now? They aren't normally late."

"They'll be here. Just give them a little more time." Nick replies. "We aren't leaving until we make the trade. That's the only thing to guarantee the safety of our city."

I keep watching and listen to their conversation. They are expecting to meet up with the vamps out here in the middle of nowhere to make a trade for safety. I can only hope they don't show up before I have the chance to give them what they are least expecting. A young girl trying to save the life of the man she has fallen in love with. That just about puts every love story I've ever been told to shame. Shakespeare can't measure up to a girl saving a boy from being eaten by vampires.

They keep shining their lights through the trees. I keep expecting a swarm of vamps to come out of nowhere to claim their prizes. All of them have their backs to me, watching the trees in front of them. I shift my eyes back to Ryder, the gun still aimed at his back. My heart pounds as I watch him shiver in the cool night air. Why am I doing something so risky for a guy I just met a few days ago? Would he do the same for me if the roles were reversed? I think he might. I think he wouldn't still be hiding in a bush waiting for the perfect moment to come out gun raised and ready to fight.

"Nick," another guard breaks my thoughts, "I don't think those vamps are coming tonight."

Nick snaps his head around and passes his friend an angry look, "They'll be here, dammit. Just give it a few more minutes."

"Well, what if they don't show up this time? What do we do with them?" the same guards asks.

Nick shakes his head, I can tell he's getting frustrated, "Then I guess we'll just have to blow the heads off these four bastards and let the wolves have them."

"Maybe we should do that now." The guard pulls a small gun from a holster on his belt and points it at one of the female's heads.

I hear her whimper and recognize Sherry's annoying squeal. There's no better time than right now to do something I'll probably regret by the end of the night, but I'm going to do it anyway.

With the gun tight in my fist, I step back from the bush and take a few short steps so I'm behind Nick's little army. They won't see me coming from this way and I kind of enjoy surprising people. I quietly make my way through the trees and walk between two oaks so I'm back on the trail. I'm a few feet away from those guys and not a single one of them notices. That is until my foot breaks a stick and the sound it makes is like a bomb going off in the woods. I grit my teeth and instantly hate myself.

Nick slowly turns his gaze my way while a few others shine their flashlights at my face. The second they see I'm not a vampire, their guns are raised and pointed right at me. It seems utterly pointless, but I raise mine as well.

"What's this?" Nick asks with a smirk on his face.

I can feel the metal shaking in my hand as I stare at him, but I keep my grip and aim strong.

"I suppose you came to save your little boyfriend, didn't you?" Nick asks, taking a few short steps closer to me.

I shrug, "I came to fight back."

He and a few of the others share a small laugh together. I don't see what's so funny, but I guess if I were in their shoes I'd probably be laughing as well.

"You really think a pathetic little girl like you can fight us?" he says.

My eyes pass over each of them. They are all *a lot* bigger than I am and probably know some crazy fight moves that I'd never be able to get away from. I'm sure all of them have seen their fair share of battle and have killed plenty of people in their days. I mean, I have too, the people I kill just aren't living anymore. How many people can say they've killed nine zombies on their own? How many people can say they've personally dragged a few vamps into the sunlight without getting a single scratch or bite? I'm sure a few others, but how many of them are nineteen year old girls? My guess, probably not a lot.

"I think I can handle it." I say, sounding more cocky than I feel.

Nick smiles, "You are a funny little girl. Don't understand why you're wasting your time with this pathetic traveler when you could be spending your nights with a man like me." He walks past Ryder and shoves him in the chest a bit. "The two of us would make a great pair, don't you think?"

I can feel the grimace crossing my face as that horrible image comes to mind, "Yeah, I think I'd rather die than let that happen."

The smile on his face goes away and he says, "You'll be making a big mistake if you don't choose wisely. Either you be with me or you can join these ingrates and be a nice dinner for the oncoming vamps."

"Hmmm," I put a finger to my chin, acting like I'm thinking about it, "that's a tough one. I think I'll have to go with neither."

"That's not an option."

"Well, neither of your choices seem appealing to me so I'm making my own choice."

"And what's that?"

"I'm gonna stop you." I say, aiming my gun right at his face.

Nick rolls his eyes and pulls his own pistol out. He doesn't hesitate when he grabs Ryder and rips the bag off his head. He presses the barrel of the gun to Ryder's left temple with one hand and wraps his other arm around Ryder's chest so he can't get away.

My heart practically skips a beat as our eyes meet. There's a small trace of blood under his nose and a cut on the right side of his face. Seeing him hurt makes me angry. Seeing a gun pressed against his head, takes me over the top.

"I'm getting real tired of you. I know you don't want to see me kill him and you know I will do it." Nick seethes. "Lower your gun and maybe I'll let him live long enough for the vamps to do my dirty work."

Instead of listening to Nick and my gut right now, I take a few seconds to think things through. I didn't come here to see Ryder get killed. I came here to get him back. Nick has his own plans of turning Ryder and the other three over to the vampires. I'm sure they have an agreement of how many people will grant them safety for one more night and I'm sure vamps aren't the kind of creature to let things slide so easily. They're the things that get pissed off and kill when they know they can win.

A smile comes to my face and I say, "Go ahead and kill him." Ryder struggles a bit in Nick's grip and passes me a frightened look. "I know you won't pull that trigger though."

He raises an eyebrow and says, "How do you know I won't?"

"Because you need him to give to the vampires to keep your precious city safe for another evening. If you don't have four people, they could take one of you, if not all of you." I reply.

He thinks for a moment, then says, "Then I'll just give them you."

I shake my head, "No, you won't. You're the kind of guy who wants to take his revenge out first hand and not give me up so easy. I'm the one who's standing up to you right now. You want the pleasure of killing me all for yourself and not let some pathetic vampire do it."

A few twigs break off to our right, grabbing Nick's attention, along with everyone else's. He whips his head in that direction and one of his men shines a flashlight at the trees. We don't see them at first, but we hear them.

"What...is going...on?" I hear a struggled nonhuman voice.

Nick keeps his grip on Ryder, but lowers the gun in his hand. My eyes turn to the creature walking toward us and the others who are right behind him. Their pale skin and white hair glow in the small amount of light coming from the flashlights. Their grey eyes stick out on their faces along with the purple veins on their necks. Most of them have blood stains all over their clothing, but the one up front looks clean and smug about his appearance.

"Zeke, I'm glad you could make it tonight." Nick says, trying to hide the fear in his voice.

The one called Zeke steps closer and says, "What...are you...doing?"

"Nothing." Nick shakes his head and shoves Ryder back with the others. "We are just waiting for you. We have what you asked for and even one more." He motions to me.

I hold my gun tighter and turn my aim to the vamp. It might not be enough, but at least it's something to slow them down if they choose to come at me.

None of the vamps even glance my way. Zeke keeps

his eyes fixated on Nick and the others are focused on Nick's men. They don't even pay attention to the prisoners.

"What are you waiting for?" Nick argues. "Just take them and keep to our deal."

Zeke cocks his head to the side, "What...deal?"

Fear instantly floods Nick's tan face and the gun falls from his hand. There's a sly smile on the face of Zeke, showing off the crooked teeth hiding behind his pale lips. There's a plan hiding behind those grey eyes of his, giving me a really bad feeling in the pit of my stomach. I hope whatever plan my little group came up with, is going to be put to play here soon.

I sort of need them right now.

***

"We had a deal, Zeke. You promised safety if we delivered so many humans every week. You *promised*." Nick pleads.

Zeke shakes his head, "I remember...no promise."

Nick's men turn their guns to the vamps. I can hear the metal shaking in their hands as they take aim. The frightened look in their eyes makes me wonder why they would bother going through with this risk in the first place. I get safety is a very important thing in the world right now, but *seriously*. Meeting up with vampires in the middle of the night when all you have to protect yourself is a gun and the hope you can aim for their heart and not miss. What the hell kind of plan is that?

A terrible plan is what that is.

"Did you really expect vampires to keep up with their end of the deal?" I say, probably more than I should have. "Did you really think this was a good idea in the first place? You can't trust a vamp with anything let alone the safety of an entire city. You have got to be the *biggest* idiot in the world."

One of the vamps turns their hideous head my way. Drool slips out of her mouth as she passes me a tooth filled snarl. Her blonde hair drapes over her narrow shoulders and her white eyes bore into my soul. I guess she didn't like what I had to say. She pushes her way past Zeke and stands a few feet away from me. She tilts her head to the side, a cracking sound comes from her neck, and smiles as she licks her lips. I can feel my hand shaking and can practically hear my heart beating in my chest. The vamp takes a small step closer to me and I jump a bit. The other vamps around her let out a raspy laugh as they watch the human fear for her life.

That laugh catches my attention. It doesn't even sound like a laugh. It's more like what an old man sounds like when he's trying to catch his breath after a short walk to the kitchen for another beer. Their laugh makes me smile and calms my heart a bit. I feel like I could take on the world. I stare at the female, she takes another step closer to me. I steady my hand and squeeze the trigger of my gun. The vamp falls backward with a bloody hole in the middle of her chest.

Thank god I didn't miss.

I turn to the other vampires, the ones who stare at me with evil in their eyes, "Who's laughing now assholes?" my turn to pass them a vengeful snarl.

I guess that doesn't sit right with them because in the next few seconds, a few of them rush past Zeke and head for Nick and his men along with myself. Gunshots blare through the woods, horrid screams are followed by the vamps as various parts of them get hit by the bullets. Another one comes after me and I'm quicker this time when I pull the trigger. He falls to the ground with his veiny hand covering his heart.

I turn my eyes to where Nick was standing a few seconds ago. Ryder is lying on the ground, backing away from a pale vamp wearing a faded red dress. His hands are still tied at his waist and he has no way to defend himself against that thing. I move closer, jumping out of the way of another vamp. *Damn thing came out of nowhere.* Their numbers seem to be multiplying while ours are staying the same.

Not sure how long we'll make it out here.

Before I can make it to Ryder, there's a sharp tug on my hair and I'm being flung to the ground even farther away from him. The world rushes by me so fast, I don't have the time to react before I crash to the ground I was just standing on. The gun is thankfully still in my hand and I stare up at the vamp who's trying to attack me. He looks like a teenager who's missing his left ear completely. Not enough to take his thirst away.

I scramble to take aim with my gun. He's moving fast and for some reason I seem to be moving in slow motion. My hands just can't comprehend the message my brain is trying to send them. All they need to do is point the stupid gun at the damn thing's heart and blow him to smithereens. What they are doing is fumbling around while my eyes keep watch on the young vamp. He drops to his knees at my feet and reaches out for one of my ankles. I finally have a shot and I pull the trigger. The bullet is lodged into his shoulder and he laughs at my failed attempt. I take aim again, but it's not my gun that makes the sound.

The vamp falls dead at my feet and I feel a large hand grab my upper arm. I'm suddenly jerked up and spun around to I can face whoever shot the vamp and saved my life.

Dwayne, may he never cease to surprise me.

"Thank you." I say.

"Don't mention it." He replies then walks away from me, joining the fight against rage-filled vampires.

Following him through the trees are the rest of my

small army. They run into this battle, shooting whatever vampire gets in their way. *Finally* I get some reinforcement and I can breathe easy again.

I turn back to Ryder. The female vamp isn't attacking him any longer. She's lying on the ground next to him, her dress is so red the blood just blends right in with it. Someone saved his life for me. Ryder is sitting up on the ground, trying to free his hands from the ropes while death and carnage is happening all around him. I take my chance and run to his side. I slide to the ground on my knees, feeling my jeans tear on one of the legs. I take Ryder's hands and go about untying the rope around them. Every few seconds, I glance up only to make sure there isn't a vamp hovering over us waiting to try a taste. So far, my little army and what's left of Nick's men seem to be handling them quite well. The other prisoners have been freed by Jim and are currently trying to get out of this madness.

The ropes start to loosen in my hand and Ryder is able to pull his hands free. He doesn't hesitate before throwing them around me and pulling my body closer to his. During those few seconds of our short embrace, the world around us seems to disappear. The screams grow faint and all I can hear is his breath. All I can feel is his skin against mine and the safely while I'm encased in his arms. This is where I'm meant to be. This is where I want to be. He is my reason to stay alive and survive this.

"I thought I'd never see you again." He whispers in my ear.

I pull away from him and smile, "I'm not letting you get away from me that easy."

Both of us get to our feet and look around us at the battle. The screaming seems to be growing and the vampires are pouring in from all directions. How we didn't see any of them on our way out here, has me completely befuddled.

"We need to get out of here." Ryder says, noticing the same thing I am.

We're not winning this thing like I hoped we would. It would take a lot more people to help us out and I know that's not going to happen any time soon. The vamps have an edge on us. They're stronger, more agile, they can take us down without breaking a sweat. We could try to outrun them, try to retreat back to the city, but they'd catch up before we could make it far at all. Even if we could, they would hop over the fence at Hatfeld like it's nothing and take rampage on the people there. I'm not one to have that sort of thing on my conscience.

"You shouldn't have come looking for me, Bridge. You should have just forgot about me and gone on with your life." Ryder says.

An old vamp with a limp comes charging at us and I quickly take aim and pull the trigger, "You really think I could have left without you?" He pulls me out of the way of another one jumping out from behind a tree, one of the others gets a clear shot at it, "I don't care if we die here tonight, Ryder. I'm not going to spend the rest of my life without you."

"You're crazy," he says, "you know that, right?"

I shrug, "That's not the first time you've told me that."

"It probably won't be the last either." He says.

"I'm counting on that." I say, as I manage to hit another vamp in the stomach, then another in the leg.

More shots are fired and I can see two vamps fall limp to the ground. That's followed by one more vamp flying through the air and landing on the man with the gun who killed the first two. I raise my gun and aim for the vamps head before he sinks his teeth into the man's neck. The bullet doesn't kill him, but it knocks him off the man long enough so he can get a shot at the vamps heart. That isn't enough to stop another one from coming at him and sinking his teeth into his shoulder.

"There's too many of them." I say.

"We need more ammo!" I hear a shout coming from one of the fighters.

"Screw that! We need more people!" another shout.

I know I'm running low on ammo and I didn't think to bring any with me. Taking the time to reload would be a death sentence anyway. A short vampire comes out from behind a tree and reaches for Ryder's leg. He quickly jumps to the side and I take a shot, hitting the creature in the mouth, then another shot to its heart.

"I'm glad you don't hesitate with these things anymore." Ryder says to me.

"Me too." I reply and fire another round into the heart of a dark skinned vamp trying to make a snack out of my new friend Seth.

Two more gunshots are fired, then the air around us suddenly grows silent. The vamps have stopped screaming and attacking the few humans who remain. They keep their eyes glued to us while they plan their next move. I look around at the humans who are left. Three men from Nick's group, not including Nick, and about seven of my own, that's including the prisoners we saved. We are more than out-numbered.

There's a woman standing a few feet from us and she looks my way, "What do we do?"

I look around, noticing more vamps closing in around us as we group together, "I don't know. We can't run and our ammo is almost empty. At least we'll go down fighting."

"Shitty." The woman says.

Ryder takes my free hand and squeezes it hard. I'm sure he's thinking the same thing I am. Wishing we were somewhere else, a place where these monsters were never even heard of, not in storybooks or in movies. A utopia designed specifically for the last of the human race. A place that doesn't and will never exist.

"No matter what happens, Bridge," Ryder says, quietly, "I'm really glad I got to spend these last few days falling in love with you."

A lump comes to my throat as I squeeze his hand right back, "Same here."

These have been some of the best few days I've had in a while. Getting to know a stranger, saving his life on more than one occasion. I'll miss the last two nights we spent together in our hotel room in Hatfeld. I'll miss his smile and how he came to trust me after just a few minutes. I'll miss everything about him.

The vamps close in on us, forcing us into a tight circle in the midst of them all. Easier for them to snack on us and harder for us to fight back.

"Fear...smells delicious." I hear a vamp speaking loud enough for all of us to hear.

His words send shivers up my spine. Any second now and this will all be over. The fear deep in my gut will be gone and every painful memory of my past erased from my mind forever. I'll never be able to see or hold Ryder or feel his lips against my own. I'll never have that feeling of being loved or cared about by a human being who isn't my family. I just got to know that feeling too.

Tears slowly drift from my eyes and flow down my cheeks. The slight breeze cools them as they slide down my face. I close my eyes and sniffle. Something doesn't seem right. A very particular aroma drifts up my nose and I open my eyes again. I could never mistake that smell.

"Zombies." I whisper.

"What?" Ryder asks.

"Zombies are coming. I can smell them." I say.

As if on cue, we hear their grunting. That horrible sound could pierce through anything. Through a small gap in the group of vamps, I see them coming. They bump into each other, banging their shoulders against the trees around them, but they don't care. They keep lumbering toward us, groaning louder than I've ever heard them groan before. The vamps don't acknowledge their growing presence. Dead blood doesn't appeal to them, they can't even smell it.

I keep my eyes on the zombies. Another threat on our lives. The rest of the humans have noticed them as well and I can hear a few silent prayers escape their lips. I don't pray for anything. I keep watching while something unexpected takes shape in front of me. A zombie, caked with dried blood and dirt is attacking a vamp. He has it pinned against a tree while he sinks his teeth into its flesh and pulls a big chunk of the pale skin off its bones. The vamp lets out a wail so loud, the others around it turn their attention to the scene.

"What the fuck?" I say as I watch in shock.

Another zombie willingly attacks a vampire, tackling the thing to the ground and pulling it apart with its teeth. The zombies seem to have no intention of coming after us. Their main focus is the vampires. Something I've never seen before, yet always feared would happen. More of them tear into their pale enemy with their teeth and fingernails, pulling their limbs from their bodies. Blood and body parts are flung all over the place while high pitched wails fill the air.

The vamps are starting to take notice. Some have even moved their attention away from us and leap through the air to fight the zombies. I watch in complete confusion as the vamps sink their teeth into the rotten flesh. The second that dead blood flows down their throats, they let go and a banshee-like shriek comes out. A few fall to the ground, their bodies twisting and turning in ways I've never seen a body move before. One falls close to us and I can see it fighting the effect of the dead blood. It writhes in pain, eyes a milky white color. The zombies' mushy blood is destroying them from the inside out and they're dying on the ground right in front of us.

Simply remarkable.

I am seeing, first hand, what happens when a vampire bites into a zombie. I am so unbelievably grateful they aren't turning into something so horrifying, my mind won't let me imagine it. I can't help but feel relieved by all of this. We finally got the reinforcement we needed.

More of the vamps turn away from us and go about attacking the zombies. Many are subdued and destroyed before they can even get in a good fight. The zombies are winning this thing for us, going against everything I ever thought to be right about them. I thought they stayed away from the vamps and went straight for those with a beating heart. Glad to know I was wrong about that.

I've noticed that more vampires are fighting the zombies and only a few are paying attention to us. Even those few are tempted to join their friends in the fight. We have a clear shot at getting away safely while the zombies do our dirty work. A few of the humans are already running through the woods, heading back to the highway that will take them to the city. Jim and Sherry are amongst them and Dwayne isn't too far behind.

"Time to go." Ryder says, tugging at my arm a little.

I nod and lower my gun. We leave the sight of the vampire-zombie war and listen only to the groans and shrieks coming from both of the monsters as they destroy each other. This has quickly turned into the most confusing, unnerving night of my life and it's not even over yet.

***

Ryder and I keep running, our hands locked together. The other humans are ahead of us, running as fast as they can and not taking a second to look back. We're all headed back to the city. It's the only place we can go where we'll be safe for the rest of the night. It's too risky to start looking for a better place to stay for a while. With zombies close by and vampires always out this time of night, no one should take a risk like that.

I can see moonlight shining through the branches of the trees above. Enough to brighten the way back to the highway. We make it through the woods, avoiding the trees and jumping over whatever gets in our way. A few logs and branches that have fallen from the trees. We have to hop over a large oak tree that has fallen in the middle of the woods. *I wonder if anyone was around to hear it.*

Forgive me for trying to think of something funny to keep my mind off the imminent death close behind us.

My lungs are burning, but I keep up with Ryder next to me. I can hear him heaving, ignoring the rules about only breathing through your nose while running. It gets kind of hard to do that when you're running at full speed trying to get away from flesh hungry beasts. No matter how hard I force my lips to stay sealed, they want to be open so I can breathe easier.

Other than the sticks cracking under our feet, I don't hear anything coming after us. I turn my head and glance over my shoulder, taking my eyes off the road ahead of me for a split second. I just need to know for sure that nothing is following. So far so good. I look back ahead of me, moving out of the way of a huge tree. Something's blocking the way in front of us. Something so horrible, we practically trip over our own two feet in order to stop running.

The vampire, Zeke, hears our stammering steps and lifts his bloody face from Nick's lifeless body. Blood seeps out of his neck and onto the leaves he's lying on. His eyes are wide open, staring up at the branches above. Zeke looks at us, showing off his yellow and black teeth in a gnarly smile. He stands and steps over his dinner toward us.

I clench the gun in my hand as I stare into the lifeless eyes of the creature before me. Hesitation can't stop me and I raise it up, forcing myself not to be afraid. After tonight, I don't think I'll ever freeze up when I'm face to face with a vampire again. My dad would be so proud of me. I take aim for the bastard's heart and take a deep breath. My finger squeezes the trigger and I hear the click.

But nothing happens.

No gunshot blasting through the air. No bullet shooting into Zeke's unbeating heart.

Absolutely nothing and it's utterly devastating.

I pull the trigger again and again. A few more times, nothing happens. Only the annoying click of an empty gun. I've run out of ammo and the rest of it is back at the hotel.

"Shit." I exclaim, lowering the gun.

Zeke takes another step closer and both of us take one backwards. Ryder holds my hand even tighter and we both watch this demon make its way to enjoy a nice meal of our blood. I was sort of hoping my life wouldn't end this way. I never really imagined how my life would meet its end, but this isn't the way I want to go. I'd at least like to be a few years older and enjoy the little things this life has to offer.

I guess fate has other plans for me.

"Stupid...human." Zeke says, "Time...to die."

In an flash of white, he bolts up to us before either of us can take a breath. All we feel is a gust of wind and he's standing inches away. He tilts his head to the side and looks Ryder up and down, examining his body. I can feel his hand trembling in my own and there's nothing I can do to calm him. There's nothing either of us can do besides wait for it to be over. Zeke turns his attention to me and smiles again. Those jagged teeth are stained black with blood and they tear into my soul as I count the seconds till everything is over. They are going by ever so slowly.

"You...first." he whispers.

I shudder and in another flash he grabs Ryder's arm and rips him away from me, throwing him a few feet in the air only to crash against a tree. I watch him fall to the ground, listening to the groan he makes as pain courses through him. I wish that would've knocked him out. I'd rather him not be awake when the vamp takes his life away from him. Zeke then grabs the collar of my hoodie and pulls me closer to his face. His hot, revolting breath caresses my skin, burning my nose and I try not to smell it. The gun slips out of my fingers as the tears swell up in my eyes. I can feel them drift down my cheeks as he shoves his nose closer to my face and takes in a big whiff of my scent.

"I will...enjoy this." He seethes and I can see the smile coming to his lips.

He leans away from me and I look into his white eyes. It kills me to know this will be the last thing I see before the lights go off in my life. His ghastly, pale, vein covered face will be the image burned into my eyes as he sucks the life right out of me. He opens his mouth and gives me another repulsive smile. He lifts me off the ground and I have no choice except holding onto his arms as he shoves me against a tree right behind me.

A terrible pain jolts up my spine as my back slams against the trunk of the tree. The pain lingers and it feels like I have a heartbeat in my lower back. I have to shove the pain aside and face what's next to come. Behind him, I catch a glimpse of Ryder gripping at his side from being thrown into a tree. He's trying to gather whatever strength he has left. Trying to force the pain from his body and be my rescuer. I can tell the pain is too much for him to bear and he can't bring himself to move more than a foot from the tree. His sad eyes look up at me while he keeps trying to fight the pain.

I hope he knows this isn't his fault. The only person to blame for any of this is lying dead on the ground a few feet away. At least he got what he deserved and was able to experience the pain he brought upon so many travelers before us.

Zeke opens his mouth and moves his teeth closer to my neck. I close my eyes and wait. This time, being so close to death brings the thought of my family to my mind. Finally something flashes before my eyes when I'm about to die.

I can see them standing in front of me. Each one has a smile on their face as they wait for me to join them. Mom has her arms draped around dad's shoulders, tears in her eyes. Charlie tosses a baseball in the air, waiting for me to play a good game of catch with him. Maggie with her arms folded across her chest, her eyes lit up at the thought of getting to see her favorite little sister again. Dad is the only one without a smile. Without the look of happiness to see his little girl again. He's upset and disappointed with the idea that I'll be joining them in a matter of seconds.

I'm not ready for this.

I'm not ready to admit to myself that I have failed every member of my family. I have broken my promise to dad about surviving in this world. I've broken that promise to everyone I'm seeing in my head. I was supposed to be the one who found a place to live the rest of my life in peace away from the monsters that haunt the world. Away from every horrible thing out there that could possibly lead to my death. How can I die knowing I have failed to do those few simple things?

I feel the tears sliding down my cheeks. Feel Zeke's breath as he gets closer and closer to my neck. Things seem to be moving in slow motion, making this dying thing so much worse.

I hear a loud grunting sound coming from somewhere around us. It catches the attention of my family in my head. All of them turn their heads toward the sound of the groans and I open my eyes just in time to see a zombie reach his arms out and yank Zeke away from me. My family disappears out of my mind and I fall to the ground at the base of the tree. I land hard on my wrist, spraining it and I wince as the pain creeps up my arm. I can get over it, though.

Zeke lets a shrill scream escape his throat and I look up at the scene. The zombie, a young man with a chunk missing out of his right shoulder and blood staining his ripped up clothing, has his arms tightly wrapped around Zeke. He has a good hold on the vamp and sinks his teeth into Zeke's neck. He tears off a good sized piece of flesh then spits it out instead of swallowing it. He goes for another bite, then tackles the vamp to the ground. Blood and tiny pieces of skin spew through the air as the zombie tears him apart.

I look away from them and turn my focus to Ryder. He's still holding his stomach, eyes glued to the zombie eating away at the vamp. I crawl across the ground, making my way to him. He looks at me when I make it to his side. I take his hand and help him sit up.

"Are you alright?" he asks, wincing with each word.

I nod, "Not really, but I will be the sooner we get out of this hellhole and back to the city. Are you alright?"

"I might have broken a rib or two, but I'll live." Ryder replies, I hate knowing he's hurt more than I can fix. "I meant what I said back there," he looks into my eyes, "I really do love you, Bridge."

I smile as the gory sound of flesh being ripped to shreds slowly dissipates, "I really love you, too, Ryder. I always thought after losing my father, I would never feel love or happiness again. You gave that back to me."

He lifts his hand and runs his fingers through my tangled hair. Our lips meet for a short, but still incredibly meaningful kiss. Probably not the best time for a kiss, after almost dying at the hands of the vampire who's currently being ripped apart by a zombie. The sounds in the background are pretty gruesome and I'm sure it's a bloody mess over there. This will, however, be one of the kisses I'll remember for the rest of my life. The kiss that truly symbolizes how two people who only met a few days ago, can fall in love even when death stares them right in the face. I'll cherish this moment forever.

There are footsteps approaching us. Staggering, unbalanced footsteps causing my heart to race once again. I peel myself away from Ryder and the two of us look up to see the zombie, blood dripping from his face and hands, standing a few feet away. The grey sweatshirt he's wearing is cloaked with mud and black blood from one of his victims. There's a slice in the sweatshirt right across the college logo. His black eyes blending in perfectly with the woods around us and the feeling of death reappears in my mind. We have nothing to stop this thing from devouring our bodies just like he did to the vamp.

He stares down at us. His lifeless eyes peering into our souls. My hands are shaking as I hold onto Ryder with all of my life. The zombie growls and I shudder with fear. He takes another step then stops and a calm look overtakes his face.

He's hesitating.

Similar to some of the other zombies I have come across. Only this one isn't weighing the options of attacking us. He's actually stopping himself from jumping on top of us and eating our flesh and bones. Something inside of him, maybe the only human part that's left, is holding him back.

I keep my eyes glued to his face and he takes a step backward. His head begins shaking from side to side giving us the notion that he isn't going to snack on us tonight. I raise an eyebrow and the fear turns into confusion. The zombie turns around and begins walking away. I follow him with my eyes until I can no longer see him through the darkness.

I look to Ryder and say, "Again, what the fuck is going on?"

He shakes his head and shrugs, "I'm just as lost as you are."

"What do you think's gonna happen to the zombies now since they ate most of the vampires?" I ask, really hating myself for that popping into my head.

He shrugs, "I don't know and I really don't want to find out."

"We should probably get out of here soon then, in

case whatever bad thing they turn into comes along." I say. "You alright to walk?"

"I should be."

I take a deep breath, then pull myself to my feet. Ryder takes my hand and it takes all my strength to help him stand. He lets out a slight grunt from the pain coming from his ribs then drapes his arm over my shoulders. He grips his stomach, holding tight to keep some of the pain at bay.

"You two alright?" I hear a deep voice coming from in front of us.

Good thing I recognize that voice, my heart has had enough of beating itself into overdrive for one night. I'm surprised I haven't had a heart attack yet. I look up to see Dwayne standing before us shining a flashlight in our faces. I squint a little when the beam hits my face and he quickly moves it away.

"I heard the commotion and came running back to make sure no one got left behind." He says.

"We're fine. *Desperately* need to lie down for a bit, but we'll be okay." I reply.

"I saw what that zombie did. Confusing as hell." He says.

"Damn right about that." Ryder adds.

Dwayne shines the light at Ryder and lingers for a moment. I can't see the look on his face, but I have a feeling I know what he's staring at. After everything that's happened tonight, I'd probably question the scar myself. It does look a lot like a bite mark and would make anyone concerned about being around him. Considering how we were all just attacked by a bunch of man-eating monsters, anyone would jump to the only conclusion their minds could come up with.

Unfortunately, Dwayne is jumping to that conclusion right now.

"What's that on your shoulder, boy?" Dwayne asks in a not so pleasant tone.

I can see the outline of his hand moving for the gun at

his waist. A prime example of someone judging another person much too quickly.

"He's not one of them." I say, simply.

"It's just a scar." Ryder says, quietly.

"Looks more like a bite mark than a scar?" Dwayne asks.

"It's just a reminder of a horrible past." Ryder states, he's trembling again.

"We all have scars, just like him." I say. "Some are just easier to see than others. He's not a monster."

Dwayne shines his flashlight at Ryder's face once again. His eyes scan Ryder's whole body looking for any sign that I'm wrong. The effects from being bit by a zombie start to show right away. Ryder would be on the ground, writhing in so much pain and agony he couldn't stand it. Blackness would have overtaken his eyes and the screams coming from his throat would be unbearable. It takes longer to change into a vamp, I know, but the mark on his shoulder isn't fresh. Still enough to get people to judge him too quickly.

At least I know the truth about Ryder and I know he's not of one them.

"You sure you're not one of those demons, boy?" Dwayne asks, taking his hand away from his gun.

"Positive." Ryder says, letting out his breath.

"Good." Dwayne lowers the light and begins to unbutton the jacket he's wearing. "Some of the others in the city might not be convinced just because you say you're not. It's better to keep a scar like that covered to be on the safe side." He takes off his jacket and hands it to Ryder. "You can give that back to me in the morning."

Ryder takes the coat and says, "Thank you."

"You're welcome, now let's get back."

Dwayne turns and begins leading the way out of the woods. I help Ryder put the jacket on and he goes about buttoning it up. It's a little big, Dwayne's huge compared to him, but it's better than walking around half naked. While he's busy with the buttons, I take a moment to search for my gun. I dropped it by the tree where Zeke had me pinned and it landed in a small pile of leaves and dirt. I rush over, pick it up and brush it off. This cold piece of metal is the last thing my father ever gave to me that isn't food or shelter. It's gotten me out of quite a few tough situations and will probably continue to do so until the end of time. I smile, thinking of all the times I've stood side by side with dad, shooting zombies and warding off the vamps. Some of the best times I've had in my life were doing those things.

"Let's go, Bridge." Ryder calls from behind me.

I turn around, swallowing the lump in my throat, and walk back to his side. He puts his arm over my shoulders and I help ease the pain in his ribs as he walks.

***

We meet the others at the gate, which the guards are mercifully opening for us. I guess seeing all of us come back in one piece is enough to get them to be decent people for once. Good thing, because I'm tired of being the mean, forceful Bridget and ready to get some sleep. I know everyone else here tonight is wanting the same thing. We've all seen and gone through too many horrifying things for one night.

So glad it's over.

The guards make sure to check us all over for bite marks or scratches to weed out any possibilities of one of us turning into a monster. I don't blame them for being worried about that sort of thing. Out of the ten of us who survived the night, none of us were injured to the point of becoming one of the undead. Still, the guards stop us from going any further into the city until they have their questions answered.

"Where's Nick and the rest of our men?" one of them shouts at us.

The three of Nick's men who survived step forward. There's Seth, the young man who helped us get to the trail in the woods. The big guy who saved my life earlier and a shorter man with a long beard. The big guy, who's name I really need to learn, moves closer to the other guards and takes a deep breath.

"He's dead and all of us would be if these people didn't show up when they did. Those vamps had no interest in staying true to their words tonight, they wanted all of us." He says.

"No more of this trading humans for safety." The short, bearded man adds in. "From now on, all of us live here in peace and fight when those beasts show up at our doorstep. Buying safety isn't an option anymore."

"And who's idea is this?" the guard asks with anger in his eyes.

The three of Nick's men step aside and look at me, "It's her idea."

"A traveler? They don't know anything about running a city like this. They don't know anything about keeping anyone but themselves safe and they can barely do that." The guard retorts.

I can hear the angry sighs and quiet comments after that remark. All of us in this small group are travelers. We've come a *long* way to get where we are today and I think we're all doing a damn good job at it. This guy, who has probably been sheltered his whole, pitiful existence, knows nothing of what we've been through to still be standing here today

I shake my head and step forward, "Then how do you explain, after five years of traveling and living on the road, not knowing if we'll eat one night and starve the next, that we're still alive? That all of us have managed to survive the hardships of this life knowing death will forever be knocking on our door when we least expect it? Explain to me how you know this and you can go back to keeping your precious city safe by whatever means you think are right."

The guard gawks at me for a moment. His mouth open as though he wants to say something, but the words just won't come out. None of those men could possibly understand what we go through on a day to day basis out on the road. They don't know how to go night after night hoping to wake up alive in the morning and not wind up as someone's dinner. They don't know the fear we have gone through or the death we have seen. The only thing these men know how to do, is ruin the lives of people who are really trying to make a difference. We are the ones who are doing our best at keeping the human race alive and ahead of the game.

With Ryder at my side, I walk away from the gate and step right next to the guard, "Didn't think you could." I say loud enough for everyone to hear, then keep walking down the street.

The rest of my group follow along with us, ignoring the guards completely as they laugh and hug each other like they've never done before. I look over my shoulder, glancing at the faces and taking in those who survived. Dwayne walks with the few survivors from our original group. The older woman crying for the loss of her friends. Two of the prisoners we rescued, walk together with smiles on their faces about making it another night.

Then, when I'm about to lose hope and think they weren't able to survive, my eyes pass over two familiar faces. Jim has his arm tightly around Sherry, keeping her close by his side. He smiles when he sees me and I smile back. Sherry passes me a huge grin and waves.

We might have lost a few brave souls tonight, but we were able to make a difference in this city. We were able to fight back and save whatever traveler who decides to come this way for a few nights of safety. I never thought I'd be able to make a difference as big or as important to the human race as this one.

It's a pretty good feeling.

***

I wake up in the morning to the sun shining through the window. The breeze flowing in through the open door of the balcony. I can hear birds chirping and can smell the fresh air creeping inside. Ryder is lying on the bed of our hotel room next to me with his arm draped over my stomach. Both of us slept in our clothes. We were way too exhausted after climbing up the flights of stairs and just crashed on the bed and passed out almost immediately.

We deserved it too.

All of the others went back to their friends in whatever that building was Dwayne lead us to. Jim and Sherry had to make a stop there to pick up Dillon then they came back to the hotel with us and went to their own room. I've never seen anyone so grateful about being alive until I looked at Sherry's face when we got back to the hotel. She gave me such a bear hug, I thought my eyes were going to bulge out of my head. Would have been worth it though.

I glance at the watch on my wrist, almost ten o'clock. Soon we'll be hitting the road again and this will all be a horrible memory. After leaving this place, I will never stay in a hotel again. Bad things seem to happen and the owners of those establishments tend to not be the kind of people I would like to associate myself with. From a man who used the monsters as a form of entertainment, to a man who chose to feed them with his own kind, hotels, or anything of that sort, are completely off my list of places to stay. I hope with Nick out of the picture from here on out, this city will be the peaceful, welcoming place the world needs it to be.

A yawn escapes me and I sit up in bed. Ryder stirs and rolls onto his back. I glance over to him and he smiles. I return the favor as my eyes drift down to the bruise on the right side of his chest. It's about the size of a grapefruit and is slightly swollen. He couldn't sleep on it at all throughout the night and I was hoping it wouldn't be so bad when we woke up. I can see that I'm wrong by looking at the purple spot on his side. I got lucky and my wrist eventually stopped hurting overnight. Doesn't even hurt when I bend it.

"You feeling alright today?" I ask.

He nods, "Better than last night. Once we get on the road and as far away from this place as possible, I'll be even better."

"Me too."

I slide my feet out of bed and set them on the floor. My boots are sitting next to our bags at the end of the bed. Ryder's shoes are there as well with Dwayne's jacket draped over his bag. We'll have to return that before we hit the road again. We'll have to stock up on food and fresh water before we leave the city as well.

I reach for my boots and slip my feet into each one, then zip them up. Ryder sits up in bed next to me and I hear him wince when he puts pressure on his side. I see the pained look in his eyes as he places a hand over his bruise.

"Are you sure we should leave today? I mean, would you rather stay until you're completely healed and able to walk without being in a tremendous amount of pain?" I ask.

He quickly shakes his head, "No, I'd rather face the

pain of walking a million miles than force myself to heal in a place where they could take either one of us away again. I don't care what they said last night. I'll never be able to trust them."

"I understand that, but I really think that with Nick out of the picture, this city will be better off. He was the one behind everything and without him, travelers shouldn't have to worry about stopping here anymore." I reply.

"I hope you're right about that, but I still don't want to take any chances." He says, "Will you hand me my bag and my shoes, please?"

I nod and reach for his things, "Then we'll leave as soon as we have everything we need. It's still a long road to Des Moines and we'll need food and everything else."

I set his bag on the bed and he takes his shoes and puts them on his feet. It takes him a little longer, but he eventually gets them over his feet and goes about tying them. He refuses my offer of helping him with his shoes even though I can see that it hurts him to bend over like that to tie them.

Stubborn boy.

I stand up, grab my bag, and walk across the room to the bathroom while he's busy getting a shirt out of his bag. I stare at myself in the mirror. It's dark, but I can still see my reflection. My hair's a disaster, in *desperate* need of attention. I reach inside my bag and pull out my brush and hair tie. I wince with every snag I hit with the brush, then pull it back in a ponytail with my bangs shoved off to the side. We'll be on the road for a while and wearing my hair down will just get in the way.

I put my brush away and zip up my backpack. I take another long look at myself in the mirror and smile. My family would be so proud of the person staring back at me. She has done some pretty amazing things over the last few days. She's saved someone's life without realizing it. She killed a ton of zombies and even a few vamps along the way, and she even helped stop a madman from killing thousands of humans in the process. That girl staring back at me is pretty awesome and I'm glad to know her on a very personal level.

With the smile still on my face, I fling my bag over my shoulders and walk back out into the main room. Ryder is now wearing a plain black t-shirt with the strap of his shoulder bag across his body and ready to go. He's holding my gun and I reach out to take it from him. We remembered to reload it when we got back to the hotel room last night. That was a necessity that took priority over sleep. You never know when something bad could happen and you don't want to be unprepared for it.

"Ready to go?" he asks.

I look around the room. We've only been here a couple of days and already made quite a few great memories in this room alone. My first kiss took place on the bed which lead me to my first act of flirtatiousness on the balcony. I fell in love with Ryder as we held each other on the floor and I felt like my world was ripped away from me when I thought I'd never see him again. This room and the memories it holds will be the only thing I miss about this place. That and the delicious blueberry pie we enjoyed when we first got here.

I turn my eyes back to Ryder and say, "More than ready."

He smiles and I follow him to the door. He pulls it open and both of us head out into the hallway. I leave the door open and walk across the dirty carpeted floor. Walking past the old drinking fountain where Ryder was so rudely taken away from me for a brief spell. Slowly descending the five flights of stairs, stopping at every other landing so Ryder could catch his breath. It's hard work to walk down all those stairs with bruised and possibly broken ribs. Without an actual hospital, we'll never know what's really wrong with him.

We get to the lobby and I let out a much needed sigh of relief when my feet hit the very last step. I've been walking across this country for the good majority of the last five years and you would think five flights of stairs would be nothing, but it can really get you winded. Especially when you're helping someone who's having problems of his own.

There's a small group of people leaning against the wall next to the exit in the lobby. There's six of them standing there and I recognize all of them. Sherry stands with her father and cousin, that raggedy teddy bear still in his grip. The big guy, *who's name I still don't know*, is standing next to Jim and Seth is right next to Sherry. Dwayne stands close to the door, a smile on his face as we approach them.

All of them have bags either on their backs or on the floor waiting to go.

"What's going on? Why are you guys just standing here?" I ask.

Sherry smiles and steps forward, "Well, dad and I were talking last night and we wanted to join you and Ryder and go north. These guys overheard and wanted to tag along."

"We're not tagging along. We're all going the same direction so why not travel together." Dwayne chimes in.

"What about the others?" I ask.

Dwayne shrugs, "Some plan on staying here to stay safe and alive. Most of the others left early this morning. The guards at the gate didn't even try stopping them."

"That's good. Those people deserve a head start on a new life somewhere and I hope they make it." I reply. "But why do you want to travel with us? We're just two kids heading for a city that might not even be there."

"The other travelers have someone they care about, either with them or they plan on finding them. We don't have anybody." Dwayne states. "Jim and his small family are all they have left and you know that. I lost my entire family when I came to this place. Seth and the big guy, Carter," *finally* I learn his name, "their families are all out there somewhere. They don't know if they're still alive and they'll never know if they stay here. Traveling with two kids to a place that is only rumored to be true is the only thing we have going for us. If it's not there, then at least we'll still be together and can look out for one another."

I smile and glance down at my feet, "I'm glad to know all of you want to join us. It will be nice to have more than one person traveling with me."

"There's one more thing you should know before we leave." Jim adds.

"What's that?" Ryder and I say at the same time.

"About those zombies from last night, the ones that ripped the vamps apart," Jim says, "some of the guards here found them on the road about a mile outside the gate. They're all dead. Every last one of them. Not by bullet wounds to the head or some physical force strong enough to bring them down. They just died naturally."

"So the poison from the vamps wasn't able to change them into something even worse than a zombie?" I ask, "That is just *awesome*. I mean, it would have been great if somehow that was the miracle cure for the zombies, but knowing they won't be walking around the planet as some mixture of both creatures makes things a lot better."

"Still doesn't explain why they attacked the vamps in the first place." Ryder says.

I shake my head, "I don't think we'll ever fully understand why they sacrificed their lives to save us. Maybe some small part of them is still human after all and they'd rather die than see the rest of our civilization crumble under the vamps. Maybe those few who I've seen hesitate before attacking a living being, are just the beginning of a change being made in them."

"I hope you're right." Dwayne says.

"Me too." I reply.

The big guy, Carter, steps away from the wall and flings his bag over his shoulder, "Enough with all that zombie and vampire nonsense. I'm ready to hit the road."

The others grab their bags as well and start to head for the door. Seth holds it open for all of us to walk through and just before leaving, I take one last look behind me. The high ceilings, the crystal chandelier still hanging in its place. The insane amount of stairs leading up to rooms that I'll never see again.

I won't miss this place one bit.

Part Three

We crossed into Iowa two days ago. It's been three weeks since we left Hatfeld and none of us have bothered looking back and it has been a *long* three weeks. First off, the little army guarding the city didn't really want us to leave. They refused to open the gates for us until Carter made it hard for them to keep us inside anymore. He is, after all, three times bigger than any other grown man I've been around and he can be quite intimidating, especially with that deep voice of his to match his appearance. He didn't hurt any of the guards at the gate, but he sure made it seem like he was going to.

Secondly, a mile away from the city we ran into the bodies of dead zombies cluttering the highway. Just like Jim had said, every last one of them who bit into the body of a vampire was lying dead on that road. I recognized the one who saved us from Zeke and I actually felt bad seeing the thing lying in a small pool of his brown, mushy blood. He saved my life and Ryder's and I'll never understand why he did it, but I'll always be somewhat grateful.

Lastly, as with every trek we humans set ourselves upon, problems naturally occurred. We thought we had plenty of food to last us a month, but we were wrong. Mainly because we didn't ration it as well as we should have and we ate more some nights than on others and that took a toll on our food. We have just enough left now for one more meal, then we're out of luck unless we make it to Des Moines soon. I'm positive my dad would've scolded me if he were around to see how much food I wasted along with these guys. Probably even smack me upside the head and I honestly couldn't blame him.

There were quite a lot of zombies on the journey north. Most of them were the same normal zombies who ran for us the second they smelled us. We took care of them without a problem. I was able to relieve some tension and shoot quite a few of them in the head. Not going to brag, but my count is much higher than anyone else's in the group. Luckily, no one was bitten or scratched during any of our encounters. A few close calls that we were able to handle without a major problem.

Then there's the zombies who hesitate and they're beginning to make me nervous. They always stare at us, like their longing for something. Probably wanting their life back. Dwayne doesn't mind when we see the hesitant ones and thinks if they leave us alone, then we should leave them alone. That maybe they are a part of some new change that's occurring and we need to let it happen. These hesitant zombies would follow us for a few miles and stop every time we turned around to shoot them. Then they would start following us again until they grew weary and decided to stand around and grunt at anything which doesn't make sense. That's just about everything.

The vamps, we had some trouble with. I'm starting to notice how some plan before they attack. They put a lot of detail into the mix and trick us. Like, a few nights ago, we *thought* we found a safe campsite. There were even signs of people camping in that spot before us. I guess the vamps knew this and took it upon themselves to keep it that way to make others feel safe. I don't know where they were hiding that night, but they picked a damn good spot. If it weren't for the stick breaking under one of their feet, they would've had us. Thankfully mother nature was there to warn us.

That was about the worst of our encounters with the vamps. Being taken by surprise can kind of make you not prepared and a little distracted. We still kicked some ass and got away bite free.

So here we are. There were eight of us when we left Hatfeld and eight of us remain. A decent number that has been able to outlive the undead at our feet. Not too many people in this world can say they fought off those demons and survived. Many of the people who've tried are one of the undead and we have to fight them off. A never ending circle of life leaving the humans toward the bottom of the food chain. One of these days we'll take our place at the top again.

It's raining pretty hard outside right now. The sky is black and it's the middle of the afternoon. Seth found us a huge house to ride out the storm in. It's one of those mini mansions that has six bedrooms and four full bathrooms. A kitchen the size of a small apartment and a living room complete with a flat screen TV taking up an entire wall. A house I've always wanted to live in yet never thought I'd ever see the inside of one.

We made sure to search the house for vamps and zombies. The main floor, upstairs, and the finished basement are completely monster free. Other than the mold growing in the corners of the ceilings and on the walls, we didn't find anything. We'll be safe here for one night.

Sherry made herself comfortable in one of the master bedrooms. She's been spending a lot of time with Seth and they're in there right now talking about their lives. I think she has a crush on him. Carter and Dwayne are in the kitchen trying to make our small amount of food last a while longer.

Jim is playing a board game with Dillon at the dining room table and they seem to be having a pretty good time by how much laughter I can hear from them.

Ryder and I are left alone in the living room. We sit on the enormous couch staring out the huge bay windows at the rain pouring in the lake behind the house. Bars have been placed over the windows, probably after the cure took a turn for the worst. At least whoever these rich bastards used to be, they took precautions to make their home safe. Comes in handy when you're traveling. Kudos to them.

Ryder has his feet propped up on the ottoman, his right hand resting comfortably across his chest. He's still experiencing some pain when he bends at certain angles, but for the most part, he's healing. I sit next to him, my feet folded on the couch next to me and my head resting on his shoulder. I watch the rain drops hit the window making it look like a waterfall on the house. It makes the outside world a little blurry.

"So, you ever think you'd be sitting in a house like this?" I ask.

"Not at all." Ryder says. "What about you?"

I shake my head and smile, "The house I grew up in wasn't even half this size. I had to share a room with my sister for ten years until my dad finished my awesome room in the attic. Even had an air conditioner up there."

"I don't think you could consider the place I grew up in a house at all. There were three bedrooms and one bathroom and a shitload of kids. Don't even remember any of their names and I was stuck sharing a room with all of them. I prefer this life much more than the one I had before the cure." He says. "What about you, Bridge?"

I'm not sure how I could answer that. There are too many things about my old life that I miss more than anything else in the world. My family being the main part of that life. I would give anything to see them one more time. To talk to them, hug them, and hear their voices. There's only one thing

I have for me to give up in order to get that again. I'm really starting to like my life right now so giving it up would be extremely hard and, not to mention, probably painful.

I sit up and put my feet on the floor.

"Bridget, I'm sorry if what I said was the wrong thing. I know you had a great family and a great life before all of this." Ryder says.

I turn to him and smile, "It's okay. I want to show you something." I reach for my bag and bring it onto the couch next to me.

The sound of the zipper echoes a little in this big house. I sift through the things in my bag and dig down to the bottom. I pull out the black album and set it on my lap then lean back against Ryder.

"What's that?" he asks.

I swallow hard and say, "This was my life before the vampires, before the zombies, before things literally went bump in the night." I open the photo album to the first page and show my family to him. "My mom and dad, my brother Charlie and my sister Maggie and then there's me." It's still really painful to look at the pictures, but I have to.

He sits up as best as he can without bringing pain to his chest and smiles at the pictures as I turn the pages, "They look like they would have been an awesome family."

"They were." I agree, hating how their lives have been transferred to the past tense. "They were always there when I needed them, even when I didn't want them to be."

"They were the kind of family you would prefer over this life and I don't blame you for thinking that. If I had something like that to go back to, I'd want to in a second." Ryder says, his eyes still looking at the pictures.

I take a deep breath, trying to keep the lump from coming to my throat as I stare at the pictures, "Being with my family was a great part of my life. Growing up with people who cared about me, who loved me more than anything else in the world, that was the best part. But, that was just the first part of my life and a part I'll never have back and I think I can be okay with that. I know wherever they are right now, they're watching over me to make sure I survive *this* part of my life. Bridget part two, I guess. This is the part of my life that makes me who I am and who I am going to be.

"Sure, I'd love to go back in time to see my family again, but I can't truthfully say I'd give up what I have in this chapter of my life to have what I had when I was a kid. I'll miss them every day for the rest of my life and I'll never stop thinking about them. I just really like what I have now, with you, Ryder. You're the best part of my life right now and I don't want to give that up. As hard as it may seem, I know my family understands that I'm doing what I know is right."

"You really wouldn't give all of this up to be with your family again? You'd really stay in this horrible world forever, instead of going back to what you had before all this?" he asks.

I take a deep breath and say, "I would, because I wouldn't want to go somewhere if I knew you couldn't come with me. I'm kinda getting used to saving you."

He smiles and says, "Yeah, you have saved my life like six different times now."

I shrug, "I've learned from the best." I motion to my family in the pictures. "These people right here, taught me everything I know, especially my dad. If it weren't for him, I'd be dead right along with them and so would you. Those zombies in that town where we met, would have had you for an afternoon snack."

"Yeah, probably." He says. "You know, you're a pretty great person, Bridget. You've been through hell and back with what this world gave us and you still stay strong. I think that's just about the best thing about you and your family would be extremely proud of you for making it this far. I know I am."

I feel a tear in the corner of my eye and I wipe it away quickly. I flip another page of the photo album and stare down at the picture on the page. Christmas, when I was about five years old. There I am, sitting on the couch next to my mom with her arm around my shoulder. She always was one for posing for the camera. Seeing their faces brings back all the memories of how things used to be. Thinking of them fills my heart with grief and sorrow and I don't want to be sad right now. I want to be happy, well as happy as I could be in a world filled with monsters.

"Hey," Ryder says, then takes my photo album away from me and closes it, "it's time to stop looking at your past and focus on your future. Like you said, the family in this book got you to where you are today, but the family your with right now, in this awesome house, is the family who will get you to where you need to be tomorrow."

I sniffle and swallow the lump in my throat, "This will be a strange new family of mine."

He smiles, "Mine too."

"Have I told you how much you make me fall in love with every time you say amazing things like that?" I say.

He nods, "Yeah, but I love hearing you say it again."

He puts his hand on the back of my neck and pulls my lips to his. I close my eyes and let the warmth of his mouth caress my own.

***

The rain cleared overnight and I had the best sleep I've had in a very long time. I might have fallen asleep with my head on

Ryder's shoulder while sitting on the couch, but I've never slept better. I think being cuddled up next to someone I feel completely safe with, makes the weight of the world disappear from my shoulders. I didn't have any horrible dreams about zombies chasing me or waking up with a vamp sucking the blood out of my neck. I didn't have any dreams at all.

The night was just perfect.

We left that perfect night back in that big house a few hours ago. With the sun shining down on us, we couldn't have asked for a better day to make it to a new city to start over. A new place to settle down in. A place where I won't have to worry about fighting bad guys or saving anybody. I'll only have to worry about waking up in the morning and making new friends and living a somewhat normal life for once. You know, the kind of life that isn't spent on the road all day, every day. The kind without zombies to kill or food to search for, because it will be provided.

The kind of life that already makes me miss the one I have now.

I'll miss sleeping in a different place every night of the week. Seeing all the wonderful sights this country has to offer. The mountains, the forests, things you can't find behind the walls of a fortified city. Searching for food and water sucks, but it's always an adventure. I think I'll even miss the constant fear of dying. The fear that at any moment a vamp or a zombie could devour me and that would be it. Call me crazy, but I'll miss it.

I'll miss being a badass and killing zombies like they're nothing. Shooting them in the head, watching their already lifeless bodies fall limp to the ground. I've gotten over my fear of confronting vampires and I'm finally able to pull the trigger without thinking about it. If I go to a city and live behind the walls they have built, I won't have any of that. I won't get the chance to save someone I didn't even know was around me at the time. I won't be able to help the human race overcome this disease the cure has brought. I'll be just another person who managed to stay alive through it all and my story of survival will be over.

I'm not entirely sure I'm ready for that.

We keep walking, going under a corroding overpass with cars piled up on either side of it. Most of them are completely totaled and only two are in somewhat good condition. The batteries are probably more than dead and the cars will never be driven again, but at least they're not completely destroyed like the rest of them.

On the other side of the overpass, we see it. A few miles to go and we'll be standing right outside the towering metal wall surrounding a city I assumed was long gone. The city where the human race is managing to stay alive. As long as they aren't doing so by trading people like us to the vampires, I might be okay with it.

Seeing this wall should make me happy. Ryder has a grin on his face as we move toward it. The others keep talking about the life they can't wait to have inside this new city. I don't feel as happy as I should. I am very grateful this isn't a rumor. This place *actually* exists. I'm glad to know humans are able to live without worrying or fear. Those walls look pretty damn impenetrable to me, which is a very good thing. There's just something wrong with me to want to believe I'll be happy there.

This has been a dream of mine and my father's for a long time. Finding a safe place to live out the rest of our lives. It's what we always used to talk about. He never told me how weird it would be actually getting to that new life.

Our little group moves faster out of sheer excitement of finding this new city and the nerves are rising in my stomach with every step I take. We cover the last couple miles and approach the gate faster than I want to. I guess I'm the only one who wants to savor these last few moments of being a traveler.

The walls are much taller this close, at least fifty or sixty feet high. Made completely of metal pieces that are welded together to seal everything in and keep bad things out. I can see people walking back and forth on top of the wall, carrying guns and keeping watch over the city. They look just like the soldiers back at Hatfeld. There's a sign outside the gate that reads "THE CITY OF DES MOINES WELCOMES YOU". I'm still not feeling as welcome as I know the rest of the group is.

One of the soldiers walking on top of the gate spots us. He orders us to stop walking, which we do, then I see him speaking into a walkie-talkie. I can't hear what he says, but it obviously gets a someone to open a large door at the base of the gate. A few men come running out, keeping their guns close at hand in case we're not as human as we look. One of the men is wearing a grey suit and tie, holding some sort of scanner attached to a laptop in his hands. The glasses on his face are thick and he squints at the screen he's holding.

They stop walking a few feet away from us. Guns aimed for our heads.

"I assume all of you are humans, but we still have to take precautions." The man with the glasses states, his voice is calm and sincere. "The device I'm holding allows me to scan your retinas to detect certain pigments in your eyes. It lets us know if you're alive or one of the undead. A few others and myself have developed this software and have saved thousands of lives."

He approaches Carter first and shines a little red light in his left eye. He reads something on the laptop, waits for a beep, then smiles at the big guy. Next he goes onto Jim and Sherry.

"We always enjoy knowing there are still surviving humans out there. You travelers are the best thing this planet has to offer." He smiles every time the scanner beeps. "You guys see things up close and personal. You know how to defeat them better than some of our own army. Believe me when I say that we more than welcome your coming here. Des Moines is one of the few fortified cities left in the country and one of the few that isn't relying on other tactics to keep safe."

"Yeah, we ran into one of those a couple weeks ago." Jim adds.

"My name is Bill Wireman, by the way." He moves from Dillon and onto Seth. "Once we're inside, you can introduce yourselves and tell us a little about you and the road you've traveled. We have a record keeper that jots the most important details down for future reference. From there, we'll find all of you a place to call home for however long you'd like."

He shines his little scanner in Ryder's eyes. It takes a few seconds, then beeps once to let us all know Ryder hasn't been infected by the cure. Lastly, it's my turn. I squeeze Ryder's hand, for some reason I'm more nervous than I should be. I know I'm not infected, but what if that thing malfunctions and says I'm dead even when I'm not? Machines are known for not being the most reliable things on the planet and I've seen them go bad hundreds of times while growing up. I stare at the red dot shining at me and hold my breath. The seconds go by like hours until I hear that little beep and I'm able to breathe again.

"See, painless." Bill says with a smile. "All of you can follow us inside and we'll take you to get settled. We have everything you'll need here, running water and electricity throughout the entire city. There's a couple thousand of us living here and there's plenty of room for more. We truly hope you will make Des Moines your new home."

Bill turns around and walks with his men back to the door at the gate. My little group is right behind them. They are much braver than I am at this moment. I've been face to face with god knows how many terrible things, but going to spend the rest of my life in a safe zone is the one thing that's tearing me apart inside.

I can't move my legs.

I'm frozen.

My mind is still trying to come up with a logical explanation as to why my life will be better being trapped behind a giant metal wall surrounding a city. I'll be stuck doing the same thing day after day, never knowing when something amazing will happen, never being part of the action. I won't be the hero Sherry likes to call me.

Then, Ryder turns around and stares at me. I look into his eyes and suddenly things start to make sense. In order to keep him in my life forever, I can't risk anything by staying on the road. I don't want to go days searching for food and only coming up with morsels. I don't want to try sleeping in a place infested with vampires. I want to be safe, with Ryder. I want to make sure both of us are alive and well each day of the week. I want to stay loving him until the end of time. Being a traveler has too many risks to make that one hundred percent possible.

"You okay, Bridge?" he asks. "You still want to stay here with me, right?"

I stare into his eyes a second longer and slowly nod my head, "You're damn right I do."

A big grin crosses his face and the two of us walk hand in hand through the gate of the city. Through the gate of a brand new chapter in both of our lives.

Through this gate is how the human race will be won.

About The Author

Tahnee Fritz lives in Iowa with her husband and their beloved husky, Baer. *The Human Race* is her first novel and the first in her zombie/vampire trilogy.

www.trfritz88.wordpress.com

www.ingramcontent.com/pod-product-compliance
Lightning Source LLC
Chambersburg PA
CBHW071133170626
46809CB00002B/602